Library and Archives Canada Catalogueing in Publication

Pilgrim, Earl B. (Earl Baxter), 1939-
Marguerite of the Isle of Demons/Earl Pilgrim.

ISBN 978-0-9783434-4-6

1. Robertval, Marguerite de--Fiction. I. Title.
PS8581.1338M37 2007   C813'.54   C2007-906135-4

Printed in Canada By Transcontinental 2007

Cover photo is of Aimee Power of Tors Cove, a local model and former
Miss Newfoundland and Labrador.
Aimee is wearing a cloak which was kindly supplied by
Abbyshot Clothiers
(www.abbyshot.com)
Cover photograph by Bob Crocker

DRC Publishing
3 Parliament Street
St. John's NL
A1A 2Y6
Phone: (709) 726-0960
staceypj@nfld.com

MARGUERITE *of*
THE ISLE OF DEMONS

Earl B. Pilgrim

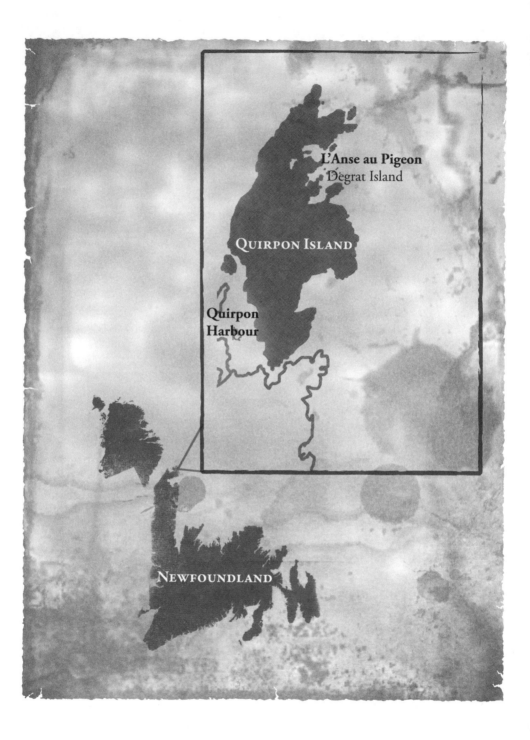

L'Anse au Pigeon
Dégrat Island

QUIRPON ISLAND

Quirpon
Harbour

NEWFOUNDLAND

TABLE *of* CONTENTS

CHAPTER 1

Preparing for the Voyage

This story began in the dining room of an old French castle located on the outskirts of Paris, France during the sixteenth century. It was a time when the New World (North and South America) was being discovered and claimed by the greedy and sometimes cruel European nations.

It was also a time when the most rich and powerful families of these countries had their eyes and minds on expanding their financial empires in the name of their royal rulers, and in doing so the kings and queens gave them a guarantee they would have their family names inscribed on cities, rivers, lakes and vast landmasses that were ready to be conquered.

So it was with the rich and powerful barons of France.

In France during this period, there was a man by the name of Baron Charles de la Rocque de Robeval who was very powerful. He knew full well the potential of the new land that lay on the other side of the Atlantic Ocean called the North and South Americas. The baron had made up his mind that he would be the first European to lay claim to this vast country of North America, in the name of France.

King Francois I of France had not yet made up his mind as to whether he should claim North America for France for fear of another bloody war. England was on the rampage and already claiming ownership of this new land. He was not interested in taking on the British in another war, however if there was another way, he was prepared to be part of it.

But this was not the case for Baron de Roberval, the most powerful businessman in France. The baron was not satisfied to sit idly by on the sideline and watch the New World slip into the hands of England and Spain. He knew that time was of the essence. The move to claim North America for France could not wait.

Some Frenchman would have to make a move in the name of France, with or without the king's blessing. Baron de Roberval made up his mind that he would be the one to do it. He decided he would put together a three-ship expedition and send it to the New World.

The baron had a few things in his favour. First, he was a very rich man. Money and resources were no obstacle. Secondly, his brother, Jean Francois de la Rocque de Roberval, was an admiral with the French Navy, had great influence with the King of France, and was the most feared admiral that sailed the seven seas. Thirdly, this would cost the French government nothing because the baron would be sailing as a private company, searching for possible riches and areas of colonization, with the protection of the French navy.

However the greatest asset the baron had in his favor was that his late wife was a relative of the king and fourth heir to the throne of France. For these reasons, the baron knew that the king would sanction his expedition without too much wrangling.

Admiral Jean Francois de Roberval was a cruel naval officer. History says he was the cruelest of his day, showing no mercy to anyone or anything. If anyone went against the orders of this tyrant they would pay. It didn't matter who it was or where they came from.

Historians say Roberval specialized in settling disputes between French, Spanish and Portuguese fishermen who fished along the shores of Newfoundland in the New World, and anywhere else. His reputation was known far and wide. Everyone was afraid of him, including the British.

Admiral de Roberval was not only feared on the high seas, he was also feared on the land, where he marched from town to town, killing and burning everything that lay in his pathway.

The baron had made up his mind. He was going to make a move on claiming North America for France and so he started the ball rolling. He wrote letters to his brother, the admiral, outlining what he had in mind and asking if he was interested. When the reply was positive he organized a dinner meeting and invited him to attend.

At the meeting in the dining room of Baron Roberval's castle, Admiral Roberval had two of his ship's captains accompany him. He didn't travel anywhere without them. When he went on a foreign voyage across the Atlantic, the ships departing for the New World would have these captains aboard. They were ferocious men.

The baron started the meeting by welcoming the naval party. "I am pleased and very excited to have the privilege of sponsoring this expedition that you are about to embark upon. I wish you every success," he said, adding with a smile, "We have the blessing of His Majesty the King."

The admiral offered his assurance that every navigational skill available to the navy would be practiced on the expedition.

The baron continued, "As I told you earlier, Jean, I had intended to accompany you on this expedition, however due to new developments that have risen within the last couple of days it will be impossible for me to accompany you to the New World."

The admiral pretended to be annoyed, but he was secretly relieved that his brother wasn't going on the expedition, as this would eliminate many problems. Admiral Roberval was like a fox, but he knew his brother was just as smart. He started to complain about not having someone on board to represent the Crown of France.

The baron held up his hand. "I know your concerns and have taken everything into consideration. The royal household will have a representative present," he said.

The admiral was surprised to hear this and wondered who it would be. Before he could ask who the royal traveler was going to be, the baron informed him that the king had commissioned a young princess to accompany the expedition to the New World.

The baron was silent for a moment as he looked at the three naval officers sitting across from him. He knew their reputations. They were veterans of most of France's later wars and had the scars to show for it. He noticed the two captains weren't looking at him. They were staring at the admiral who sat motionless, with his arms folded and his face expressionless.

"I am sending my daughter Marguerite on this expedition," the baron continued. "As you know, she is the fifth heir to the throne of France and will be a very good representative of our country. She is a champion swordswoman, having won the French national fencing championship twice in a row. She is also a marksperson in archery, having won several titles."

The admiral and his captains were silent.

"The king will be sending the papers concerning her commission tomorrow," said the baron. "Preparations are being made now for her departure. She will be accompanied by a trusted servant who will remain with her for the voyage."

The admiral said nothing as the baron continued, "My daughter is a seasoned sailor with great knowledge of the sea and is skilled in the art of sailing."

"I hope you know what you are getting your daughter into," said the admiral, as he shifted restlessly in his chair. "It's a man's world out there on the high seas. To send a woman on such a voyage is not a very good idea. We can offer protection, but being on a long voyage and away from her family for such a long time might not suit her. She may not be able to withstand the stormy ocean the same way as a man does." The admiral appeared to be very concerned, yet he was glad that his niece and not his brother would accompany the expedition to the New World. His young niece would fit better into his plan.

The baron looked at the three men. "My daughter is young and full of life and can take care of herself," he said. "And to tell you the truth, I will not be worried about her because I know I can trust her. I had a long talk with His Majesty a couple of days ago."

He paused to take a sip of wine from one of the glasses in front of him. "I told the king that we were going to send Marguerite with you on the voyage. He was very pleased, and said he knows she can make the trip successfully."

The admiral was not a fool. He knew that his brother had not been talking to the king. The king was at a secret meeting away from Paris and even if he wasn't away, Admiral Roberval knew that His Majesty would never discuss sending his naval ships on any kind of expedition without having him present.

However he said nothing more to his brother in the presence of his two most senior naval captains. If truth be told, he didn't care who went on the expedition as long as he or she behaved themselves and as long as his brother financed the trip. The admiral was anxious to get off the land and under sail, especially on a voyage to the New World.

"When will we start preparing for the voyage?" he asked his brother.

"You will start immediately, as early as tomorrow. It is hoped that you will return to France before the first fall of snow," said the baron.

"I'll have to have a meeting with the Admiralty at once," said the admiral.

"Yes," agreed the baron. "We will travel together to Paris tomorrow. I will send a carriage to pick you up in the morning."

"Good," said the admiral. "We will then talk further about Marguerite going on the voyage with us. We will also discuss the land that you will acquire for France in the New World."

After dinner, the four men drank to the voyage and shook hands before taking their leave of each other.

It took two months for Admiral Roberval to get his three ships ready for the voyage to the New World. Many things had to be gathered and taken care of for the twelve to eighteen months they would be gone. The captain of each vessel was responsible for outfitting his ship with everything from the dishes on the tables to the sails that flew on the masthead. Everything from the food the crews would eat to the water they would drink would be stored on board in its proper place. Stores of clothing would be brought aboard and put in storage. Ships' carpenters would stack tools and repair materials in the vessel's warehouse. It was a busy two months making the ships ready.

The admiral recruited new men and officers for the voyage. He took care to select a crew able to fight if the need ever arose. Accompanying him as well would be a contingent of army soldiers who were highly trained and carefully selected.

There would be a commanding officer (major) and two lieutenants in charge of the soldiers, all of whom took their orders from the supreme commander, Admiral de Roberval.

Baron de Roberval was also a very busy man during this time. He had to oversee the group he had put in place to get things ready for the long Atlantic voyage that his daughter Marguerite and her maid would be taking to the New World.

It was a very exciting time for the baron. He could hardly sleep at night, thinking about the vast land beyond the sea that would have his name stamped on it forever. Just imagine, generations to come would write about and live in the nation of Roberval!

The baron knew his daughter would be the one who would put a brand on the whole of North America for France. And his name would stand out in history as one of the greatest Frenchmen of all times. For these reasons, the baron spared nothing in making his preparations.

At the naval yard in St Malo, where the ships were being made ready, he had a group of men build a specially designed boat for taking Marguerite ashore. It was twenty-two feet long and nine feet wide with sides four feet high. It was constructed of oak and fully equipped.

When the baron designed this after-boat he had it loaded with enough supplies to last many months, just in case there was ever a need to abandon ship. Lockers built along the sides of the boat held an assortment of tools. The baron made sure nothing was forgotten in the event they might have to abandon ship.

He also had one of his long time employees assigned to the voyage. Violet Chalifoux was a woman from the west country of Normandy who had nursed Marguerite from the time she was an infant. She cared for her as she would her own child, never letting her out of her sight for a second, teaching her manners and helping her with all aspects of life, especially with her education. The baron trusted Violet to look after all the needs of his daughter on the expedition.

As well, Violet had the responsibility of writing a private daily diary, which she would deliver to him upon the return to France.

Admiral Jean Francois de Roberval gave orders to his captains that the crews of every ship under his command would be aboard a week before sailing. This was to make sure that each sailor and soldier learned what was expected of him, and was familiar with the workings of everything on the ship. The admiral's order applied to Marguerite and her maid too. There were no exceptions and the baron knew that.

Anyone new aboard was made aware that Admiral Roberval didn't tolerate any misbehaving on his ships. Everyone knew he had a reputation as the cruelest man that ever lived.

Meanwhile, the baron put everyone in his castle to work at getting his daughter ready for the expedition to the New World. He hired the best people he could find to put together what she would need, including clothes and footwear for all occasions. She had the finest of everything. Marguerite had clothing enough to last for a year; her maid had the same. The baron made sure his daughter had all she needed to ensure her comfort and safety on the long voyage.

Marguerite was the only child born to Baron Charles and Lady Cynthia de Roberval. When Lady Cynthia died after giving birth, Baron Charles named the baby Marguerite after her great grandmother. That was her mother's final request.

The baron did not re-marry.

The night before Marguerite left Paris to head for the naval port of St. Malo in the English Channel, her father asked her to come to his inner chamber. He said he wanted a private talk with her. When they were seated he told her that he had something to give her. A package sat on the table in front of him wrapped in a purple velvet cloth. It was obvious to Marguerite this was something she had never seen before. She looked at it in wonderment. What could it be?

Her father talked to her about her long voyage, and warned her about the dangers of the sea. "You're not a child any more, indeed if you ever were. We have always said that you were all grown up from the time you were ten years old," he said. He wondered if she knew what he was trying to tell her. "You are going on a long voyage with hundreds of young men, all of whom will likely be attracted to you, so be very careful."

"Papa, I am not a child and I can take care of myself," Marguerite said indignantly. "I know the rules aboard these naval ships, especially on the ships that Uncle Jean commands."

The baron had confidence in his daughter and said no more.

Marguerite realized her father hadn't called her into his office to tell her to be careful; she had heard all that before. She knew there was something more.

The baron cleared his throat. "Marguerite," he said. "There is something I have to give you before you leave." He reached for the package on the table and she watched as he carefully unwrapped it. When the velvet cloth was removed, it revealed a golden jewelry case. "This has not been opened for many years, cherie," he said, "not since your mother died."

When he opened the cover of the jewelry case, Marguerite saw a beautiful golden ring inside. It had one large diamond in the centre and three on each side. It was the most beautiful ring that she had ever seen. "It's yours, cherie," her father said as he pushed the jewelry case towards her. "Take it, and put it on."

Marguerite was speechless as she stared at the ring. "Papa," she finally asked, "Where did this come from?"

"It's your mother's ring. I gave it to her the night she promised to marry me. It belonged to my grandmother. My mother wore it, then your mother, and now it's yours." The baron paused for a moment before continuing, "No one knows for sure where it came from. There's an inscription in Latin, but the lettering is so worn that no one has ever been able to read it."

Marguerite took the ring out of its case and put it on her finger. It fit her perfectly. "There's a saying that goes with that ring, Marguerite," said her father. "My grandmother used to say that if you are wearing that ring when you die you will go to heaven."

"Well, in that case I will never take it off," Marguerite said in a serious tone of voice.

"The ring will bring you back to me safely and with a job well done. Wear it for my sake," said her father, as they got up from the table and left the room.

The carriage carrying Marguerite and Violet arrived in St. Malo late in the evening. Marguerite led the way followed by three cargo carriages, each loaded with hers and Violet's travel luggage. When they arrived at the pier they were greeted by a group of drunken soldiers and sailors, all whooping it up on the dock next to the gangway.

As they drew nearer, they heard fiddle music and the loud singing of an old French ballad. Some sailors were dancing wildly, while others were clapping their hands and yelling for the dancers to pick up the pace. Marguerite noticed that some of the dancers were soldiers. She suspected they were members of the crews that were sailing to the New World with her uncle.

The carriage drivers felt quite comfortable leaving the women amongst these men. It was well known that every man who sailed with Admiral

Roberval was fearful of his harsh discipline and would obey his orders without question. The drivers knew there would be no trouble from the admiral's men.

As the four carriages pulled up to the side of the ship, the music and dancing stopped. The men stood and stared as the carriage drivers dismounted. No one knew that two women, one a young princess, would be sailing with them on their long voyage. Only the captain and his officers knew anything about it.

The sailors were shocked when they saw the women climb from the carriage, but no one spoke. The women were met by two stewards and the captain, and escorted aboard.

Marguerite had a great quantity of luggage. She had five large trunks and two barrels packed with just about everything. She also had three cases and a wooden crate filled with linen such as had never been seen in the New World. There was as well a large box filled with gifts for any natives they might possibly encounter.

A long line of men formed, and in a very short time the carriages were emptied and all the freight was loaded aboard the ship. The music and dancing then started up again.

This story here takes on a different twist, and as it is with every true and adventurous tale drama seems to be the rule of the day.

In the northeastern part of France, in the great city of Lille, there lived a very successful businessman who owned a chain of tailor shops. Henry de Val Cormier designed clothes for all the rich and famous in France. He was well known, rich, and highly respected.

He had one son known as Pierre de Val, and this young man was a bit of a rabble-rouser. When Pierre was a boy he learned to play the fiddle just like his father, and at the age of ten he knew every sea ballad sung in France. When Pierre was still a young lad his father sent him to Absam in Austria to learn how to play the violin properly.

After he returned Pierre became well known around the northeastern part of France, singing and playing at the huge garden parties that were held around the countryside. Some called him a highwayman because, even though he was never known to rob anyone, he was familiar with everyone who rode with the outlaw gangs.

His singing and playing made him very popular, especially with the ladies. Young Pierre was having a grand time around the northern part of France. But his freewheeling ways soon made him very unpopular with the older generation.

One day, his father sat him down and had a man-to-man talk with him. It was put forth that Pierre should leave home and venture out into another field for a while rather then work in one of the tailor shops. This would hopefully slow him down and prepare him for the day when he would take over his father's business.

It was decided that Pierre would go into the military, the army. He agreed, and off he went to military college to become an officer.

After a year's training, he was a well-trained soldier, and graduated as a first lieutenant in the French army. He became highly skilled in archery and was quite a swordsman. He still played the fiddle and sang, and continued to be a very popular figure wherever he went, especially with the ladies.

It is not known if his commanding officers were intimidated by his popularity, or were just plain jealous of him. All we know is that he was assigned to the Roberval expedition, bound for the New World as a young army lieutenant.

Lieutenant Pierre de Val Cormier arrived at the port of St. Malo, on the north coast of France. The man-of-war he was joining was tied up at the pier. He walked along by three or four ships until he came to Number Three pier. He gazed at the huge hulk all decked out in flags and wondered if it was a national holiday or if something else of interest was going on. Then he noticed the beehive of activity around the ship and realized it was being prepared for a trip across the great Atlantic Ocean.

His orders stated he was to join a navel contingent and would be going to the New World for a year. He would be one of eighty soldiers, taking their orders from Army Major George Jacques. Pierre carried a duffle bag and a packsack with a pair of leather boots tied to the outside.

The naval guards at the companionway saw the rank on his shoulder and saluted him when he came to the rail. He didn't salute back. They asked to see his papers and his sailing orders. Pierre put down his duffel bag and produced the necessary paperwork.

One of the guards recognized his name and asked him if he was the fiddle player from Lille. Pierre said he was, and was surprised when the guard told him that he was from the same city and had heard him play.

The guard asked Pierre if he had his fiddle with him. He said if he did he was looking forward to hearing him sing and play. "I certainly do have my fiddle with me," laughed Pierre. "We won't be seeing a woman for more than a year so I might as well have my fiddle." The guard laughed and said no more as Pierre went aboard the ship.

The great wooden ship that loomed in the sunny afternoon was a sight to behold. Pierre was used to seeing horses and wagons and equipment carried and pulled around by men and horses. But this massive ship had sheets of iron plating bolted to the sides and large cannons lining the sides.

When he stepped aboard, he was met by the duty officer who welcomed him, escorted him to his living quarters, and followed up with a tour of the ship.

"This will be your home for how long we don't know," the officer said when they arrived back at Pierre's quarters. The young army lieutenant said nothing as he went in and closed the door.

The flagship of Admiral de Roberval was a busy place. The crew was assigned, doing whatever was required to get the ship ready for the ocean voyage.

The admiral had not yet arrived; he usually came aboard a day or so before the ship sailed. However, no one could trust Roberval. He was known to steal aboard ship just to test the sentries. If he got aboard without being challenged, someone's head would roll.

Pierre de Val went to the officer's mess after he had his bags unpacked. He met the army major he knew and had served with. They were glad to meet again and shook hands.

"I'm happy to once again meet the famous tailor's son," Major Jacques said as he invited Pierre to sit at his table.

Pierre laughed. He was aware that most of the army officers knew about his womanizing but chose not to talk about it.

"I don't know if the old man is famous or not," he said, "but there's one thing I can say about him and that is he has produced many undergarments for well known French women. If that makes him famous, then so be it."

There was a roar of laughter from almost everyone in the mess. Then a young navy lieutenant sitting not far from Pierre's table made a wisecrack.

"If making women's drawers makes your father famous, then what makes you famous, sonny?" he asked with a smirk.

Everyone was silent. Pierre looked at the officer for a moment, and then said, "I get my fame from personally delivering the drawers at night."

Everyone laughed again, everyone except the young navy lieutenant.

"We're going on a long voyage, Sir. You may regret that remark," he said as he rose from the table and stood and stared at Pierre de Val.

Pierre said nothing. Major Jacques heard what the officer had said and so did the rest of the officers. The young naval officer looked mad as he stomped angrily out the door.

Word spread quickly throughout the ship that Pierre de Val was aboard and going on the Atlantic voyage. Most of the crew wondered if they would hear him sing and play his fiddle.

The soldiers had their quarters up front in the bottom of the ship. This was not the best place aboard ship. When the vessel got into rough weather, these soldiers would get quite a rough ride. The army major and the other army lieutenant slept with the rest of the naval officers in quarters just below deck at the centre of the ship. Pierre requested a bunk with the lower ranks in the head of the ship and his request was granted.

After dinner was served and the day's activities had settled down, the troops asked Pierre if he would play some tunes on his fiddle. He agreed. The captain of the ship asked if they would go on the dock instead of staying aboard, saying it would be a better place for a hoedown on a warm summer's evening.

Some carpenters were put to work making a small stage, and word was sent to the other two ships that Pierre de Val from Lille was doing a show and everyone was invited to come and join in.

Pierre had no fear of crowds. He was used to playing and singing for a large audience. He could sing most of the sea shanties and country ballads popular around France at that time. He could, in fact, play any tune he'd ever heard.

The show started around seven with a rousing fiddle tune, followed by an old country ballad about a highwayman running from a sheriff along the French countryside.

Everything was going full swing until around nine-thirty when the carriages with Marguerite and her maid arrived. It was quite a surprise for Pierre and everyone else to see two women going aboard the ship that was preparing to sail across the Atlantic.

Pierre didn't stop playing, but from the corner of his eye he watched the women climb out of the carriage. His eyes feasted upon beautiful Marguerite as she stepped down onto the wooden dock. Everybody was looking at her and at her maid, a very elegant looking lady.

Pierre strummed soft music as Marguerite's eyes met his. She smiled at him and he smiled back and nodded. He realized he was hooked on this raving beauty, whoever she was.

The captain and several officers, including the young officer Pierre had words with at the officers' mess, were there to meet Marguerite and help her aboard ship. They practically carried her aboard in their eagerness to help.

Pierre de Val knew that this young lady was not just another officer's daughter going on a voyage to keep her father happy. He knew this was someone of great importance for the captain and officers to be waiting for her arrival. But who could she be? He would have to find out.

Marguerite went to her quarters as the sound of the violin played on. She was attracted to the violin music and the man playing; she had made eye contact with him.

Her quarters were at the rear section of the ship and on deck level. Marguerite and her maid occupied two bedrooms, a dining room and a lounge with a small kitchen off the dining room. Shuttered windows opened to the side of the ship giving them lots of light whenever weather conditions allowed them to be open.

Their luggage was put into a storage room next to their living quarters. Everything was set up for the convenience of the two women going to the New World.

Marguerite took off her long riding boots and short coat. She asked the steward who helped with her luggage to open a window and let some fresh air into the rooms. As he opened the window the sound of violin music came floating in. She went to the window and looked out at the huge crowd on the dock.

"Who is the man on the fiddle?" she asked the steward.

"That's Pierre de Val from the city of Lille. He's with the army," he answered.

Marguerite had heard of Pierre de Val as he was popular in Paris as well as in the north of France.

"Is he going on this voyage with us, I mean on this ship?" she asked.

"Yes, Mademoiselle. He is part of the fighting force the admiral has with him just in case we have to fight the British after we get to the New World," said the steward.

"The New World should be a very interesting place," said Marguerite with a laugh, feeling a thrill to be part of it.

The music and singing went on till late in the night.

After she and Violet were served a late dinner in their dining room, Marguerite sat by the window out of sight of everyone and listened to the music and singing. There was no doubt she was intrigued by the young army lieutenant with the fiddle. She had high hopes of meeting him.

CHAPTER 2

Pierre de Val Cormier

Those who manned the three ships that Admiral de Roberval commanded were picked from among the many thousands of sailors making up the French navy. They were experienced men, seasoned and reliable.

They were all aware that the admiral was a cruel and merciless man. He was also a tough man who cared for nothing or nobody. There were no idle times aboard the admiral's ships. When the men were not carrying out their shipboard duties they were training or taking part in various competitions. And so it was, as the three ships were tied to the naval dock in St. Malo, competition was the order of the day.

Pierre de Val was a fearless man with a sword. He had taken part in many fencing duels in the French army and had won.

It has not been documented, but it is suspected that Admiral Roberval had heard of him and had the army high command post him aboard his ship for the voyage. Pierre would fit in with the admiral's plans.

Everyone, especially the military, enjoys competition. Whether it's farming, fishing or fighting, people always want to compete against each other and it makes no difference if it is in peacetime or in wartime. And now, with two fencing champions aboard the admiral's ship, everyone was looking forward to seeing them compete.

Marguerite told Violet she wanted to meet the fiddle player. She said she didn't want anyone to know about their meeting, and it would have to be done secretly.

"Somehow I will have to get word to him and arrange a meeting place," she told the older woman. But she didn't know how she was going to do it. Anyway, this wouldn't be the night because she and Violet were busy unpacking and making their quarters look as much like home as possible.

The first night they spent aboard ship was a comfortable one. They were tired and slept soundly. The next morning they awoke to the sun shining through their window.

At 8 a.m. they heard a bell ringing. Violet went to the door and found it was the steward. "The captain wants to know if you ladies would like to have breakfast with him and some of his officers in his private dining room," he said.

Violet invited him to step inside and said she would ask her mistress.

"Yes," said Marguerite. "We will have breakfast with the captain. It will be a good way to get to meet some of the people aboard."

Violet told the steward they would meet him at nine. She said they would like to have an escort because they weren't familiar with the ship. He told them there would be an escort at their door to take them to the captain's dining room a few minutes before 9 a.m.

Just before nine, the two women arrived in Captain Fonteneau's dining room, but he wasn't alone. At the table sat Army Major George Jacques and two naval lieutenants.

"Good morning, ladies," said Captain Fonteneau. "It is our pleasure to have you dining with us on such a fine morning."

The captain told the women how beautiful they looked, especially among a group of rugged military men. The group laughed.

"We will be looking forward to having you gentlemen dining with us between the Old and the New World," said Marguerite.

"It will always be a pleasure," said the captain.

The steward arrived to take their orders. They all ate a very good breakfast and chatted occasionally.

After breakfast, Major Jacques asked Marguerite if it was true that she was the fencing champion of France.

She told him that it was true, "I have been in competition for over five years now and have done quite well," she said.

"My, what a coincidence," he said. "We have the army fencing champion here aboard ship with us."

The captain was surprised and spoke up quickly, "Who might that be?" he asked.

"Why of course, none other than the fiddler himself, Pierre de Val," said Major Jacques.

"The fiddler, you mean the one who sang and played the fiddle last night, is the French army's best swordsman? Are you serious?" said one of the young naval officers.

"I certainly am serious," said the major.

Everyone looked at Marguerite, who was smiling.

"Maybe we could match up Her Highness and the fiddle player for a fencing duel," said the captain jokingly.

"It might be fun," said Marguerite. "If I am asked I would certainly accept the challenge."

Major Jacques looked surprised. "Have you met Lieutenant Pierre de Val, Your Highness?" he asked.

"No I have not," she replied.

"Have you heard him play and sing?" the captain asked.

"No," Marguerite replied.

"Last night he played on the dock and drew a large crowd that included townspeople. It's good for publicity," said the captain.

Major Jacques laughed and said, "If you are serious about having a match with him then maybe we could arrange it."

"We have to be careful, gentlemen," said the captain. "I don't think the admiral would be in favor of a duel taking place without his consent."

"We wouldn't be able to have a match today because Lieutenant de Val has gone out with his company on an exercise. He left for the countryside early this morning," said Major Jacques. Turning towards Marguerite, he asked, "Are you a horseman, or I might ask, are you a horsewoman?"

The captain and officers laughed.

The major quickly spoke up. "I mean, Your Highness. Are you familiar with horseback riding?"

"Yes, I do a lot of riding, my father owns a stable with good breeds. We ride all the time," said Marguerite.

"Well then," said Major Jacques, "In about an hour I will be riding out to visit the fiddler, as everyone calls him, and his company. If it pleases the captain, you can come along with me for a ride. It's better than being cooped up aboard ship all day. At least you will have another day on land."

The captain looked at Marguerite and saw her eyes light up.

"It will be entirely up to her, she will be under your protection, Major," said the captain.

"Thank you, Captain, thank you Major, I will go immediately and get dressed in my riding outfit. I brought it with me," Marguerite said as she quickly stood up. She told Violet to stay and visit with the captain. She said she knew where her things were and could take care of everything herself. She then excused herself and left the table.

Two saddled horses waited on the dock as Major Jacques and Marguerite walked down the gangway from the ship. All eyes were upon her. Word had spread throughout the ship that she was a princess and was going to the New World.

15

The two men holding her horse were preparing to help her mount. She told them this was not necessary. "I can get on this horse myself, thank you," she said as she took the reins, quickly putting one foot in the stirrup and mounting with ease. It was obvious to everyone that this young lady was quite familiar with horseback riding.

The major got on his horse with a little struggle, but in less then a minute they were out of sight, trotting through the city of St. Malo, watching the activities around them. It was a beautiful morning; the sounds and sights were great to behold.

"Where are you stationed, Major?" Marguerite asked.

"In Paris, at the garrison," he told her.

"I suppose you do a lot of horseback riding?" she said.

"I did at one time, but in the last few years I haven't done as much due to office duties," he said.

"How far do we have to go to meet your men?" she asked.

He looked at the countryside ahead of them, then at his pocket watch. "Oh, I would say about a forty-five minute ride," he replied.

As they rode along, watching the cattle grazing in the fields, he told her about the different battles that had taken there years ago.

"There is a little country inn further up the road where we have to stop, if it's all right with you. I have to pay the lodging bill for some of the troops who stayed there a few nights ago while enroute to the ship," he said.

"It's quite all right with me, Major," she replied.

"Good," he said. "We should be there in about ten minutes."

As they rode to the inn, he told her it was owned and operated by a lady named Madame Frances Palchier whom everyone loved. "We can trust her," he said. "She knows how to keep her mouth shut."

In about ten minutes they turned off on a side road that was almost covered by overhanging trees.

They rode on for about two hundred yards when Marguerite saw a brightly colored brick building with a sign over the entrance that said, "St. Malo Country Inn."

"This is the place, Marguerite," said the major. "We have to go to the back of the building where the hitching rail for the horses is located."

They went to the back of the building and dismounted. The major took the saddlebag containing his papers from his horse and placed it over his arm.

A pleasant looking woman in her thirties came to the door and opened it after hearing the sound of the horse's hooves.

When she saw the major she called to him. "Bonjour George, how are you this morning? Good to see you again." Coming over with outstretched arms, she hugged him and kissed him.

When she saw Marguerite she stepped back, puzzled.

"Who is the lovely lady?" she asked.

"Madame Palchier, I want you to meet Her Highness Marguerite de la Roberval," said Major Jacques.

"It is a pleasure to meet such a beautiful lady," she said.

"Thank you, Madame Palchier," said Marguerite.

"Come in, please come in," she invited. "Have you had breakfast yet, Major?" she asked.

Jacques replied that they had.

"Then you will have a glass of wine. Please sit down and make yourself at home and take off your coats."

The major and Marguerite removed their coats. They were warm after being in the saddle for about an hour and it felt good to take their coats off.

While the innkeeper was getting the wine, a young girl came into the dining room with a large fruitcake on a tray and placed it on the table. She brought plates and cutlery for three. Madame Palchier returned with the wine and poured three glasses full.

"Please help yourself to cake," she said as she seated herself next to the major.

Marguerite could tell by the way the innkeeper rolled her eyes at Major Jacques that they were more than casual acquaintances. When Marguerite wasn't looking directly at them she could hear them whispering quietly to each other.

"Major, tell me, where is the young fiddle player, is he back aboard the ship?" asked the innkeeper.

"No, he's not far from here. He's just down the road at the range, doing an exercise," said the major.

"We love his music and singing. He should come back before he leaves," she said.

"I don't know about that because the admiral will be here soon and then no one leaves the ship," said the major.

"Let him come before the admiral comes, just for one night," she begged.

"We will see," said Major Jacques.

Madame Palchier looked at Marguerite and asked, "Do you like the fiddle player's singing and playing, Your Highness?"

"I have never heard him sing or play, as I just arrived here late last night. I may meet him aboard ship as we go on our journey," said Marguerite.

"You will love him, he's a darling," Madame Palchier said with a giggle.

After they had finished their wine and cake, Major Jacques opened his saddlebag and gave the innkeeper several coins to pay for the soldiers' lodging.

He and Marguerite thanked Madame Palchier for her hospitality and promised they would return.

As they were leaving the table, Madame Palchier asked the major to come inside for a minute. He excused himself and did as she asked.

Marguerite put on her coat and prepared to leave the dining room. In a couple of minutes, Major Jacques hurriedly returned and followed Marguerite outside.

CHAPTER 3

Meeting the Cavalier

It only took fifteen minutes on horseback for Major Jacques and Marguerite to reach the firing range where the company of soldiers was having an exercise. There was a tent pitched near the entrance of the range. The two stopped there and dismounted.

Some soldiers saw the major and saluted. When they observed Marguerite with him they took a second look and smiled.

One of the soldiers, a sergeant, came over to where the major was standing.

"Good morning, Sir" he said, as he saluted.

"Bonjour, Sergeant," the major replied with a salute.

"We have been busy all morning, things are going well. We have sent a platoon up into the hills scouting the area as you suggested. It should be a good exercise. Lieutenant Balfour has gone with them," said the sergeant.

"I have some new orders here for the company. Is Lieutenant Pierre de Val around?" said the major.

"Yes Sir, he is not far from here, I will get him," said the sergeant.

In a few minutes Pierre de Val came into view, heading towards them. He was in uniform and had been working hard all morning. As he got closer it was obvious he was staring at the woman standing next to the major.

"Good morning, Sir, good morning, Mademoiselle," he said as he saluted.

"Bonjour, Lieutenant," said Major Jacques, returning the salute.

"Bonjour," said Marguerite in a friendly tone of voice.

Pierre could hardly keep his eyes off her because she was so stunningly beautiful.

"Lieutenant, this is Marguerite de Roberval. She is a member of our expedition, and, Your Highness, this is Lieutenant Pierre de Val," said Jacques.

Pierre took off his gloves and shook hands with her.

"How do you do, Your Highness?" he asked.

"I am fine, thank you, and how are you?" said Marguerite.

"Wonderful, a good morning to be alive, thank you," said Pierre.

Marguerite looked Pierre over from head to toe. Ever since last night when she saw him playing the fiddle at a distance, she had seen him every time she closed her eyes. And now here he was standing only a few feet away, looking at her.

"Lieutenant, I have brought some new orders with me that you should take a look at," said Major Jacques.

"Good," said Pierre.

The major walked to his horse to retrieve his saddle bag and was surprised to find that it was not there; he looked a second time and found nothing.

"Where is my saddle bag?" he asked, sounding concerned and puzzled. He looked at Marguerite for an answer, but she had none.

"I must have lost it along the way," he said.

"I think I know where it is, Sir," Marguerite said after a moment's thought. "You left it in the Country Inn. It was on the back of the chair next to where you were sitting."

"You may be right, but I am not sure. I am going to have to go back and see where it is," said the major.

Pierre could hardly look at the major for laughing.

" Major," he said, as Jacques went for his horse. "You stay here and I'll go to the inn and take a look. I can ride faster than you."

"Alright," replied the major. "And be sure to have a good look along the road just in case I dropped it."

"I can go with you if you'd like. Four eyes are always better then two," said Marguerite.

"Certainly, if it's okay with Major Jacques," said Pierre.

"It's fine with me," the major said.

Pierre went to the back of the tent area and got his horse. It was a large black stallion, all saddled and ready to go.

"Major, you can rest in the tent. We shouldn't be long," said Pierre.

Pierre could hardly believe what was happening. Here he was riding in the countryside with this beautiful girl by his side.

When they were out of sight, Pierre stopped and held up his hand. Marguerite stopped also.

"Do you think the major left his saddle bags at the Country Inn, Your Highness?" he asked Marguerite.

"Are you talking to me, Lieutenant?" she said. "If so, you will have to call me Marguerite."

"And you can call me Pierre," he said.

She nudged her horse closer and held out her gloved hand.

"Take off your glove," Pierre said.

She removed it.

Pierre removed his glove and held out his hand. She took it and they shook hands. When he leaned over and gave her a hug she did not resist him.

"You were asking me if I thought Major Jacques had left his saddle bag at the inn. I am most certainly sure that he did because when he returned from the back room he came directly to where I was standing holding his coat and ready to go," said Marguerite.

Pierre started to laugh. "That old dog still thinks he's in his twenties. And Madame Palchier is still in love with him," he said.

"I heard them whispering behind my back, and I thought I saw him pulling his hands away from her when I turned around," Marguerite said gleefully.

"She is a good woman and you can trust her with your life. That's why we go there whenever we are here in St. Malo," said Pierre.

The two of them continued on their way to the inn.

When they arrived, they saw Madame Palchier standing in the doorway. She was smiling and waving for them to come in.

They dismounted and went inside.

"Pierre de Val," said Madame Palchier as she ran to greet him with a hug. "I love you. But where's Major Jacques? I thought he would be back for his saddle bag."

"The major is getting old now, cherie, he can hardly do anything anymore," said Pierre with a laugh.

"Ah, ah, you speak for yourself," she said, grinning.

She looked at Marguerite with an embarrassed look.

"Don't mind him, Your Highness, he always has a wisecrack when he sees me," she said.

Marguerite smiled. "Please call me Marguerite from now on," she told the innkeeper.

Madame Palchier went into the kitchen and brought out the saddlebag and placed it on the table.

"Marguerite, would you like to go to one of the rooms and freshen up a little?" she asked.

"Yes, I think I would like that," Marguerite answered.

"I am going out to the garden for a few minutes, so Pierre, help yourself to some ale," said the wise old woman with a wink.

"You are a saint, Madame," said Pierre.

She left immediately with her watering pot, just as Pierre and Marguerite headed for the stairs.

CHAPTER 4

Heading Out To The New World

Admiral Roberval stood on the bridge of the flagship viewing the three-ship expedition. All was going very well this morning, under a gray sky. The wind was partly in their favor with a stiff breeze blowing from the northeast.

"If this wind keeps up all day in the same direction, we should be away from the English Channel by sunset, and out into the Atlantic Ocean," said the admiral.

Captain Fonteneau nodded his agreement. "I wonder if the English are on the rampage again in the north?" he asked.

Admiral Roberval didn't care to answer. He was heading for the New Found Land, as it was now called, and no one was going to catch him.

He knew what he had to do. He would sail to the southwest coast of Ireland near Mizzen Head, just south of Bounty Bay, and steer a straight course of 51.5 degrees dead west. If he kept the ships on course with him they would sight the northern tip of the New Found Land.

If all went well, in three to four weeks they should see land. He had been there before.

Pierre de Val was spending a lot of his spare time playing his fiddle and singing, entertaining the soldiers and sailors aboard ship.

Everyone was having a grand time, including Marguerite. At night when everything was quiet, Pierre had a way of sneaking into Marguerite's bedroom. He was trained in reconnaissance by the military, and was an expert in moving around at night. He had a passage from the front section of the ship, where the women's quarters were, all the way back under deck to the rear.

This continued for some time. Violet knew what was going on and on several occasions she warned Marguerite about what would happen if the admiral found out.

"You know what your uncle said, Marguerite, when he came aboard? He said he wouldn't tolerate anyone disobeying his orders. And you know he has done cruel and unforgivable things to people who disobeyed his orders," said Violet.

"Pierre won't get caught. He knows what he is doing. He's an expert at moving around silently without being seen," said Marguerite.

"But, Marguerite, that's not where the problem lies. The thing is, there are young officers aboard who are attracted to you. I have seen them looking at you and jealousy is a deadly weapon."

Marguerite knew Violet was right. But how could she not see Pierre every night?

"I suppose I'll have to tell him not to come anymore," she said.

Violet observed the young woman; she was as concerned about her as if she was her own flesh and blood. She knew this young Lieutenant Pierre de Val was daring, handsome, talented, and everything a young woman desired.

"Marguerite, there is something that I must discuss with you that you may not agree with," said Violet.

"Yes, what is it?" asked Marguerite.

"Suppose you become pregnant? There are no physicians, nurses or midwives in the New World," said the worried Violet.

For a moment Marguerite said nothing. She knew that Violet was right; she was playing a dangerous game.

"Okay," she said. "I'll tell Pierre he will have to stop coming until we get to the New World, for our sake and for his."

Violet was glad Marguerite was going to put caution ahead of all else.

The young naval officer who'd had the argument with Pierre de Val was watching every move that Pierre made. He watched him morning and night. He had his eye on Marguerite and was determined to get her attention one way or another, but Pierre stood in the way and something would have to be done.

For some time he had been setting the trap.

He watched and waited until he saw Pierre going to Marguerite's room, then he made his move. He went to the captain and told him what was going on.

"I have proof," he told the captain. "Others are aware of it too," he lied.

The captain knew he would have to tell the admiral before another crewmember did. If the admiral learned of the courtship before he told him about it he knew he would be in trouble. What could he do? He was fond of the young fiddle player and didn't want to do him any harm. But the young naval officer was mad with jealousy and determined to cause trouble. So, the captain knew he had only one choice.

There was no doubt that Roberval would be a very angry man. The admiral was more than capable of throwing the two women overboard, right into the cold Atlantic.

But the captain knew, to save his own neck, he would have to do something.

He called the young naval officer into his quarters and had another talk to him about the situation.

"Are you aware of what could happen if the admiral decided to do something out of the ordinary to that army officer?" he asked. "Pierre de Val is a very popular man and it could start a riot aboard ship. Suppose the admiral decided to throw him overboard?"

The young naval officer was dead set on causing trouble; he didn't care. If he couldn't have Marguerite, then the army lieutenant wouldn't get her either. He said if the captain did not go to the admiral then he would report the matter to him personally. With that said, Captain Fonteneau felt he had no other choice but to go to Admiral Roberval and report what the officer had told him.

CHAPTER 5

Caught in the Act

Although he was downhearted about what he had to do, the captain went to the admiral's quarters. He found him sitting in his chair, reading.

Roberval had a good view of the ship, because all of the housing was at the rear. The admiral worked and lived on the right side of the upper section; Marguerite's quarters were directly below his.

Captain Fonteneau was invited in and told to sit at the oak table that served as a chart table, a card table and a dining table. The table stood in the center of the room.

The admiral knew the captain was there to see him on business. Turning towards the table, Roberval put down his book and placed his glasses on top.

"State your case, Captain," he said.

The captain was nervous, but nevertheless stated his case. He knew that Marguerite was the admiral's niece and the end consequences could be drastic for someone.

"I have had a report brought to me by one of our officers that there is a problem below decks, Sir," said the captain.

"A problem below decks. What is it?" the admiral demanded.

The captain didn't know for sure how the admiral was going to take it, so he decided to clear himself and make sure the blame for reporting this went to the right person.

"One of our officers came to me and told me about an incident. He threatened that if I didn't report it to you, he would," said the captain.

"Keep talking," said the admiral, sitting up straight.

The captain continued, "He says Lieutenant Pierre de Val, an army lieutenant and fiddle player, is having an affair with Her Highness, Marguerite de Roberval, Sir."

It is now very important to stop this story and go back to a meeting that Admiral de la Roberval had with an important French general a few months before leaving Paris. During the meeting, they discussed the possibility of driving the English out of Newfoundland for good. The general asked Roberval if he would be interested in making an attack upon the English colonists in Newfoundland instead of going off on some kind of expedition with a couple of women waving a flag and driving down a stake.

"We will be made fun of around the world," said the general. Roberval laughed and agreed with him.

The general was pleased that Roberval agreed, especially when it was his brother, "the great baron," as he called him, who was financing the voyage. But, before deciding anything, the general knew he would first have to meet with the French king.

Before the two men departed, the general asked Roberval how he would carry out an attack with two women aboard his ship. "How will we be able to explain this to the baron when we come back to France with Marguerite?" asked the general. "If the baron is not pleased, then someone's head will be on the chopping block."

"You leave all that to me, General," said Roberval with a grin. "I learned a lot from the Indians when I was in the New World."

The general later met with the king and, as he knew, King Francois was delighted about the plan and gave his blessing.

Now, talking to Captain Fonteneau, Roberval knew that this was his chance to get rid of the two women and anyone else who wanted to go with them and he set out to make a master plan.

"That army dog, the fiddle player," he sputtered.

"Yes, it's the fiddler, Sir," said the captain.

The admiral thought for a moment then stood and went to the window and looked out. He realized he would have to play the game if he was to get rid of the two women. He would have to be careful because the sailors and soldiers with him could talk when they got back to France.

When Roberval turned around, the captain saw a very angry looking man. The admiral walked over to the table and slammed his fist down hard and swore bitterly.

"What proof do you have, Captain?" he asked.

"I don't have any proof, Sir, only what the officer is reporting to me. He's saying that half of the ship's company knows about it."

"Go and get that officer and bring him to me immediately," shouted the admiral.

The captain went out the door, realizing that the admiral was a dangerous man. He was terrified of him.

The captain went to the bridge and called for the duty officer. When he arrived he told him to ask Naval Officer Marten to come to the bridge immediately. The duty officer rushed below and soon arrived back with the young man in tow.

"You and I have to go and see the admiral immediately, Officer Marten," said the captain.

"What does he want to see me about, Captain?" asked Marten.

"You know what it's all about; don't pretend otherwise," said the captain.

The four men on duty and the duty officer looked at the captain and then at the officer with puzzled looks.

"Button the front of your jacket and straighten your hair. You're going to see the admiral of the fleet," the not-so-happy captain told Marten.

"Yes Sir," answered Marten.

"Now," said the captain, "step over there for a moment while I talk to the duty officer."

Captain Fonteneau asked the duty officer if he had heard anything about an affair between one of the army officers and the young Princess Marguerite.

The duty officer looked puzzled and replied that he had not heard of anything and, as far as he knew, no one else had either. "We are certain nothing is going on," he said.

The captain and Officer Marten left for the admiral's quarters. When they knocked on the door, an unpleasant voice told them to enter. They came in, saluted, and stood to attention.

The young officer never thought he'd see the devil himself until the moment he looked into the face of Admiral de Roberval.

"Now, do you have a message for me, young man?" demanded the angry admiral.

For a moment Marten didn't know how to answer the question. "Message…Sir," he stammered.

"You reported an incident to the captain. Tell us about it," said the admiral.

"You mean about the lieutenant and Her Highness…well, yes Sir."

"Yes, Yes." The admiral nodded impatiently as he urged Marten to continue.

"I only know what I heard, Sir," said Marten. "Everyone is talking about it, that is, all the sailors down below are talking about it."

"Captain, when you left my quarters, did you ask anyone if they had heard anything about this matter?" asked the admiral.

"Yes, Sir. I asked the duty officer if he had heard anything and he told me he had not. The other men on bridge duty said the same," replied the captain.

"You go down below right now and bring up Madame Violet. Tell her I want to speak to her," yelled Roberval.

As the captain was leaving, the admiral stopped him and said, "No forget that. We'll watch for them and catch them in the act, because the Madame will deny it anyway. We'll only be wasting our time talking to her."

Marten was relieved but still frightened.

"You get out of here as fast as you can," the admiral said to him. "And Captain Fonteneau, I want you to confine this officer to his room until we get further information about the matter."

"Yes Sir," replied the captain, as Marten saluted and left.

"Now, Captain, you go and get Madame Violet and bring her up here to me immediately. I have changed my mind about speaking to her," Roberval said angrily.

The captain saluted and left.

When he was alone, Roberval sat in his chair and thought for a few moments. He knew there might be trouble. From what he'd seen and heard since he came on board, he knew that this Pierre de Val was a very popular man and well liked.

However, he wasn't going to let anyone run him. He figured the ships would be in sight of land in a week or less if the weather and wind stayed in his favour.

If he could get a confession from Violet, then he would decide what to do. This was playing right into his hands; he now had the opportunity to get rid of the two women.

It only took a few minutes for the captain to bring Madame Violet to the admiral's door.

"Come in," Roberval roared.

The door opened and the very distinguished looking Madame Violet entered with the captain.

For a moment Roberval was set back; he had not expected to see such an elegant looking lady.

"This is Madame Violet," said the captain. "And this is Admiral de Roberval, admiral of the fleet."

"My pleasure, Admiral de Roberval. I have heard your name at the castle many times," said Violet.

Roberval nodded curtly.

"What do you want to talk to me about, Admiral?" she asked.

"You are fully aware what I want to talk to you about, Madame, but I will get right to the point," said the admiral.

Violet looked at him with eyes that showed no fear, then asked, "Yes, my Lord Admiral, what is it?"

For a moment, the captain thought the admiral was going to hit her.

"I want to know what in the devil's name is going on right under my nose," Roberval said in a loud voice.

Violet looked surprised. "What is it you want to know, Admiral?" she asked.

"It has come to my attention that Pierre the fiddler has been sneaking into Marguerite's bedroom at night. Is this true? Tell me the truth?" the admiral roared.

Violet paused as she tried to find the right words to answer the question. She had heard how rude Roberval was and what he was capable of. After a moment, she looked at him and said, "Whether I admit it's true or false, obviously you have already decided that it's the truth."

The admiral folded his arms and looked at this woman. There was no doubt about it, she had all the answers. However, he wasn't finished yet.

"Let me ask you this, Madame, has the fiddle player ever been in your quarters...I mean in the rooms down below... since the two of you came aboard this ship?" he asked.

"Yes," she replied.

"And what was he doing there, may I ask?"

"We invited him to come and play his music, and it has been more then once," Violet said.

"Are you aware that there may be something else beside playing music going on between him and Her Highness?" asked the admiral.

"I cannot say that for fear of tainting someone's character, Sir," said Violet.

"I'm not going to ask you any more questions about this matter. I know what's been going on down below," the admiral said in a rage.

Violet didn't answer for fear of what he might do. She knew about his reputation as a mad man who was capable of anything.

"If this incident involved my sailors, do you know what I would do to them?" he said. "I would have them thrown into the ocean."

Violet did not reply for fear of getting the same treatment.

"You and that harlot are not going to get away with it. I'll decide what to do with both of you. The same goes for that army lieutenant. So now get out of my sight," he said as he leaned over and almost spit in her eye. "I don't want to see you again."

Violet said nothing as she turned and walked out the door.

After she left, the admiral went into a terrible rage. The captain just stood and watched as Roberval kicked over his big armchair, then picked up a vase and smashed it against the wall. There was glass everywhere.

"Bring me that army dog, bring me that army dog!" he yelled.

The captain didn't know what to do or say. He held up his hand to get the admiral's attention. "My Lord Admiral, may I say something, please?" he quietly asked.

"What do you want?" the admiral asked, straining the cords in his neck.

"Are you asking me to go and arrest the army lieutenant and bring him to you immediately?" asked the captain.

"Yes, go get him and bring him here to me now. He won't live to see the sun go down," said the angry admiral.

Captain Fonteneau was very concerned. He had never questioned the admiral's orders before, but this order had to be given some thought. The admiral was asking him to go and arrest a member of the army, which was not under his jurisdiction. Suppose the lieutenant refused? There were ninety troops aboard this ship, all trained soldiers of the French army and fully armed. They were specially picked men, and were accompanied by their commanding officer, Major George Jacques, who was a distinguished senior officer. What would happen if the lieutenant refused and was backed up by the rest of his men? Would they be facing a revolt or a mutiny?

The captain was alarmed at the admiral's rage. He would somehow have to talk to him. "Sir," he said, "we will have to talk before anything else is said or done about this matter. It has gotten very serious."

"Gotten serious? It's a disgrace," said the admiral. Roberval paused for a few seconds then said, "Are you questioning my orders, Captain? Or what is it you want?"

"You are telling me to go and arrest an army lieutenant and bring him to you for playing his violin in the room of the two ladies down below – after he was invited in to do so. We have no other proof that anything else happened. This Pierre de Val is a very well liked army officer aboard this ship. Suppose the major orders him not to report to you and says that he will deal with the situation instead. That is the chain of command. I would be very careful in dealing with this situation for fear of some kind of a revolt, Sir," said the captain.

For the first time, the admiral quieted down a little and listened.

"Before I go and carry out your orders, it may be better for you to get the major up here and have a talk with him. He might be able to straighten this out," said the captain.

The admiral thought for a moment. He wasn't used to being questioned about any orders he gave. As well, he did not want the matter straightened out. "Are you saying that there could be a mutiny, Captain?" he asked.

"No Sir, I'm not saying that, but we can't jump the gun, as they say."

"I don't like it, Captain," said Roberval as he ran his fingers through his hair. "I don't like the army well enough to have that major step into this room. You go and have a talk to him and tell him I want the fiddler arrested and put into the brig, in stocks, and held there until further orders."

Captain Fonteneau was about to say something else, but he was stopped by the look in the admiral's eyes. The captain saluted and said, "Yes Sir," before leaving the admiral's quarters.

CHAPTER 6

Marguerite is sentenced

The captain left the admiral's quarters in disgust. There were no other words to describe Roberval, only that he was insane. "What a way for an admiral to conduct himself over such a small issue. Smashing up furniture and pottery, what a fool," he whispered to himself.

Captain Fonteneau returned to the bridge and told the duty officer to go and get Major Jacques and have him come to his quarters right away. "Yes Sir," said the officer, as the captain left the bridge and went to his quarters.

After the captain left him, Admiral Roberval rang a bell for his steward to bring him something strong to drink.

He then took out his logbook and began to write:

"Due to a serious breach of orders that has come to my attention by the officers of this ship, I have come to no other conclusion then to take strong disciplinary action. Marguerite de la Roberval and Madame Violet have conducted themselves as harlots aboard this ship. It has been unanimously decided by the officers aboard that they will be put ashore on the first land we see when we reach the New World, and will be picked up again on our return voyage to France in the fall. We have decided that to continue any further with them aboard will only bring us a heavy burden, disloyalty and bad luck.

The army lieutenant involved with them will be burned at the stake in the name of France for disloyalty to his country when we reach our destination unless it is decided otherwise."

The admiral called in a member of his staff and had him write a letter to the captain using the same wording he had put in the logbook. "Mark it classified," he told him.

He issued orders to have a party prepare the boat his brother had put aboard for landing Marguerite when she went ashore. It would be used now to get her off the ship at the first sight of land.

In a letter to Major Jacques, the admiral also issued orders to have Lieutenant Pierre de Val put in stocks below, out of sight, and held there indefinitely.

The captain met alone with Major Jacques to talk about what was going on. "I want to talk to you in strict confidence, Major," said the captain.

"I give you my word that everything you say will be strictly between the two of us," said the major.

"First I want to say that I am of the opinion that Admiral de Roberval has gone crazy," the captain said, speaking very quietly. "I just came from his quarters and he is so mad that he is smashing up furniture and anything else he can get his hands on."

The major looked puzzled, not knowing what to say.

"It's all about Lieutenant Pierre de Val having an affair with Princess Marguerite aboard this ship," said the captain.

"Good God in heavens, Captain, what next?" said the major, shaking his head.

"That is the report given to me by a naval officer who threatened to go to the admiral if I didn't do it first. Naturally, I had to take the report to him," said the captain.

Major Jacques was a wise man who could see through steel. He had been in action in many different wars during his career. He could see right through what he was being told. "I bet the report came from someone who was jealous," he said now.

"You said it right, Major," answered the captain.

"What do we have to do to straighten this thing out?" asked the major.

"Straighten it out? There's nothing that can be done to straighten this out, only throw the two women and the lieutenant over the side. When the old man gets himself riled up and makes up his mind to do something, look out," said the captain.

"Does he want to see me?" asked the major.

"No, he doesn't want to see you. He told me to tell you that you have to place Pierre de Val under arrest and have him put in the stocks below and held there," said the captain.

The major could hardly believe it. Pierre de Val was an officer of the Crown, a lieutenant in the French Army who had broken no laws as far as he was concerned. He was an officer in good standing, well disciplined, and well liked by all ranks.

Major Jacques got very upset. "What else did the admiral tell you about this situation, Captain?" he demanded.

"The only orders he gave me were for you to go immediately and have Pierre de Val arrested," the captain replied.

The major took off his hat and scratched his head.

"I don't know what the troops will say when I tell them that the lieutenant has to be arrested and held in stocks," he said.

"I am at a loss for words myself," said the captain. "However, you have no other choice but to follow orders. If not, I will have to arrest you, you know that." He paused, and then continued, "We have fifty armed naval guards aboard and every one of them has to obey orders."

The major knew the captain was right. Orders were orders and that was it. The admiral was in charge of the ship and everyone aboard.

"Maybe I should go and see the admiral myself. I might persuade him to change his mind," said the major.

"No, he told me not to let you come to his quarters. He doesn't want to see you," said the captain.

"Can you imagine the admiral of the fleet, I mean, one of the head men in the French navy, going out of his mind because he suspects that a man and a woman had an affair aboard his ship? Good grief, Captain, I am the commanding officer of troops aboard this ship and I am not allowed to go and see the admiral about a problem that is supposed to involve one of my officers," said the major.

"There is nothing I can do about it, Major, only deliver the admiral's orders and see that they are carried out," said the captain.

"I will go and do as the admiral ordered, and have Pierre de Val arrested and held in stocks. But you can tell the admiral that we won't allow him or anyone else to do any harm to the lieutenant as long as he is under my command," said an angry Major Jacques.

"I won't tell the admiral that, Major, because that is treason. He could have you arrested and shot," said the captain.

"I know, I know," said Major Jacques. "You and I will have to work something out as we go along. We will have to work together."

"I will keep you posted on every detail, especially about what he plans to do with the women," said the captain.

"Okay, make sure you do," said the downhearted army major as he turned and went out the door.

Captain Fonteneau didn't know what the admiral was going to do when he went back to his quarters to see him. He had known him for years, and had sailed with him on many voyages. One thing he knew was that the admiral hated anything going on behind his back aboard his ships. And if it were right under his nose, as this was, he would have no mercy. It didn't matter who was involved.

When the captain got to the bridge he met the duty officer just coming to get him. "I have a message for you, Captain, from the admiral," said the duty officer.

The captain took the folder containing the message and sat down. He took out the handwritten sheet of paper and read the message. He let out a puff of air and then folded the paper and put it in his tunic pocket. He told the duty officer to come below to his quarters right away.

"We should see land in about two days if the weather holds and the wind stays in the same direction or close to it. The men in the crow's nest saw pieces of Arctic ice just a couple of hours ago," the duty officer told the captain when they were seated in his quarters.

The captain instructed the duty officer to go to Her Highness Marguerite de Roberval and inform her that she was to start packing up all her belongings. He said to tell her to be sure to have everything packed by tomorrow night, because at the first sight of land she and Madame Violet would be going ashore. He told the duty officer to say that was the admiral's orders.

The duty officer did not know what to think of such orders, especially given to two French women whom everyone aboard ship respected. 'It is unimaginable. Dumping them off in a land filled with pure savages, with no one to turn to and nowhere to live," he thought, as he saluted the captain and went to do his duty.

Roberval called the captain to his quarters. "I want you to go and signal to the other ships," he said. "Tell them I am having a meeting as soon as the wind drops to a moderate breeze."

The captain informed the admiral that the wind was dropping, and if this kept up for an hour there should be no problem to get from ship to ship safely.

"Okay, you call the shots," said the admiral.

In about an hour, the ships started taking in their sails and slowing up. This was during the late afternoon.

The three ships came close to each other and hove up side by side about one hundred yards apart, with their heads into the wind. It was a spectacular sight.

The two ships accompanying Admiral de Roberval in the *Valentine* were the most powerful ships in the French navy, the *Anne* and the *Lechefraye*.

The boats were soon lowered, and in a few minutes the two naval captains came to the side of the flagship. The admiral was on deck to meet them. They were the same men who had been with him when he met with the baron over dinner. The captains accompanied the admiral to his quarters and sat at his table. Captain Fonteneau of the *Valentine* was not invited to the meeting.

"All plans are set to go, gentlemen," said Roberval. "But first I want to know how things are going aboard your ships?"

Both captains reported a smooth voyage with nothing worthwhile to report.

"We are having a smooth voyage too, except for preparing to cast off the two women at the first sight of land."

They laughed. One of the captains, a man in his forties, said he would volunteer to be put ashore with the women if the admiral wanted a volunteer. They all laughed again.

"I already have a volunteer," said the admiral.

The captains asked him who it was.

"Do you remember the young army fiddle player? Well, one of our naval officers got jealous and turned into a spy and caught the fiddle player in bed with Her Highness. That gave me the justification to put them ashore. The fiddle player will be going ashore with them. He doesn't know it yet, so you don't have to volunteer," said the admiral with a laugh.

"If that's the case," said the captain, "I guess I won't be going."

"No, you definitely won't be going ashore with the princess," said the admiral with a grin.

"What is our next move to be, Admiral?" the captains asked.

"We will get Captain Fonteneau to come to the meeting in a few minutes and brief him on what we plan to do. I haven't told him anything about the plans, because I was afraid word might leak out and cause confusion."

"What is the plan now? Do we still split up when we reach land?" asked one of the captains.

"When we reach land, or when we get into the area where we see the first icebergs, we will go about getting the two women and the fiddle player ready to go ashore. One of our ships will go south along the coast for about ten furlongs and then return. The other ship will go northwest into the Strait of Belle Isle and remain there until this ship catches up. When we get close to the land, I am going to get aboard with you and go on up into the Strait of Belle Isle with you, and let Captain Fonteneau put the people ashore," said the admiral.

"When do you plan to come back and pick them up again?" asked one of the captains.

"Oh, don't worry about that, Captain, we intend to give them a year's food and lots of rope they can use to hang themselves."

The three men laughed.

"What if the women refuse to go ashore, Admiral?" asked the youngest captain.

"Don't worry about that. They will be going ashore and if not we will be looking for a new captain when I come back aboard. Fonteneau knows that," said the admiral.

"How far up the St. Lawrence river do we go?" one captain asked.

"We'll go up to where we left the Indians last year. If we go up past there we could run into trouble," said the admiral, and then he added. "We should be able to get the Indians on board again somewhere around there."

One historian wrote that Roberval went to an area somewhere along the St. Lawrence River and took aboard some very cruel and bloodthirsty Indians, as he wanted to strike terror into the hearts of English colonists on the Avalon Peninsula of Newfoundland.

"Are there any more questions, gentlemen?" the admiral asked.

The two captains indicated there were none except ones about icebergs and that was pretty straightforward.

When the captains left, Roberval rang a bell and a steward came into the room.

"Yes my Lord, you rang for me?" he asked, as he saluted.

"Yes, I want you to go and tell the captain I want him," said Roberval.

"Yes, Sir," was his reply as he saluted again and left.

In a few minutes, Captain Fonteneau came to the admiral's quarters and was briefed on what was going to happen regarding the attack on English colonists in Newfoundland. The captain was surprised to hear the new orders and said it was a good plan, although he didn't want to even think about it.

When he was told about the plan for the women he was shocked, but not surprised.

"I have changed my plans for the fiddle player. Instead of dumping him over the side or having him burned to the stake, I am going to have him put ashore with the two women. He should enjoy himself; he will only have two to look after. Major Jacques should be pleased with this. He won't have to see his fiddle player burned at the stake, after all," the admiral said, laughing.

The captain knew the laugh was an expression of hate.

"They will only have to stay there for a short time, maybe a month or so, then we will come back and pick them up again and go on our journey," said the admiral. He looked through the window at the gray sky and added, "When we get a short distance from the first land we see, I will be transferring to one of the other ships for a day, going ahead along the Strait of Belle Isle. We want to see if there are any British warships up that way. You will be in charge of putting the party ashore, so it's all in your hands."

The captain did not ask any questions for fear of getting orders restricting him as to what he should send ashore in the boats.

Just then, they heard bells ringing from the other ships, indicating that their captains were back aboard and ready to sail again.

"Okay, Captain, get going and deliver the orders," said the great fighting Roberval.

When word reached Marguerite and Violet that they were to start packing up everything to move ashore, they were completely devastated.

Marguerite began to cry. She thought there was some mistake. The duty officer told them the orders were from the admiral himself. He said he could not change a thing.

"It will just be for a couple of months and you will be picked up again, after the battle with the English is over," he told them, trying to soften the shock of the news he had just delivered.

"How much time do we have to pack?" asked Violet.

"I don't know, but we expect to see land tomorrow evening and the captain says there will be no time to spare when the time comes to put you ashore," said the duty officer.

"Please go and tell the admiral I want to see him at once," said Marguerite.

The duty officer said he would pass her request to the captain and then he left. When he was gone, the women sat at the table and looked at each other.

"I just can't believe it," said Violet, wringing her hands. "I am forty-two years old and have always been sensible in life. I've never hurt a soul, not even a fly. Now I am going to be put ashore in a foreign land among wild animals, and maybe savage Indians, to fight for my life, and for yours."

"Ever since I was a young girl I've heard how cruel my uncle was to the prisoners he captured and of the torture he inflicted, but we never believed it. Maybe all the stories we heard were true," Marguerite said bitterly. "But why would he want to kill us?"

"If someone had told me this before we left the castle I would not have believed it. This must be an awful dream," said Violet.

"It's not a dream," said Marguerite, as she stood up and looked out the window at a group of sailors uncovering the new after-boat, which was tied down on the deck. She was supposed to use the boat when she reached her destination and was ready to claim the New World for France.

"They are getting our boat ready to put us off so it must be true," said the frightened young woman. "Do you know something, Violet?" she said, after she'd recovered a little. "I have been a fool, or my father has been a fool, all this time."

"What do you mean," asked Violet.

"This has been a planned plot all along. Uncle Jean is using my father's money to finance an attack upon the English colonists in the New World. Did you hear what the steward said about having a battle with the English?" asked an angry Marguerite.

Violet thought for a moment then said, "Let's you and I go to his quarters and tell him we know the whole scheme, and we will go and tell the king about it when we return home."

"No, we can't do that. If we make him aware that we are on to his scheme he will never come back and pick us up," said Marguerite.

Violet wrung her hands. "I will never be able to survive in the wilderness of the New World. It will be too much for me. I think the cold will kill me," she said, as tears rolled down her face.

"We have no choice but to start packing immediately," said Marguerite.

"What will we take with us?" asked Violet.

"Everything we brought aboard, and more if we can get our hands on it, because Papa paid for it all," said Marguerite.

The women started packing, putting blankets, sheets, pillows, and clothing in their trunks. Soon, everything they could get their hands on was packed and ready to go ashore.

Captain Fonteneau called Major Jacques to his quarters and told him about what had taken place.

"The lieutenant will be put ashore with the two women," said the captain.

"Well, at least he will die a natural death on the land, I suppose," the major said after a few minutes. "That's better than getting burned at the stake or dumped alive in the ocean." The major appeared very distressed.

"I have been put in charge of getting the party ready and put ashore, so we will try and get them all the supplies they will need to set up a household ashore for – say one year. Although the admiral says we will be back for them in three or four months." said the captain.

"I suppose there is little point in me shouting and screaming about the matter because I can't change a thing," said Major Jacques. "The only thing we can do now is try and help them survive while they're living there, however long that may be."

"That's the way I feel about it too, so we should get together and draw up a list of things they will need," said the captain.

"I wonder if there's a forest near where they will be put ashore. They will certainly need lots of firewood," said the major.

"If we are on course, and I think we are, according to the bearings I made last night, we should see Cape Degrat by noon tomorrow if the wind stays in our favour," said the captain. "The men in the riggings are starting to see pieces of ice in the distance."

"Are there any charts of this area?" asked Major Jacques.

"No, none, but I have been here before and know the area," said the captain.

"Are there any fishing rooms nearby?" asked the major.

"No, none within hundreds of miles. There are some Beothuck Indians in that area and they say there are a lot of Eskimos around there. We never saw any, but we saw tracks of them around Cape Degrat and places where they had tents set up. We suspect that Grat Cove is their tenting area," said the captain.

"What do you think could happen if we put them off there? The natives might attack them and kill them for taking over their land," said the major.

"You might be right. But I know of a place where they could go. There's a small harbour about a mile from Degrat Cove called L'Anse au Pigeon. It's a good place to get ashore with deep water and a brook running out nearby," said the captain.

"That sounds good if we strike that area," said the major.

The two of them thought for a moment then the major asked. "What will they live in, will we have to make them a tent?"

"No, we won't have to make a tent. They have a house up there on deck," said the captain.

Major Jacques looked puzzled. "What are you talking about, a house on deck?" he asked.

"That new after-boat that's up there, the one that's built like a tub. It was put aboard for the women to go ashore. The baron had it specially built as a survival craft. What we will do is take it ashore in a good safe place and build up a rock wall about three feet high and turn it bottom up on the wall. All they will have to do then is put a canvas sail over it and sod it in and they will have a comfortable shelter. The Vikings used to do it all the time," said the captain.

"What about a stove and pipes?" asked Jacques.

"There's a special stove being made for them in the forge," answered the captain, "and they're even putting an oven onto it to bake bread in. We've got plenty of stovepipe on hand. I have that all taken care of."

"Well, there is a possibility they could survive for a couple of months if they do the right things," said the major.

"They could be there for a year or more, Major. The admiral has all the power and it's up to him whether or not he comes back to pick them up," the captain said.

The major knew that was true.

"Make sure three or four bags of heavy salt goes ashore, just in case they have to salt fish or seal, or anything else that has to be preserved," said the major.

"We have all that taken care of, I gave them a list," said the captain. "When the admiral goes aboard the other ship we will be able to send ashore whatever we want."

"I think I should go and tell Pierre de Val that he will be going ashore with the women. He doesn't know it yet, and once he does know he can get his luggage ready," said the major.

"You can tell him about it, but don't let him out of the brig till after the admiral leaves the ship," said the captain.

"Has anyone told the women that Pierre is going ashore with them?" asked the major.

"No, we haven't told them. As far as they're concerned, they're going ashore themselves," said the captain.

"I think that's too big a worry on them, thinking they're going ashore by themselves. We should let them know that Pierre is going with them," said the major.

"Yes, but we have to be careful. You know how the admiral acts, he could lose his mind again," said the worried captain.

"I'll take care of that, no one will find out," said the major, adding, "I will pack up two flint lock guns as well as powder and shot for them to take ashore. At least they will have something to defend themselves with."

"Okay, you take care of that," said the captain.

"If anything else comes up please make sure to let me know about it," said Major Jacques.

That night, Marguerite received a note from Pierre de Val that said, "I have been notified that I am going to be put ashore with you. Don't worry, cherie, everything will be fine."

Marguerite lay on her bed and thought of the last words her father had said to her, about her mother and her grandmother. She twisted the gold diamond ring her father had given her before she left, and remembered what he had said about always wearing it. She knew she was never to take it off for fear that something awful would happen to her. But now, here she was, being abandoned in the New World among wild Indians, with her ring still on her finger. "What does this mean?" she asked herself. "Maybe I should take it off, it's bringing me bad luck."

She and Violet felt relieved that a man would be coming with them, and especially that it was Pierre. Marguerite seemed happy after receiving his note; however she was in no mood for singing.

The women sat at the table and talked about how their lives were about to take a very drastic turn. They wondered what the New World would have in store for them. They had heard about wild Indians scalping women and children in this land and that made them shudder. They had also heard of these natives taking women and carrying them away and using them in ways that they didn't want to even think about. They were certain Pierre would have a gun or two to defend them.

"Poor Pierre de Val, I wonder what they have put him through," was the thought of both women.

As they sat in the dark, Marguerite suddenly looked at Violet and said, "There is something I have to tell you."

The older woman looked at the young woman with curiosity.

"What is it, cherie?" she asked.

"Violet, I think I am pregnant," said a sorrowful Marguerite.

"My God in heaven," said the older woman as she put her hands to her face.

CHAPTER 7

Going Ashore

Just after dawn the next morning, the man in the crow's nest sounded his horn. "Land ho, land ho on the horizon, dead ahead, Captain," he shouted.

The men on the bridge called back, "Land ho, got the message."

Captain Fonteneau was quickly notified.

The man in the crow's nest called again, "Icebergs straight ahead four miles, another berg to the right about five miles, steady as she goes."

In a few minutes, the captain was on the bridge wearing a heavy coat to protect him against the cold, almost freezing, air. He talked to the bridge master. He had the information confirmed.

"Ask him if he can give us a distance estimate of land sighted," said the captain.

The man in the crow's nest came back with the information that it should be approximately thirty miles. The captain knew that this land should be Rangellet Mountain. (Rangeley Head is the local name). The captain spoke to the bridge master. "If he can see land and it's about thirty miles away, then he should see land looming to the right a few degrees," he said. "It's an island called Belle Isle. Ask him if he can see anything else."

The bridge master went back to the crow's nest with the message, and was told to stand by. In just a few minutes the message from the crow's nest was that land had been spotted to the right, about ten degrees northwest.

"We are right on course, gentlemen. You have done a good job, congratulations," said the captain. He told the signalman to alert the two ships to the rear that land had been sighted ahead. He told the duty officer to take a message to the admiral and stand by for further orders. A reply was sent to the men in the crow's nest that their message had been received.

It was early noon when the three French warships took in their sails and hove too about a mile off L'Anse au Pigeon.

Sailors in the front of the *Valentine* were throwing lead weights attached to lines overboard. They were sounding the depth of the water as the ship moved closer to land. The ship had dodged several large icebergs on the way in. Most of the men aboard had never seen an iceberg before and could hardly believe what they were seeing. The captain gave orders to let down one anchor and watch closely in case the ship drifted with the tide.

It was a sunny June day in the New World. Sea gulls and kittiwakes were everywhere, skirting the ships and screeching for something to be thrown overboard. Shore ducks were seen by the thousands, flying close to the land and low on the water.

"You can smell the fish in the water, " one sailor commented.

On shore, the hills were turning green.

The sky showed signs that a sunny day was in store.

Very few waves rolled on the ocean where the flagship lay in wait for the ship the admiral would board to go on to the northwest, scouting the Strait of Belle Isle.

The admiral again reminded Captain Fonteneau about the task he had to do. He also told him that he could not delay the ship forever getting the women ashore. He said their main objective would be theIndian Nations, far to the west in the Gulf of St. Lawrence.

The captain assured Roberval that as soon as he put the landing party ashore he would be on his way to meet him.

There were three boats used to transfer the admiral and his party from the flagship to the other ship that was waiting with its gangway hanging down along the side. Sailors were everywhere, standing to attention, as the admiral drew nearer to the ship's side.

The bells started ringing when the admiral stepped onto the gangway and started walking up towards the deck. Everyone saluted and gave three cheers for Roberval.

As soon as the admiral stepped on board, the anchor was taken up and the sails were hoisted. A light breeze carried the ship slowly forward and away from the flagship that was about to dump Marguerite onto an island, near the shores of the unforgiving Labrador Sea.

This was an honourable person who was being thrown to the mercy of Mother Nature. She had lived a good life, caring, loving and very active, and was a worthy representative of her country. Now, she was about to experience something that not even the scholars of France during this period would ever dare write about. Their imagination would never be able to comprehend the hardships that lay ahead for her and Violet and the young army lieutenant, Pierre de Val Cormier.

When the three boats returned from transporting the admiral, Captain Fonteneau and Major Jacques had thirty sailors and soldiers ready and waiting to go ashore with the landing party.

When Pierre de Val walked out onto the deck, the rays of the sun hurt his eyes. He was dressed in his full lieutenant's uniform. He wore his brass sword and brass helmet and a breastplate made of brass. He was a sharp looking soldier.

All the troops and sailors standing around let out a roar and cheered for him. "Play us one more tune before you go," they pleaded. They asked the captain if this was permitted and he gave his permission.

Pierre opened his duffle bag, took out his violin and bow, and started playing a tune. It was a tune that had never been played before or since. It was a tune that he had put together while he was below in the stocks. It wasn't a fast tune and it wasn't slow either. It was a tune that pierced the ocean underneath the ship and struck the land in the distance. It was also a good-bye to all on board. The playing did not take long.

When he was finished, Pierre shook hands with his commanding officer, Major Jacques, and with Captain Fonteneau, and thanked them both. He also cursed Admiral Roberval and all he stood for. Then he used the deck to wipe the dirt off his feet and stepped aboard the boat that would take him and the women ashore.

As Pierre got on the boat he spotted Officer Marten standing near the ship's rail. "One moment, please," he said, as he quickly jumped out of the boat and leapt towards the naval officer. Pierre punched Marten in the mouth, knocking him down before he had time to defend himself. While he had Marten on the deck, he kicked him in the ribs, making him wince in pain. "That one is for the admiral, you weasel," he said, as he jumped back into the lowered boat. "Stop that man," roared Marten. But no one heard him as Pierre disappeared.

The history books only tell so much about incidents that happened to those who get dealt a cruel injustice, especially those in the military. It appears the country involved in this incident didn't want the details spread abroad for fear of diplomatic embarrassment. The incident where Marguerite got driven off the French naval flagship and put ashore on a barren island in the north Atlantic was one that should have caused an international crisis, even in the mid-1500s, but it didn't. The incident was talked about in France for years but very little was done.

When Marguerite and Violet came on deck that afternoon, there were no flags flying or cheers given. The only indication of a departure were the tears of pity in the eyes of hardened sailors, who watched with horror what was taking place. Some men cursed when they looked at the barren land and at three of their own being herded ashore like cattle to endure hardships no one could predict.

With tears in their eyes, the women shook hands and said a farewell to the men and officers aboard France's greatest warship, the *Valentine*. Marguerite, wearing a black cloak with a red lining, and Violet, in a gray cloak, were then helped down the gangway and aboard the boat that would take them ashore.

As the boats carrying the party rowed toward shore they had to pass a giant iceberg near the entrance of the little harbour. The iceberg cracked and shone in the June sunlight so splendidly that the thought of being removed from civilization left the minds of the women for a few moments. They had never seen anything like this before, not even in their wildest dreams.

Before the boat carrying the women reached the little harbour of L'Anse au Pigeon, thirty men were already at work digging a three-foot hole and building a rock wall to put the after-boat upon.

One army sergeant, who was an engineer, knew exactly what to do and he was put in charge as he had done this kind of job before. He took all the measurements of the after-boat before leaving the ship. This was an easy job to do because the beach rock and sand were easy to move and there were lots of good flat rocks close by for the walls, and plenty of black mud and sods to insulate the rock wall and use as plaster.

The plan was to dig a hole down three feet in loose rock and sand, then build a wall three feet high out of rock and plaster the outside with mud and fill it in around the sides. Sods would be cut to put on the outside. The after-boat would be turned upside down on top on the rock wall with boulders on each side to keep it from slipping off. A heavy ship's sail would go completely over the boat and it would be ballasted down with rocks to prevent it from blowing away. The sail would make the structure waterproof. If possible, the men would dig down a foot in the centre of the house, making it five feet deep. They would cover the floor with flat rocks and cover everything with a heavy canvas tarp.

In less then two hours after the site was selected, the thirty men had the rock wall completed, and the hole dug out. They also had a frame made and put in place for the five-foot door they had brought with them.

When the after-boat carrying the women arrived, it was unloaded and picked up by a group of strong Frenchmen who put it in place on top of the rock wall. It fit perfectly.

Before the after-boat left the ship, the captain had the boson launch a twelve-foot long rowboat. It was fitted with oars and an anchor and was to accompany the landing party. The captain told his men to leave the rowboat on shore for the castaways to use.

The last thing the army engineers did before they left was to install the stove and pipes and put the flange in place.

All the tools they had brought ashore to use in construction, including shovels, picks, axes, hammers, saws, buckets and extra ship's canvas, were left on shore for the castaways' use.

Just before they left, Pierre took out his violin and played a tune of farewell for the men and comrades he loved.

"We may never meet again," he told them, "and if we don't, we want you to tell our story to all of our countrymen in France. Tell how Admiral de Roberval cast us off in the wilderness of the New World."

The men in the three boats were grim faced as they slowly rowed out of L'Anse au Pigeon harbour, with the sound of the violin playing a final farewell.

Pierre, Marguerite and Violet stood on the little hill near the beach as the light wind slowly moved the *Valentine* out of sight and past L'Anse au Pigeon Point. The last they heard was the plaintive sound of the ship's bell as the vessel slowly disappeared, forever.

CHAPTER 8

The New World

The three castaways sat on the little hill, not far from where their dwelling was to be, overlooking the small harbour of L'Anse au Pigeon. They slowly looked around for a few minutes before saying anything.

Finally, "Well, here we are in the New World," said Pierre.

Marguerite was silent as she continued to look around. At last she said, "Everything looks so beautiful, and peaceful." She closed her eyes for a few moments then added, "I wonder what the future has in store for us?"

Pierre began to laugh as he looked at the women. He appeared to be carefree in his attitude.

"When I was working with my father in the tailor shop cutting cloth to make dresses and underwear," he said, "I kept saying, 'Father, I am not going to stay here with you all my life because there is no freedom here. I always wanted to be out in the wilds. Do you know what my father used to say? He would say, 'Pierre, the day will come when you will wish that you were back in this shop, you just wait and see," Pierre laughed.

The women said nothing.

Pierre continued, "I would rather be here now than be aboard that stinking ship, down in the prison cell with my hands and feet in stocks."

"Yes, so would I. At least here we don't have the threat of a mad man hanging over our heads. We can now do as we please," said Marguerite.

"Let's not talk about that savage any more," said Violet. She looked at the two younger people. "We're here now in this beautiful little harbour and I like it. Let's get to work and get our house in working order."

With that, the three of them jumped to their feet. Rushing over to the overturned boat that would be their home, they started sorting things out.

The items brought ashore included everything from a ten-gallon keg of molasses to dried fruit. They even had a turning stone for sharpening axes and knives; that would be a valuable tool for them to use.

There were two fifty-pound cloth bags of sugar and a hundred pound bag of beans, the same for peas. There were three five-gallon barrels of lard, and two thirty-five gallon barrels of brown flour, each one weighing one hundred pounds. There were as well a couple of jars of ale.

They had plenty of food to last them for a year if they were careful. The sailors had also unloaded twenty pieces of plank. They had as well several boxes of candles and flint for starting fires.

Violet told Marguerite and Pierre that she was not to be called 'Madame' any more. From now on, or until they got back to France, she was to be called 'Violet.'

"Pierre, there is something important you should do this evening," said Violet.

"Yes, what is it?" asked Pierre.

"You should start and dig a trench all around the wall and fill it with loose rock just in case it starts to rain. That way, there will be no water coming down through the centre and on to the floor of our kitchen. It will all run away in the ditch," said Violet.

Pierre agreed and started digging with pick and shovel while the women put the stores away. He dug the trench around the side of the building and out to the water's edge where any water getting in could run away.

The after-boat was twenty-two feet long by nine feet wide in the middle. In other words, they had a fairly big house to live in. But it wasn't big enough to hold all their stores; they would have to make a place out of the sail they had left. This would have to be done later. In the meantime, they would cover their stores with the sail.

During the summer of 2006, I was in the abandoned community of L'Anse au Pigeon where I have a cabin. As I looked around, doing research on the story of Marguerite, I came upon an area close to the shoreline that looked like historians had written about. The size of the honeycomb area on the ground would fit perfectly with the size of the after-boat that Marguerite came ashore in. I went to some of the old timers who were born there, and knew about the markings to which I am referring, and they told me people had known about the honeycomb markings for generations, but always thought the Vikings made them. Norman Tucker of St. John's, who is now eighty years old, says he played there as a small child and was told it was a Viking house. But since he learned the story about Marguerite and how she was put ashore there, he is convinced that this is the very place.

Late in the evening, after things were stored away and made ready for the night, Pierre and Marguerite went looking for firewood and fresh water.

They walked up around the rocky beach for about a hundred yards and to an area that leveled out into a flat plain.

There were trees not far from them at the foot of a large hill. This would be a good place to cut firewood when it was needed.

As they were walking along the side of the inner pond they were surprised to see tracks of people in the grass.

They stopped and stared.

"There are more people here than us," said Pierre. "It must be natives, according to what they have on their feet. See, the tracks are smooth and round."

Marguerite looked more closely. "I think some of these smaller tracks belong to women and children," she said.

They picked up several pieces of driftwood and filled the kettle with fresh water from the brook before returning to the houseboat with the news that they had seen tracks of other people. Violet was surprised to hear this and wondered if it was safe to leave their stores outside the houseboat for the night.

They figured the tracks belonged to Indians, and made plans to construct a rock house onto the side of the houseboat the next day.

Pierre got the fire going and put the kettle full of water on the stove. As it got dark, Marguerite lit two candles and placed them on the large trunk in the center of their quarters.

"We have to figure out where we are going to sleep," said Marguerite.

The three looked at each other, waiting for someone to comment. Of course there were no beds or bunks, so what was the plan?

Outside, under the sail were four cloth bags of hard bread.

Thick, oval-shaped coarse biscuit, baked without salt and kiln-dried, hard bread was used aboard vessels going on long voyages. It was packed in fifty-pound bags and, when used, it was put in water and soaked for twelve hours to make it soft. It was then brought to a boil, and served with cooked salt fish or beef, flavored with fried salt fatback or pork and onions and sometimes gravy.

It was decided that the four bags of hard bread would be brought in and used as a bunk in the forward part of the boathouse, making a bed for Violet. This would also be a good dry place to store the hard bread.

It was decided too that they would bring in the bags of beans and peas to make a bunk for Marguerite, and probably Pierre, if Violet approved. After a discussion, which included some persuasion, it was agreed that Pierre could share the bunk in the kitchen with Marguerite.

The bunk in the kitchen could be used as a seat while eating. One of their large trunks could be used as a table and another could be put near the stove to stack pots and dishes on.

It was also decided that they would use one of the dark blankets to make a screen to partition off Violet's sleeping quarters.

When Violet and Marguerite packed their belongings in France they put in two chamber pots to be used aboard ship. When they again packed to leave the ship, they took the pots for use in the New World. These would serve them well now, especially Violet, who would be rooming in the front of their small confined dwelling.

They had two candles burning as they got their things settled away; however it was decided that they would never light more then one candle at a time and that their wick lamp would be used whenever possible.

As the kettle began to boil, the three castaways sat and stared at the fire in the stove through the half-open door.

Pierre gazed at Marguerite and saw that she looked beautiful with the reflection of the fire on her face and a long heavy sweater tucked tightly around her body.

He knew she came from a very wealthy family that was well known throughout France. He thought about her father's castle, and all the things she had at home. Now, here she was, through no fault of her own, set ashore on a desolate shoreline in the wilds of somewhere called the New World.

For the first time, he realized that Roberval would never come back for them again. The admiral had no intention of facing the consequences that would result if Marguerite returned to France and reported the incident to her father.

Pierre took out his violin and started to play as the two women sat and listened. When he finished playing, he told Marguerite this would be a good place to teach her how to play the violin. He then showed her a couple of chords, and demonstrated how to hold the bow.

"I would say this is the first music lesson that was ever held in the New World," he said, as all three laughed and forgot where they were for the moment.

Pierre went out into the chilly night air to look around. When he stepped outside he heard a splash in the water just a few feet away. He looked closer and saw more splashing in the water all around the little tickle near the beach.

The tide was high and running into the inner pond. He knew by the splashing and the rushing sound that it was fish of some kind, and that they were going into the salt pond with the rising tide. "What a place for us to set our net tomorrow evening," he thought."

He came back and told the woman and they were very excited as they talked about going fishing in the morning.

The three had a very good night, although Violet and Marguerite found the bed hard to lie on. Pierre had no problem. Being in the army, he was used to sleeping on the ground.

Pierre knew what they would do the next day. They would take the clothes out of the trunks and place them on the bags for a mattress. That would make the bags softer to sleep upon.

During the night, Violet called to Marguerite and Pierre and told them they had forgotten to bring one of the most important tools they would need – a broom! She said, "I know how to make them out of a certain kind of low growing hardwood. We called them birch brooms back in Normandy. I will make a couple tomorrow."

At dawn, on their first morning in the New World, Pierre got out of bed and went outside. When he pulled up the canvas and looked out he got the shock of his life. The cove was full of ducks. There were thousands feeding in the little harbour. When he stepped outside, the ducks started to quack and began to fly away. He noticed they were white, black and brown in colour. He had never seen anything like it before, he told the women when he went back into the boathouse.

"If I had my gun in shooting order when I went out I would have killed at least twenty or thirty of these ducks," he said.

Pierre lit the fire and told the women to stay in bed while the boathouse warmed up. He put the kettle on and went outside again.

He noticed that the tide was out, leaving the inner pond almost dry. He intended to walk to the inner pond and cross over to the other side. He would then walk up the hill over there and have a look around while the kettle was boiling.

He put on his boots, told the women where he was going, and set out. He had only taken a few steps when he thought about his gun. "I had better take my gun with me," he said to himself. "I might see a few ducks or something around the cove that I could kill for food."

Pierre went back to the boathouse and got his gun. He loaded it with powder and shot. All he had to do then was put the flint in place on the firing pin, aim it, and fire.

As he walked up to the inner pond he could see tracks of people in the sand. He also saw schools of fish trapped in a pool inside. He put down his gun and stepped out into the water. He began kicking fish ashore.

"The like of this has never been known before, especially back home in France," he said.

He examined the fish closely and saw that while they looked like trout, they were a more silvery color and bigger. *Pierre did not know and would never know that the fish were Arctic char.*

He took the fish and carried them back to the boathouse.

The women were out of bed and getting dressed when Pierre came in with the fish. They could hardly believe what they saw.

"This is really the New World," said Marguerite.

"If you don't mind, ladies, I would like them cooked for lunch," said Pierre.

After breakfast, which was bread and jam that the cook on the ship had packed for them, the three of them decided to walk around the Pigeon – *what we will call the little harbour from now on* – and see if anything was around there.

As they walked around the area they could see tracks that belonged to people all over the place. They realized those other people could be looking at them at that very moment.

They crossed over the small peninsula to a sandy beach in a deep cove. Here they saw small fish by the thousands rolling on the beach. It was fish they had never seen before. *These were capelin ranging from four to six inches long, and they come to the sandy beaches around the coast of Newfoundland to spawn during the month of June.*

Again, the same as before, Pierre walked out into the water and kicked some of the fish ashore. The women picked the fish up and examined them; they looked beautiful. They planned to take some back to the boathouse when they returned.

They walked along the beach, and then crossed a large soft bog, which was covered with white flowers. *They were not aware this flower was in the first stage of growing into a berry called bakeapple or cloudberry.*

After they crossed the bog they walked up a small hill overlooking the plateau now called Degrat Cove.

Just about two hundred feet from shore was a beautiful island, Degrat Island, with a huge iceberg close by.

While they were there they saw smoke rising about half a mile away. They did not know what to think of this. They knew someone had to be there. As they sat and watched, they saw what looked like tents on the shoreline near the fire.

"It must be natives," said Pierre.

The three sat and watched in wonder.

"The natives must have seen us come ashore yesterday," said Marguerite.

"Maybe they are the same people who were over at the inner pond near our place catching fish," said Pierre.

The women agreed.

"What do we do now?" asked Marguerite. "Do we try and make contact with them?"

"No, not now, they are probably watching us," said Violet.

Pierre was carrying his gun and didn't want to frighten the natives. He thought they may have seen a gun before and it might have been used against them.

"We have to make friends with them in a different way," said Pierre.

They looked around Degrat Cove and decided to put the rowboat in the water later and row over to the tent area.

In the afternoon, Pierre took the axe and went up the side of the hill behind the boathouse and cut two sticks of firewood and brought it down. When this was done he put the door in place in the boathouse and nailed leather hinges to it. He dug a ditch from the boathouse doorway down to the beach.

Violet busied herself making three loaves of bread and baking it in the oven. It turned out fine. Pierre told her he was surprised she knew how to make bread and cook.

"I was cooking when I was ten years old, I cooked for the baron before you were born," she told him. Pierre laughed, but he knew it was true.

In the evening, Pierre opened the wooden box and found a complete fish net about fifty feet long, ready to be set in the water. He was happy about this but had never seen a net set before.

"I know how to set it out," Violet told him. "My father was a fisherman. I know how to set a net and cut and clean fish."

Pierre asked her how it was done.

"You tie one end of the net to the shoreline and, using the boat, you set the net straight off from the land and put out an anchor. In this case, we don't need an anchor. All we have to do is go on across the cove and tie a rope to the other side and pull it tight," said the older woman.

Pierre and Marguerite started laughing. They were glad that Violet knew so much about fishing.

Violet and Pierre launched the rowboat, put in the box containing the net, and rowed to a spot about two hundred feet out the harbour where they set the net. While they were setting the net they saw fish in the water under the boat.

Their net was only in the water for a few minutes when they saw the cork floats on it moving, an indication they had a catch of fish.

This time, Pierre and Marguerite got in the boat and went out to the net. They lifted the edge up over the side and pulled up on the linnet. Large fish were tangled in the net. Pierre had never seen such fish before. Violet was standing on the shoreline not far away. He held one of the fish up for her to see.

"That's a codfish," she said as she looked at the fish. "I've seen them before when father brought them home from fishing, only they were not as big as that one."

As Pierre was taking fish out of the net more were getting in. He had to let the net go, then go to the other side and untie it and pull it into the shore for fear of it sinking with fish.

It is to be noted that when John Cabot first came to Newfoundland in 1497 the codfish were so plentiful he and his men reported they could lower baskets in the water and fill them up with fish. Now, this was approximately sixty years later and fish were still very plentiful.

It took several hours for Pierre and Marguerite to clear the fish from the net.

Violet showed them how to clean the fish and salt some of them. They only cleaned and salted the large fish; the rest were thrown away.

"After three days in salt we have to wash the fish out in clean salt water and put it out to dry," Violet told them. "We can get some branches from the trees you cut down and make a flake. We will spread the fish on the flake and let it dry in the sun. After four days in the sun, we will have salt dry cod. It will keep for years if it doesn't get wet. We will have fish to eat whenever we want it."

"Thanks for the training session," said Marguerite and Pierre.

"Before we get out of here we will need all the training we can get, in more ways than one," said Violet.

CHAPTER 9

The Storm

After the castaways had been in the Pigeon for close to a week, enjoying the sunshine and combing the beaches, they were introduced to one of the summer storms that sweep through the Labrador Sea when the forces of nature decide to cause trouble.

The storm started in the afternoon with heavy clouds pulling themselves into motion. Pierre walked up on the high hill behind the boathouse and saw black squalls of wind pitching on the water about half a mile off the harbour. He knew it was going to blow.

He rushed down and asked the women to help him pull the rowboat further up into a safer place behind the boathouse because he knew the wind was coming on. In a few minutes, the sky was heavily overcast and the wind pitched, and then came the rain.

Fortunately, they had their dry fish and everything else they needed to keep dry in under the roof of the boathouse.

By late afternoon the wind was at gale force from the southeast, blowing straight into the Pigeon.

There was only one thing protecting the castaways from being swept away, and that was the point that jutted out into the harbour about three hundred feet further out from where they were settled.

The breaking sea came in through the harbour's mouth like mountains. The salty spray covered their dwelling with hurricane force winds and slammed against their door, but it held.

The boat on top of the rock wall shook and shivered as if it was going to lift off, and it probably would have if the ship's sail had not been in place and weighed down with tons of rocks, preventing the wind from getting in under the edge.

Pierre decided they should make up a bed on the floor near the rock wall in case the boat blew off its foundation. At least they stood a chance if they were close to the floor.

It was after midnight when the three of them got into the bed on the floor. They had a lot of clothes under them to cover the rock floor that was, in turn, covered by the ship's canvas.

They huddled on the floor in the roar of the wind and rain, and the mighty rolling waves close by. Pierre and Violet made Marguerite lie between them, protecting her.

"Pierre," said Marguerite. "Can you hear me?"

"Yes, cherie, I can hear you," he said.

There was a silence.

"Pierre, can you hear me?" she asked again.

Torrents of rain poured all around. The salty spray from the ocean swept by their doorstep as if it would wash them away.

"Yes, Marguerite, I can hear you, what do you want?" asked Pierre.

"There's something I have to tell you, are you listening?" she asked.

"Yes I'm listening, what is it?" Pierre said, as the wind roared.

Just then, they heard a loud clap of thunder. It seemed as though it hit the cliff behind their hut. Then a flash of lightning lit up the Pigeon like the noonday sun. But the three could not see the lightning in all its brightness, only a little glimmer showed through a seam at the top of the door.

For a moment, the two women put their arms around Pierre and held him tight. He told them that there was no need for them to be frightened, "Everything will be all right in the morning, it's just a test of our boat, although it is bottom up," he said, laughing.

Marguerite was silent as the thunder roared.

"You were saying something, cherie," said Pierre.

"Yes I was, but you wouldn't listen," she said.

"I'm listening now so go ahead," he said.

"Pierre, I am going to have a baby, I'm pregnant," she said.

Pierre sat up straight, the sound of the thunder and roaring wind silenced by the thoughts that flew through his mind.

He slowly lowered himself down again into the bunk near Marguerite. He lay there very still. He felt a hand and then an arm come around him. He knew it wasn't Marguerite's arm, it was Violet's. She'd heard Marguerite tell Pierre about her pregnancy, and knew that while it was a shock to him, it was not something totally unexpected.

Violet knew that Pierre de Val Cormier was a very reliable man. He had a reputation for being a ladies' man and a rabble-rouser, but Major Jacques had told her that he was a good soldier, a good leader, and a hard worker, someone whom he could depend on. "Of all the men I know, if I had a choice to pick anyone, I would choose Pierre de Val because he could get the job done," he'd said.

"Marguerite, it makes no difference what we go through here — and we don't know our future — but I'll protect you for as long as I have a breath in my body. And the same goes for you too, Violet," said the weary young lieutenant as he lay there, holding the hands of the two women, while wind, rain, lightning, thunder, and the mighty sea beat down upon their doorstep.

Marguerite went to sleep with Pierre holding her closely.

When she awoke it was almost daylight. She opened her eyes and looked at the shadowed ceiling.

Pierre was up and had gone outside.

She listened for the sound of the wind and rain but all was quiet. Then she heard a sea gull calling, breaking the silence of the morning. The storm was over; the sun was going to shine.

Pierre walked around the beach in the salt pond area. The tide was out and the sea was beginning to quiet down.

He was amazed at all the fish that had come into the large pool. He knew thousands of them would die from lack of space. He looked at them, but walked on across the now dry seabed.

He knew last night's storm was not the only one that would come their way, and he knew too it was not the worse one they would see.

There was no way he could risk living there in that spot. It was too risky. The sea had come too close for comfort last night. If the storm had gotten any worse, they would have been swept away. They were living too close to the ocean. Last night had been a frightening experience, especially for Marguerite, now that she was expecting a child.

He knew there was only one thing for him to do and that was to move to a safer location on higher ground. He had made up his mind last night. If they were to survive until this morning, he would begin the process to move.

Pierre walked across a low marshy area near the seabed. It was mainly long grass and he could see where the sea came in over the land, in a place that people who lived there in 1890 called The Bond. Pierre walked up to the top of a little hill and looked at the area. Not far from where he was standing, he saw a beautiful place, back clear of the ocean. "This is where I am going to move the houseboat," he said.

He knew he would have to do the impossible in order to dismantle the set-up they had now and move everything to the new location by himself. But he had made up his mind. He was going to move one way or the other.

CHAPTER 10

Moving The Houseboat

Pierre went back to the houseboat where the women were cooking breakfast. The sun was shining clear and bright on this late June morning. Before he arrived at the houseboat, he saw a bunch of yellow flowers growing in a little grove not far away. He picked two bunches and went into the houseboat. The delicious aroma of fresh fish frying filled the air even before he got to the door.

"I can only say three words and that is, good morning ladies," he said as he handed over the flowers.

The women were glad to see him and gave him smiles that made his heart leap.

"Good morning, Pierre," they said together.

"The smell of food struck me even before I reached the door," he said.

"We were watching you over there on the other side of the harbour," said Marguerite.

"You were?" he said.

"Yes, and I bet we can tell you what you were doing over there too," said Violet.

Pierre figured the women had the same thing in their minds this morning that he had, and that was moving to a safer place.

"Yes," he said, thinking out loud. "It will be quite a task but it has to be done, one way or the other."

The women knew then what he had in his mind, and that was to move across to the other side of the harbour, to higher ground.

While they were having breakfast, they talked about the frightening experience they'd had overnight.

"I thought we were going to perish," said Violet.

"Yes, so did I," said Marguerite.

Pierre knew the women had been scared when the salty spray and the waves started striking the door.

"If we hadn't had the ship's sail covering the complete boat, there was no way this boat could have stayed upon the rock walls," he said.

The women nodded in agreement.

"But we won't be staying in this location for long," Pierre continued. "I was over on the other side and looked around. It's perfect over there. There are lots of flat rocks to build a wall to put the boat on, and there's a good place to put a ditch."

The women looked at him with a lot of questions in their minds.

"How will we move this boat from here to the other side of the harbour, and put it on a new foundation?" asked Marguerite.

Pierre thought for a moment, then said," I don't know, but the three of us should be able to come up with a plan that will get the job done."

"It took thirty men to put the boat in place. How do you suppose one man and two scrawny women can move it, and still keep it intact?" asked Violet.

"I don't know, but it has to be done," said Pierre.

The three finished breakfast and decided to do their chores. Pierre went for two buckets of water up at the brook. Marguerite put whatever clothes were wet out in the hot sun to dry, while Violet prepared to clean the dishes and get the bunks put back in place.

When Pierre came back with the water, he asked Marguerite to help him put the rowboat into the water.

"You and I will go over and have a closer look at where I think we should move," he told her.

The rowboat was almost full of rainwater that had fallen in the night during the storm. After bailing out the water, they rowed across and landed on the rocky beach where they tied the boat onto a boulder.

"We would never be able to get that big boat up over here. It's too steep and rocky," Marguerite said, looking around.

"You're right," said Pierre, as they walked up to the level area near two big boulders at the base of a cliff. "But this is a perfect place, right here where we are standing. We can look out the harbour and no sea will never hurt us here, no matter how big a storm comes along."

Marguerite agreed.

They sat down on a rock and looked all around. They could see hundreds of different kinds of sea birds. And fluttering in the grass were many songbirds that they had never seen before.

"Everything looks so beautiful after the storm," said Marguerite.

Pierre looked at her and saw that she was smiling. Her long dark hair hung loosely over her strong shoulders. She had the prettiest face he had ever seen. He fell in love with her all over again this morning, right here in the Pigeon. Reaching out, he took her in his arms and kissed her.

"Cherie, I will never leave you again," he said as he kissed her and told her he loved her, and said he was glad she was going to have his baby.

"What will we do, Pierre, if they don't come back and pick us up. Have you ever thought about that?" she asked him.

"At the moment we are too busy to even let that thought come to our minds. We will get back to France one way or another," he told her.

"We are depending on you for everything," she told him as she leaned over to kiss him once again.

Pierre set his mind to the task of coming up with a plan to move the houseboat to the new location.

It was around noon when the three sat down to have lunch. They had leftover fish that had been cooked for breakfast, as well as Violet's home-made bread to dip into the liquid the fish was cooked in.

"The food is delicious, Violet," said Pierre.

Violet thanked him for the compliment.

As they sat eating their meal, the talk was about moving the houseboat to the other side.

"I want to ask you something, Pierre?" said Violet.

"Yes, what is it?" he asked.

"Tell us how you intend to move this boat from here to the new location you have picked out?"

Pierre hardly knew what to say as he looked at Violet and wished she had not asked the question.

"I will do it somehow," he said.

"Can I tell you what should be done?" she asked.

"Yes, go ahead, we want everyone's opinion," said Pierre.

Violet brushed back her long hair and sat down at the trunk they were using for a table.

"As you know, this is our home, it's the only one we have in the New World," she began. "In fact it's the only shelter we have to our name. There are no other places where we can go to stay while we are moving. If all goes well, it will probably take us a week to move this boat from here to the other side and put it in the place you've selected. From what I can see, there are only two ways you can do it and both involve cutting it in half. You can either cut it off across the middle or you can slice it in two long-ways and move the two sections. I have been thinking about it. It's too risky for us to even attempt to move the boat intact across the harbour for fear of something going wrong. Suppose you injure yourself. What will we do then?"

Pierre said nothing, only listened.

"The job is too much for us, if anything happened to you, you know that," Violet said.

"In other words, you are saying we should leave the boat here like it is and take our chances," said Pierre.

"No, I am nor saying that. What I am saying is that we should move the boat, but not over to the other side of the harbour," said Violet.

"And where do you think we should move it?" asked Pierre.

Violet motioned for him and Marguerite to come outside.

Once outside, she said, "As you can see, the sea came in as far as this last night." She pointed to where debris had come in along the shoreline at the high water mark.

"From where we stand and look out that way, this place is protected by that point jutting out," she gestured toward the point. "The waves coming in from the open ocean cannot reach us if we move the boat back about another twelve feet or so."

Pierre realized that what she said made sense.

Violet walked to the back of the rock wall where the boat sat bottom up.

"There's plenty of room behind here to move the boat back. All we have to do is extend the wall firmly for about twelve feet or so. We can lift the boat with a hand-prise, then put a couple of planks across to prevent it from fall- ing off the rock wall, and push it back in place. We don't even have to move out," said Violet.

Pierre went and sat down on the little knoll not far from the women. He knew Violet had a good plan; what she said made sense.

"You're right," he said. "That is the only thing we can do without taking any chances of losing our shelter."

"We can leave the wall we have there now in place, and put a canvas roof over it. This wall will give us extra protection from the sea, and we can store our firewood there for the winter if we have to," said Violet.

Pierre agreed. It was an excellent plan and he was willing to get at it right away before another storm came along.

He and Violet immediately went to work on the rock wall. Margue- rite was not allowed to do any heavy lifting due to her condition. Pierre brought the rocks up from the shoreline and Violet put them in place. Pierre grinned as he told her she could work better then most of the soldiers he knew.

Before dark, they had one wall and part of a second built.

"If all goes well, we should have the walls built and the boat moved in place by tomorrow evening," said Violet.

As twilight cast its shadows over the little harbour of L'Anse au Pigeon, the three sat together and ate their supper.

Early the next morning, before the sun came up, Pierre and Violet were out at the rock wall. They knew this was a job that had to be done as quickly and as perfectly as they could do it. They started by bringing the flattest rocks they could find to put in the wall. After they had so many gathered, Violet stacked them into the wall while Pierre continued to bring them to her.

Around 9 a.m. Marguerite called them in for breakfast. She had salt fish that had been soaked overnight and boiled with soaked hard bread. It was not what they would serve at the castle in France, however, considering their situation now, it was a wonderful meal.

"By noon, we should be ready to move the boat back to a new position on the rock wall," said Pierre.

"Are you going to take the ship's sail off the top of the boat?" asked Violet.

"No, we are only going to loosen it on one side and roll it up, then we will rise the boat up and put at least three of the planks across the rock wall, and slide the boat back on them," Pierre said.

"Yes, that's a good idea. But we have to roll the canvas up on both sides, because the flange that the stovepipe is coming up through is nailed to the other side of the boat. That way, the ship's sail has to travel with the boat as we move it," said Violet.

"You're right, that's how it has to be done," said Pierre. He turned towards Marguerite. "I want you to start and take all of the things out of the lockers in the sides of the boat. It will make it much lighter when we go to push it back," he said.

"That's a good idea," said Violet.

After breakfast, Violet and Pierre started bringing mud and sand and all the small rocks they could gather. They threw everything along the rock wall. The mud was easy to shovel this morning; it was still damp and soggy from the rain that had fallen the night before last.

When this chore was done, they started lifting the back of the boat and putting planks underneath on the rock wall.

This was not an easy task, but with the help of the planks that they used for a hand-prise they got the job done without too much difficulty.

Pierre and Violet tried to push the boat back by hand but could not move it. However, Pierre knew how to rig a hand-prise that would move the boat a foot each time he put it in place.

By early afternoon they had the boat pushed back twelve feet on the rock wall. It was now in a much safer place. The next thing they did was secure the ship's sail back over the boat and throw a lot of rock and mud onto the edge to weigh it down to the ground. They put two heavy ropes over the sail and anchored them down in order to make the boat extra safe against storms.

The heavy ship's canvas on the floor was moved further back to cover the new area of the floor. The next thing they put in place was the stove. It was heavy and hard to move.

When the stove was secured, Marguerite lit the fire and put the kettle on. She began to make a supper of leftovers from lunch.

After they had finished eating, Pierre and Violet started making a frame out of the plank over the rock wall that had previously been part of their house. When the frame was done, they put the last of the canvas over it and ballasted the edges with rock, mud and sand.

Their living quarters were now complete and as good as they could be with the material they had to work with. *From now on, we will refer to the houseboat as their "hut."*

After the middle of July, the berries started to get ripe.

All the bogs and around the edge of the barrens were covered with bakeapples. *Considered by some to be the most delicious berries that grow, bakeapples can be eaten from the plants where they grow, or cooked to make jam. The berries can be eaten as dessert with a little cream or sugar or made into a liqueur and preserved for years. Bakeapples contain vitamin C. The barrens were also filled with blackberries, berries that can be eaten from the plants, but leave a black inky stain in the mouth. When cooked, blackberries make excellent jam. They also contain vitamin C.*

"We might as well start picking a whole lot of these berries and start preparing them for the winter," said Pierre.

The number one topic now was 'what would happen if they weren't rescued?' How would they survive during the winter in a hut on the edge of the mighty ocean? They had no idea.

One day, Violet told Pierre that they should begin getting firewood ready for the winter. She said she had a feeling Admiral Roberval would never come back for them.

"If I was in the admiral's place," she said, "I would never come back and pick up people I dumped off in an isolated land instead of carrying out the job I was commissioned to do, for fear they would go to the authorities when they got back. Without them, I could always make up something to satisfy the people in control."

Pierre and Marguerite knew she could be right. As far as they were concerned, they were doomed unless some other ship picked them up.

Almost every day, Marguerite would go upon the high hill behind their hut and watch for ships out on the wide ocean. She had that job because of her condition. She was getting bigger every day. She told them she thought she would deliver her baby around the middle or the last of January.

Pierre had the job of catching fish and cleaning them. Violet was responsible for putting the fish in salt and spreading them out to dry.

One day in late July, Pierre got a net full of large salmon. There were too many fish for them to handle, so what they did was clean the largest and sprinkle them with a little salt. They then hung the salmon over round poles to dry in the sun to preserve them. It worked quite well.

Almost every day Pierre would cut and bring firewood to the hut. He now had a large stack, enough to last all winter.

He decided to set up the sharpening stone and show the women how it was used. He was quite familiar with it. He had taken a course on how to sharpen swords and knives and maintain the stone.

CHAPTER 11

The Caribou Kill

One morning, Pierre got up early and went for drinking water. Because the tide was out he walked along the shoreline. After a hundred feet or so, he came to a place where he had to go in around a little cove. As he walked along, he thought he saw something close by the side of the trees.

He stopped and stared and saw it was some kind of animal. He looked closer, crouching to avoid being seen. The animal was feeding on moss and shrubs. He knew it was a type of deer, but had never seen anything like it before. It had huge antlers and stood very high on legs that were light in colour.

As he stood watching, he was surprised to see two similar looking animals walk out not far from the one with the big antlers. "Good Lord," he said. "There's enough fresh meat there for a whole year, if only I had my gun."

He dropped his buckets and started to crawl back to the water's edge. "I've got to go back to the hut and get my gun," he whispered excitedly.

Pierre rushed back to the hut and burst through the door with eyes bulging. "Shh," he whispered to the women as he put his finger to his lip. "There are three large deer not far from here. If I can get close enough, I should be able to shoot them."

The women were excited. "Can we come with you?" they whispered.

"Not right now," he said. "But get ready and come as soon as you hear the shot fired."

Pierre's gun was loaded with grapeshot (*a kind of shot, consisting of a cluster of iron balls*). He put the flint in place on his gun and left.

The women came outdoors and watched as he slowly crept along the shoreline, looking keenly as he went. When he got so far, he peeked up over the cliffs that lined the shore. He looked for a moment then went further.

He could see where he had left his water buckets. He moved further, watching carefully. Then he saw the stag. It had not moved far from where he had first seen it. He moved a little further along the shore, keeping out of sight so the animal would not see him and get spooked.

He reached the spot where he'd left his water buckets. He looked carefully around and saw all three animals. He knew if he was to get a good killing shot at them he would have to get much closer.

He sized up the terrain and saw where he could get closer, But first he would have to go back and approach by a different route near the tree line. He again looked the area over and moved back. The three animals did not move from where they were feeding.

Pierre worked his way quietly along the edge of the trees at the bottom of the slope without the animals seeing him. When he got to the point of trees where the open barrens started, he was not more than thirty feet from them.

He checked his gun. Everything was ready. He pulled back the hammer and took aim. There was a loud roar as a cloud of black smoke rose from the gun.

The large stag dropped immediately. One of the does started running. It fell and got up and ran for about fifty feet more before falling again. The other doe ran and disappeared over the barrens about a hundred yards away.

Pierre put down his gun and walked over to the stag. There was no doubt he had killed it dead. Grapeshot had entered its head and lungs. He went to the downed doe. It was not dead, but it was obvious it would die soon.

He saw Marguerite and Violet coming as fast as they could.

They were excited when they saw the big animal lying on its side and amazed to see such large antlers. Pierre said it was a stag, and the other now dead animal was a doe. Violet said these were the largest deer she had ever seen.

"The skins will make two fine mattresses for us to sleep on," said Pierre.

The women agreed.

Taking out his knife, Pierre cut the throats of the two animals in order for them to bleed out.

"You stay here while I go and have a look for the other deer. I think I hit it too," he said.

"No, we're coming with you," the women said, hurrying to catch up with him.

"Look over there," said Marguerite, pointing to a spot on the barrens, not far away.

"Yes, I see it," said Pierre.

It was the other doe, dead and lying on its side.

They could hardly believe what had been accomplished with just one shot from the gun.

"We have enough meat to last us for a year," said Violet.

"Now, we have to get all of these animals cleaned and skinned," Pierre said as he cut the doe's throat.

Back at the hut, they got things ready. Violet suggested making a handbarrow to carry the meat back.

"What are we going to do with all the meat? It might spoil before we can eat it," said Marguerite.

"We can salt about a barrel of the meat. That way, it will keep until the frost comes," said Pierre.

Marguerite did not want to talk about the frost coming. She hoped to be back in France by then.

"Where are we going to get a barrel to salt the meat in?" she asked.

Pierre did not know, and he did not answer.

When Violet was growing up in her little village in Normandy she learned every trick there was. She saw her father and mother make a living from things around the countryside that most people threw away. Her father used to say, "Always cut the garment to fit the cloth, and you have to rob Peter to pay Paul."

Now she looked at Pierre and Marguerite and said, "We have one barrel full of flour outside and one open here in the hut. We will use one of the barrels and salt it full of deer meat."

"What will we do with the flour that's in the barrel?" asked Marguerite.

"There's no worry about that, cherie," said Violet. "All we have to do is take one of the fancy dresses in your trunk and make it into a bag. Then we'll empty the flour that's left in the barrel into the bag. Voila! We will then have an empty flour barrel."

Marguerite and Pierre laughed as they looked at the older woman with admiration.

"Here's your job, Marguerite," said Violet. "In my sewing kit, you'll find a cobbler's needle and heavy line. You chose the dress you like the least and I will show you how to cut it so as to make the bag strong enough to hold the flour that's left in the barrel."

The women went to work making the bag while Pierre busied himself cleaning and skinning the deer. In a couple of hours, he started bringing the meat to the hut. The first thing they did was put on a frying pan full of the delicious meat and have a feast.

Afterwards, they filled the empty flour barrel with meat and salted it.

They sprinkled the animal skins with light salt and laid them out in the hot sun to cure.

"It will take a couple of days for them to dry out," said Violet. "After that, they should be fine to sleep on."

During the month of August, much time was spent improving the hut. More mud and sand were added and sods were cut and laid over the mixture.

They had enough fish caught and dried and stored in the hut to last them all winter. The hut smelled like a fish store because of the dry fish in the lockers.

By now, their hopes of being rescued this fall started to fade.

Marguerite was getting bigger every day.

Some mornings, she was too sick to get out of bed. Her legs were often swollen and she was puffy around the eyes.

Violet said she thought eating too much salt and no milk products caused the problem. Marguerite was, however, eating plenty of wild berries and the dried fruit they had brought from the ship.

During the last week in August, the three castaways experienced another terrible storm.

The wind came on from the southeast and blew for three days and nights with heavy rain, thunder and lightning. Brooks were running everywhere, but there was no water on the floor of their hut. Then the winds switched around to the northwest as a gale.

During this time nothing was done, except for Pierre entertaining the women by playing the fiddle and singing old country ballads.

They were very careful with their food supplies and made sure that nothing was wasted.

Pierre added a shed he built out of round sticks onto the side of the hut to store supplies they couldn't bring inside. He used round sticks to make a roof that he covered with sods. This would prevent wild animals from eating the meat stored there. The roof worked well, and the shed didn't leak when it rained.

He also decided to pile firewood against the side of the hut, figuring it would be easier to get at when the snow came.

Up until this time, all was going fairly well for the three castaways. They were working hard every day to gather enough food to last them through the winter. And the hut was almost completely covered with sods and mud.

Pierre and Violet spent many days bringing mud and sand to cover the roof of the piece they had built on. After this was done, it took very heat from the stove to make the place warm. Their biggest problem was darkness. There were no windows in the sides of the hut. The only light they got was when the door was opened.

Violet asked Pierre if he could saw out part of the boat's stern section and make a hole so that they could have light in the kitchen area. Pierre wondered what he could use to cover the hole.

Violet thought for a moment. "I have an idea," she said. "Cut the hole big enough to let in enough light so that we can move around the hut and see to eat our meals. I would say the hole should be about two feet square. Then, we can take the cover off one of our trunks and make a shutter. We won't need the trunks anymore after we are picked up, or at least I won't need them. All I want to do is get aboard a ship and head for France."

"Yes, me too," said Marguerite.

Pierre looked at the older woman with a twinkle in his eye. "Violet," he said with a grin, "You should be the leading training officer for all of France's military."

Marguerite laughed. "Why do you think Papa employed her for twenty-two years?" she said. "Maybe if he had listened to her in the first place we would not be here now."

Violet was silent.

"I will start right away and cut the hole," said Pierre.

In a couple of hours, the job was completed. Now they had light in the kitchen.

Early one morning during the first week of September, Pierre opened the door in the porch and stepped outside. He looked around to see if there was anything unusual happening.

His eye caught sight of movement just across the tickle. Whatever it was, it was on the rocks, not far from the edge of the water.

He looked closer and knew at once that it was some kind of a seal, but it was very large. He slowly and quietly stepped back into the hut. He woke the women and told them what he'd seen.

"I am going to have a shot at the beast," he said.

Violet jumped to her feet. Wearing just her nightgown, she went to the porch and peered across the tickle.

"There's enough fat and oil on that animal to keep our lamp burning for over a year," she whispered.

Pierre was getting the gun ready. It was already loaded with grapeshot and powder.

He put the flint in place and crept out to the porch. He estimated the distance to be about forty yards. Perfect for a sure killing shot.

"Go outside, Pierre. If you shoot in the porch you will fill the hut with black smoke," whispered Violet.

Pierre moved, catlike. He saw the sleeping seal and was about to take aim when he heard Violet whisper, "It's a walrus, it's a large walrus. I've heard of them."

Pierre took aim at the animal's head and pulled the trigger. The kick-back from the gun threw him back against the rock wall.

There was a loud explosion and the walrus made a terrible leap. But, instead of going into the water, it went on the land, on the grass. The walrus had received a deadly wound. Blood poured from its head.

"Come on, Violet, let's get the boat in the water," said Pierre.

"You get the boat. I'm not dressed," she shouted.

Pierre ran for the boat and pulled it down to the water's edge. "Get the axe and some rope," he called, as he looked towards the floundering walrus. The animal was still on the edge of the grass.

Violet grabbed the axe and a piece of rope and threw it into the boat just as Pierre pushed off. In a few minutes, he was on the other side of the tickle. He pulled the boat up onto the rocks and grabbed the axe. He dashed to the dying walrus. It was a massive animal.

He saw that several pieces of the grapeshot had gone into the animal's head and neck. He swung the axe with his entire might and hit the walrus in the forehead. The blow would have killed the animal, even if it had not been wounded by the grapeshot. The walrus floundered a few more times, and then went still.

Pierre took out his knife and stabbed the animal twice to make sure it was dead. He looked the walrus over. "What a beast," he said. "I want you to come over and take a look at this," he called across to the women.

Jumping in the boat, he went back across the tickle where he got rope from the hut. His idea was to tie rope to the walrus and pull it across in the water.

The women came with him to take a look at the dead walrus. Its two tusks were more than a foot long. None of them had ever seen anything like it before.

Violet said it was better to clean and do whatever they were going to with the animal on the spot. "It will make a terrible mess around the hut area if we cut the walrus up there. We should do everything here. The gulls will carry away anything we don't need," she said.

"You're right again, Violet. We will leave it here," agreed Pierre.

There were four inches of solid fat next to the skin of the walrus.

They got wood and made a fire between two rocks not far from the carcass. They put the big iron boiler on the rocks over the fire. They filled the boiler with chunks of fat and rendered it out, leaving them with a light yellowish coloured oil.

After removing the rendered fat, they boiled the oil for two hours and removed the debris. This gave them clear oil, with no odour.

"Where will we put the oil?" asked Marguerite. "We can't leave it in the boiler."

"I don't know where we can put it," said Pierre. "Violet, where can we store the oil so we can make another five gallons?"

"What about the sugar tubs? Can't we do the same with the sugar as we did with the flour?" Violet asked.

Pierre and Marguerite laughed. "We knew you would have a solution for the problem," said Pierre.

"We can handle twelve gallons of oil in the containers we have," said Marguerite.

As Pierre was cutting the fat off the walrus's skin he cut himself with the razor sharp knife. It was a cut more than one inch long across the thick part of the palm of his hand.

The women looked at the cut and the blood as it oozed out. It was not a deep cut, but one that was about a quarter of an inch deep. Pierre wiped blood and grease away from the cut and continued cutting up the fat and meat.

Violet was uneasy about the fat and oil getting into the wound. "This could be serious," she said. "All that grease getting into the cut could cause infection so please stop right now."

Pierre told her he would be fine and continued working.

The three castaways were all living dangerously in the New World. They had no medical equipment or medicine whatsoever. In the case of an accident, they had to manage the best way they could.

After ten gallons of oil had been rendered from the walrus fat, they went back to the hut. Violet made a bandage from some cloth that she tore from one of Marguerite's dresses. She washed the cut and bound Pierre's hand. She knew he had a bad cut that would have to be attended to with extreme care. Pierre, however, did not think it was serious.

Late that evening the cut started throbbing and Pierre began to complain. Violet took the bandage off.

Marguerite lit a candle and looked at the cut, noticing that Pierre's hand and arm were swollen. He said his hand and arm were very painful.

Violet took a look and decided to boil hot water and soak his hand in it.

"I will add a little salt to the boiling water," she said. "That usually kills any germs."

The women made Pierre put the infected part of his hand into the hot salty water. He did so only after a lot of persuasion.

Afterwards, Violet made another bandage out of some clean linen. She put his arm in a sling and told him to try and get some sleep. Pierre lay down near Marguerite and soon fell asleep.

Early in the morning, he awoke with a terrible pain in his arm. He woke Marguerite, and she told him to try and sleep until daylight. He said he would try and suffer it out until then.

As he lay there in great pain, Pierre de Val did not know and was not aware that he had what Newfoundlanders called a "seal hand."

Seal hand is inflammation and swelling of fingers and hand caused by an infection from handling seal pelts or carcasses. When someone is cleaning or handling seal meat or seal fat, the grease from the animal gets in the cut and causes a deadly infection. If this wound is not treated immediately, it can cause permanent damage or even death. In the old days aboard sealing ships, whenever a sealer got a seal finger it would have to be amputated. In other words, the captain of the sealing ship would cut the finger off with a sharp knife and a hammer. If this was not done the sealer could die of blood poisoning. The sealer who refused to have his finger or hand cut off soon became so delirious and insane from the infection that he sometimes jumped overboard or ran away from the ship on the rough ice. Read the book "The Greatest Hunt in the World" by George Allen English.

The women were up at daylight. Marguerite had kept the fire going all night. She had not slept at all.

If Violet had nurse's training and some medicines to work with, she probably could have stopped the infection that was causing all the pain in Pierre's hand and arm. His hand was swollen and red, and had to be elevated to ease the pain. A red streak went halfway up his arm, indicating blood poisoning.

"I am going to make a soft bread poultice and put it on the cut," Violet told him.

She knew some of the old remedies used in France at the time, but had no knowledge of poisoning from seal grease.

She did know, however, that if someone had dirt in a wound, the remedy was to make a bread poultice out of bread, add a little ash from the stove, and put it on the infected area. This was supposed to draw out the debris from the wound and it would heal. In this case, she was dealing with seal grease in a cut, not dirt in a cut, and she had to be careful not to poison it further, or make it worse.

She had Pierre put his hand on the table. When she took his hand out of the sling, he screamed in pain as the blood flowed into it. She took the bandage off and revealed a terrible looking hand. It was badly swollen and very red. She noticed that infection was starting to set in the cut.

"I am going to bathe your hand in hot salt water. That will ease the pain," she told him.

Marguerite held Pierre's other hand to lend him support. She knew he had a fever; she could feel the heat from his body.

Violet held his hand down in the hot salty water as he screamed in pain. "Help me, blessed Virgin, help me," he shouted. "You're going to scald my hand," he yelled, looking at Violet.

"I'm trying to save your life, so you can scream all you want," she shouted back.

Violet continued to clean the wound. She ordered him not to take his hand off the table while she was dressing the wound.

"I think I'm going to pass out," said Pierre.

"Get a cold cloth and put it on his forehead," Violet ordered Marguerite.

Marguerite got a cloth, which she put in cool water then wrung it out and placed it on Pierre's forehead. That made him feel better.

By now, all the feeling had gone from his hand. The hot scalding water had deadened it.

Violet took his hand out of the water and dried it, then examined it. "You've got a nasty looking hand, Pierre. We've got to give it great care," she said.

She took some ashes from the stove and put them on a plate. She took a knife and separated all the dirt from the white part of the ashes. She took soft wet bread and wrung it dry. She placed the ashes on the bandage and spread it out. She then put the soaked, minced hot bread on the ashes and carefully spread it in a thin layer. Pierre opened his hand as Violet applied the poultice.

"This will help kill the infection," she said.

Pierre winced as she bandaged his hand. The poultice eased his pain, but it was still throbbing.

"Violet, cherie, you are a saint," he said as he put his arm around her and thanked her.

"Marguerite will get your breakfast now. You will feel better soon," said the worried Violet.

Pierre lay back on the bed and talked about the oil that had entered into his wound. "I wonder what kind of germs are in that oil?" he asked.

"There may not be any germs in it at all. It's just that the grease in the animal's body doesn't mix with the blood in your body, and when it does it causes an infection," Violet told him.

After Pierre had eaten his breakfast he went to sleep.

Marguerite and Violet went outside and sat down near the water's edge.

"I am very worried about his hand," said Marguerite.

"Yes, so am I," said Violet. "There's not too much that we can do, only try and kill the germs with hot water and salt. We are not medical people and we have nothing to give him, so we just have to wait and see what happens."

Marguerite was frightened. She knew that Pierre had been in great pain, and she didn't like the red streak that was creeping up his arm.

"What do you think of that red streak going up his arm?" she asked.

"It's blood poisoning. I've seen it before. It could be fatal if it's not taken care of." Violet gave her the blunt truth and Marguerite's face filled with grief. "We'll see what happens when he wakes up. If the swelling has gone down we will soak his hand in hot salty water again and bandage it. We will have to continue doing that until the infection clears up."

Sometime around noon, the women heard Pierre talking. "I believe he's awake," said Marguerite.

Violet went inside the hut. She saw Pierre still lying on the bunk. His eyes were closed and his arm was in the sling. He wasn't making any noise. He looked as though he was sleeping.

"He's still sleeping," she said quietly.

She and Marguerite saw that Pierre was breathing heavily and there was perspiration on his forehead.

"He really is still sleeping," whispered Marguerite.

Violet looked closely at his arm and saw that his hand was still swollen, perhaps even more so than earlier.

"We should wake him. He's been sleeping for close to five hours," she said.

Marguerite put her hand on Pierre's shoulder and gently shook him. He rolled his eyes and moved his legs. She shook his shoulder again, and he opened his eyes.

"Pierre, how are you, cherie?" she asked with concern.

He mumbled something she couldn't fully understand.

She asked him again how he was. He opened his eyes and looked at the girl he loved. "I think I am dying, or I'm going to die," he said in a weak voice.

Marguerite looked at Violet who was watching closely and with great concern.

"Do you have pain in your hand?" Marguerite whispered to Pierre.

He tried to move his hand but couldn't. "I have a lot of pain in my arm and in my hand. I can hardly move it," he said.

"Stay still and we will get you a drink of water," said Violet.

"Help me up," he implored.

Marguerite put her hand behind his back and helped him to a sitting position. He swung his legs over the bunk and sat up straight.

"There's so much pain in my hand and arm that I feel like crying. It feels like it's on fire," he said.

'We're going to take a look at the cut and see if the bread poultice drew out any dirt or infection," said Violet.

Pierre's whole body ached.

"I need to go to the bathroom," he said.

"Marguerite will help you outside," said Violet.

Marguerite helped him outside and closed the door. He could hardly stand on his feet.

"This is the first time that anything like this has ever happened to me," he said. "I feel so helpless, Marguerite. The pain is killing me."

"You'll feel better when Violet changes the bandage and bathes the cut again," said the frightened young woman.

"I dread to go through that again," he said.

"If that's what it takes to make your hand better we will tie you down and do it," said Marguerite, as they came back into the hut and sat down at the table. *The table was one of Marguerite's large trunks. Pierre had put four legs underneath it to make it higher. It stood in the middle of the kitchen area and served them well.*

Violet took Pierre's sling off very slowly, but even this slight movement made him wince in pain. She put his hand on the table and gently removed the bread poultice.

She and Marguerite were alarmed at what they saw. Pierre's hand was at least three times its normal size. It was swollen up to his elbow. There was a red streak all the way up his arm. Violet felt his armpit and the side of his neck, below the arm. She could tell the infection was rapidly working its way upward.

She felt helpless, not knowing what else she could do. The only thing she knew was to bathe the hand and arm in hot water and salt. It was her only hope.

The bathing was continued again with much groaning on Pierre's part. When the pain caused him to faint, he had to be revived with wet cloths placed on his forehead.

When the ordeal was over, the women helped him lie down on the bunk and covered him with a blanket. He immediately fell asleep.

He lay motionless, but every now and then he quivered and made unintelligible sounds.

Violet told Marguerite to expect the worse.

Marguerite became frantic with grief and started to cry.

"Can't we do something to stop the infection?" she sobbed.

"We have done all that we can do. I don't know anything else to do, except wait," replied Violet.

The women kept a vigil all night, stoking the fire and keeping a lamp burning.

Early in the morning, Marguerite tried to wake Pierre. His breathing was very heavy, and his hand was turning very dark. It was swollen out of shape.

After daybreak, Marguerite shook Pierre again. This time, he opened his eyes and looked at her.

"How are you, cherie?" she asked.

He told her he felt very sick and wanted a drink of water.

She helped him sit up and put a mug to his mouth. "Do you have any pain in your hand now," she asked.

"Yes, and a terrible pain in my neck. My neck is so stiff I can't move it."

"Would you like to have breakfast?" Violet asked him.

"Yes," he said.

"I will make you some," said Marguerite.

She sat near him, holding him upright. Finally, he put his head on the table and groaned in agony.

Violet told him she was going to put another bandage on his hand. He said he was afraid to have her touch it because of the pain.

"You're going to have to grin and bear it because that's the only way it's going to be cured," Violet said, with a firmness she didn't feel.

Pierre said nothing as he turned to Marguerite. "How are you feeling, cherie?" he asked. "Do you think the baby is going to be okay?"

"Yes, the baby will be fine, and I will be fine," she assured him.

"Marguerite, if you have a boy and something happens to me, will you be sure to name him after me?" he asked.

"Nothing is going to happen to you, Pierre, because Violet is going to cure your hand," Marguerite said, as she forced herself to smile.

"I think I'm going to faint," he said, as he tried to lift his head up from the table.

Marguerite helped him to the bunk where he lay shaking, with perspiration covering his forehead.

Violet came with a cool, wet cloth and placed it on his forehead. That seemed to revive him again.

After a few minutes, he sat up.

"There's no need to put a new bandage on my hand, Violet. I'm not going to survive," he said.

Marguerite put her arms around him as her eyes filled with tears. "You will survive, Pierre," she said. "You have an infected hand, that's all, and we are going to cure you."

"Your breakfast is ready. You can eat now, and after that you will feel better," said Violet.

Marguerite dried her eyes.

Pierre tried to lift his cup but couldn't get it off the table.

"I am too sick to lift the cup," he said.

"I'll lift it for you," said Marguerite.

She lifted the cup of water to Pierre's lips and he took a sip. He had the water in his mouth for some time before he swallowed it. As soon as it was down, he vomited it up on the floor.

"I can't eat," he said with a sigh.

The women didn't know what to do or say.

"I want to lie down again, Marguerite. Will you help me lie down?"

Marguerite helped him to the bunk and he lay there quietly.

Violet looked under Pierre's sling and saw that his arm had turned dark, all the way up to his elbow. She didn't tell Marguerite.

Pierre appeared to be asleep, but his body was twitching. This was not a good sign. Violet went outside. She couldn't bear to stand there and watch him suffer.

Outside the hut, she saw a storm was brewing. The clouds were wild in the eastern sky and the sea birds were silent. At this time, however, Violet was not concerned about a storm. Her mind was preoccupied with the condition of the young lieutenant, Pierre de Val.

She leaned against the woodpile as tears came to her eyes.

She knew Pierre was fading fast. She could see no hope for him. There was nothing more she could do for him, only pray that he would die easy.

Hearing Marguerite talking to Pierre, she went inside and saw the young woman leaning over her lover. He was telling her something, but Violet couldn't hear the words.

She stood near the table and watched. In a few minutes, Pierre went back to sleep.

Marguerite covered him with a blanket and tucked him in before turning to Violet and motioning her outside.

They walked to the woodpile and stood there as if in a trance.

"He just told me that he is going to die," Marguerite said, with tears in her eyes. Violet held her close, just as she had when she was a child in France.

"Don't worry, Marguerite, I will be with you no matter what happens," she said as she patted her back.

"If anything happens to Pierre, what will we do?' Marguerite asked the older woman.

"We will survive, Marguerite. We will survive." she reassured her.

Marguerite dried her tears. "What is your honest opinion, Violet?" she asked.

Violet knew there was no point saying something that wasn't true. Marguerite was going to have to face reality, just like her.

"I don't have any hope," she sadly said. "It looks like gangrene to me, and it has taken over. His arm is black up to his elbow."

Marguerite knew she was right.

"What was he telling you, Marguerite?" asked Violet.

The younger woman started to cry again. She covered her face with her hands and couldn't answer.

Just then the wind blew from the southeast and a few heavy raindrops fell on the heads of the women. The storm was coming on, as the morning sun hid its rays and the shadow of doom settled in.

The women went inside and secured the doors. Violet knew there was nothing more she could do for Pierre.

In the semi-darkness, she opened her trunk and took out her Bible. It had been there, wrapped in a cloth ever since they left France.

She opened the Bible, and then found a candle wrapped in the same cloth and lit it. She opened her diary and wrote in it. Then, picking up her rosary beads, she silently began to pray. She continued praying till Marguerite called her.

CHAPTER 12

Sorrow and Tears

The exact date when the storm came sweeping into the harbour of the Pigeon on that day is not known, but we do know that a young army lieutenant lay dying in the first dwelling ever constructed in that area by white people.

Sorrow and grief were written on the faces of the two women sitting in the shade of a flickering oil lamp. Both women were weeping as they sat at the table watching Pierre de Val gasping for breath. The sea roared as it swept past the outside door. Lightning flashed and thunder roared as the overturned after-boat covered in a ship's sail shook in the heavy gale.

Around midnight, Pierre opened his eyes and sat up.

"I have to go to the bathroom," he said in a voice that was little more than a whisper.

Before the women could get to him, he staggered to his feet and stumbled out the door. In a matter of seconds, he was outside in the wind and rain.

Marguerite ran out behind him. She was followed by Violet.

"Where is he, where has he gone?" asked the wide-eyed Violet.

"He said he had to go to the bathroom."

"Grab your coat and stay in the porch," Violet said to her.

Pierre wasn't near the front of the hut.

Violet called his name but he didn't answer.

It was very dark, the sea was not far away, and she could feel the salty spray.

She called him again, and then crept in around the woodpile. She thought she heard him. She called a third time. She heard him not far away. Violet felt around in the darkness, walking slowly. Without warning, she suddenly tripped over Pierre's body and fell to the ground.

"Pierre, Pierre," she screamed above the driving wind.

He did not answer.

She saw that he was lying on his face in a puddle of water. He was covered in mud and sand. She turned him over and yelled at him, but he didn't respond.

She pulled him towards the woodpile and left him there. She felt her way back to the porch and found Marguerite there, weeping.

"I found him. He's out near the woodpile," she told her.

"Is he all right?"

"Get me a heavy blanket, Marguerite."

The younger woman rushed in and got a blanket. She gave it to Violet, who dashed out again. She groped her way to the woodpile and found Pierre. Once again, she tried to rouse him but got no response.

She spread the blanket on the ground and rolled Pierre in it. She pulled him along to the door. Marguerite kept the door open as Violet pulled the lifeless body inside and to the kitchen, where there was enough light to see him.

His sling was gone and his arm was dangling by his side. The women knew at once that it was over for young Lieutenant Pierre de Val Cormier. He was dead.

The two women had a terrible night. They cried for hours, holding one another.

Towards dawn, they lifted Pierre's body up on the bunk and removed his wet clothes. Violet looked at his hand and arm and could hardly believe how much the infection had spread in just three days.

"The cause of his death is blood poisoning that turned to gangrene," she told Marguerite.

They dressed Pierre in his army uniform and laid him out. Violet took a piece of cloth and tied his mouth together.

Marguerite was broken-hearted as she sat near the table and wept.

The following morning, the storm was over and the tide was low. A light westerly wind blew out of the little harbour of L'Anse au Pigeon.

During the night, Violet had lit a candle and gone into her part of the hut and pulled over the screen. Taking her Bible from her trunk, she turned to the index in the back where she looked up deaths and burials. If it were possible, she would try and give Pierre a decent burial. She marked the place where a priest would usually read from the Bible and pray. She would read the passage, but she would not be able to pray. Again, she wrote in her diary.

She and Marguerite brought Pierre's body out to the porch and covered it with a part of the ship's sail.

They decided they would bury the body wrapped in the sail, because there were no boards to make a casket.

Violet left Marguerite in the hut as she walked around the inner pond area, looking for a decent place to dig a grave for their departed loved one. She took the shotgun in case she encountered wolves along the way.

Her plan was to wait until high tide when she would load the body aboard the small rowboat and carry it as close as she could to the gravesite. She would then take the sail-wrapped body, drag it to the grave, and bury it.

Violet returned to the hut and got the shovel and pick, then walked back to the gravesite. She thought about her situation as she walked along. She was in a place where she had to carry a gun to a gravesite for fear of being torn to pieces by savage wolves. "What will happen next?" she cried.

She wasn't sure if there was enough soil for a grave until she started digging. The site, however, was suitable and she dug a hole a little over two feet deep and two feet wide and about six feet long.

She wept as she dug, for she had loved Pierre as a son.

But she knew she had to control herself for Marguerite's sake. If Marguerite had a miscarriage because of stress, Violet didn't know what she would do.

When she had finished digging the grave, she decided to walk up the high hill not far away. She wanted to look out over the ocean for a few minutes, to collect her thoughts.

Atop the hill, she thought again about what Roberval had done. He was the cause of Pierre's death and perhaps of that of her and Marguerite as well. "But only God knows that," she said as she looked up at the sky.

Violet thought if there were some way she could put a curse on Admiral Jean Francois de Roberval, she would do it immediately.

She banished the thought as she headed back to the hut.

Violet told Marguerite how she planned to get the body to the gravesite. "When the tide comes in after midnight, I am going to move him," she said.

Marguerite still couldn't believe it. "Pierre is dead," she said, as she put her hands to her face and wept.

"We have to keep going, Marguerite," said Violet. "Pierre was like a son to me and his death is breaking my heart. But we have to go on and try to survive another day."

The women had a little lunch. Afterwards, Marguerite opened her trunk and took out a beautiful blue dress she'd thought she might wear on some special occasion. She never dreamt she would be wearing it to a funeral, especially to the funeral of the man she'd loved.

She had a problem getting into the dress due to her condition. Her stomach was starting to swell large with the developing baby. She wept as she realized Pierre would never see their child.

After Marguerite had finally managed to put on her finest gown and was ready to go, she sat at the table and tears ran down her face at the thought she'd never again hear Pierre's voice.

Violet came back inside and told her the tide was high. "You can stay here while I take the body to the gravesite. I'll come back and get you."

"No," said Marguerite, "I want to go with you."

Before they left, Marguerite went to her trunk and took out Pierre's sword as well as his helmet and breastplate. This was his ceremonial dress, worn on special occasions by French army officers.

"Do you remember him talking to me when you were outside yesterday? He told me if he died, he wanted to be dressed in this, and his sword put in his right hand," Marguerite spoke through her tears. "He also said, 'If you survive, Marguerite, and get back to France, make sure you take my violin with you and give it to my father in Lille. Tell my father what the admiral did to us and he will go to the king.'"

Marguerite carried Pierre's belongings to the boat and laid them gently atop his body. With the body of the young lieutenant in the bottom of the boat, the women rowed to the gravesite.

They landed within fifty feet of the grave that Violet had dug.

Marguerite helped Violet take Pierre's body out of the boat and place it on the grass. Violet dragged the body close to the side of the grave, where she untied the sail, and uncovered it.

Marguerite carried the sword, helmet and shield to the gravesite. She put the helmet on Pierre's head, the breastplate on his chest, and lastly she placed the sword in his right hand.

She wept as she said a final farewell to the man she loved.

She put her arms around Pierre's neck as she kissed his cold lips for the last time. Violet had to pull her away.

Violet wrapped the body again and lifted it gently down into the grave. There were no flowers placed on the body of this fallen son of France.

"Pierre was a good soldier and was loyal to his country," Violet began in a quivering voice. "He was well liked by all who knew him. He has fallen at the hands of a cold-blooded murderer, Admiral Jean Francois de Roberval."

She tried to say more but her voice failed her and she began to cry. After a while, she got herself under control and said a prayer, holding her rosary beads in her hands. She picked up some earth and said, 'Ashes to ashes, dust to dust. I commit you to the ground, one of France's finest soldiers."

Violet picked up the shovel and covered Pierre's body with earth, then walked back to the boat, with her arms around the weeping Marguerite.

The women returned to their hut and closed the doors behind them.

The fire was still burning and the kettle was hot on the stove.

They sat with their elbows on the table and looked at each other, emotionally drained. Sorrow was everywhere.

"I hardly know where to begin," said Violet, as she wiped her eyes.

Marguerite stood up and started to take off her too tight dress. Going to her trunk, she opened it, then folded the dress and carefully put it away. She came back to the table and poured glasses of ale for herself and Violet.

"I have to tell you something very important, Violet," she said.

"Yes, what is it?" asked Violet as she looked at the young woman with watery eyes.

"I am going to live to get back home to France. Come hell or high water, I'm going back. And you know what I'm going to do? I'm going to get revenge for what my rotten, murderous uncle has done to us. He will never sail the ocean again after I get back home. He murdered Pierre De Val and he will pay for that," said a very determined and angry Marguerite.

Violet heard the determination in Marguerite's voice and knew she meant what she said.

"It's true," she said. "If the admiral hadn't put us ashore, Pierre would still be alive."

As the women drank their ale, they talked about how they would manage without the young lieutenant.

The codfish had moved out of the harbour and offshore to the fishing grounds, but there was still plenty of trout and char in the big pool at the inner pond, waiting for the big rain to raise the water to let them get over the falls.

The women knew they would have to catch more fish to help with their supply of food for the winter. Their hopes of seeing a ship close enough to attract attention and get picked up before winter closed in were fading.

Every day, they watched from the hills.

Once, they saw three ships come out of the Strait of Belle Isle, but they headed out into the Atlantic in an easterly direction.

Every day, they kept themselves busy, improving their hut for the coming winter.

One day, Violet told Marguerite that she didn't think the porch walls were strong enough to support the heavy snow that could come in the winter.

"We'll cut round sticks and stud the porch around, and lay round sticks close together on the roof. Then we can put the sail on top. That will keep the snow and rain from coming down through the roof," she said.

Marguerite agreed, but she knew there was heavy labour involved in ding the work, which included putting a post up in the centre of the hut.

Violet began to work, cutting the material and carrying it on her back. In a week, she had the task completed. She then started cutting wood and carrying it to the hut. She chopped all the wood into stove lengths and packed the porch full.

In late November, the snow was on the ground and ice was forming along the shoreline.

By this time, Marguerite was heavy with child, but that did not stop her from using the flintlock gun. One morning, Violet peeked out through the door and saw a large flock of shore ducks in front of their hut. She quietly went back and told Marguerite who got the gun, put the flint in place, and cocked it. She crept out onto the porch, opened the door, and went outside. She hardly had to take aim. She just put the gun to her shoulder and fired. The impact from the gun hurt her shoulder, but she killed many birds. Violet launched the rowboat and picked up twenty-five.

The women spent two days picking and cleaning the birds.

There was no problem preserving them. They hung them outside in the porch to keep them frozen. They could use them anytime they wanted.

They secured their rowboat at the rear of the hut for the winter. All their food was stored inside, and they figured there was enough to last until spring. Violet thought there was sufficient firewood to last them for most of the winter, but she planned to add more and stack it outside.

The women had no idea how much snow would fall during the winter, or how much ice would build up in front of their hut, which was close to the windswept ocean. But the greatest fear to come their way and frighten them out of their wits was the arrival of polar bears.

Around the first week in December, Marguerite wasn't feeling very well. There were days when she didn't get out of bed. The women slept together in the bed near the table. It was closer to the stove for Violet, who had to keep the fire going night and day. The women were fortunate because they had a good stove that could burn almost any type of wood. At night, they filled the stove full of wood and closed it off, and it would slowly burn for more then ten hours, giving them enough heat to keep the hut fairly warm. They also melted snow in the big boiler, which gave them a supply of fresh water for their needs.

"You have to get lots of rest, Marguerite, and make sure you don't lift anything heavy," Violet cautioned.

Marguerite didn't expect the baby to arrive before the last week in January or the first week in February. There were times when she thought she was having labour pains.

Marguerite had no one to talk to about labour pains. Violet had never had a baby and had never seen a baby being born.

The women talked about what was going to happen when Marguerite went into labour. Violet told her she'd heard many women talking about having babies, and was confident she could deliver the baby.

During December, fierce storms swept the area. There were days when the women never opened the door to look outside. One evening a terrible blizzard started and lingered for two days, and snow drifted in through the cracks around the outside door. Violet got strips of rag to put in the cracks to stop the drifting; she got an old blanket and hung it inside the door to stop drafts.

Spray from the sea covered their hut and caused ice to form on everything outside. Violet thought it would be better not to use the outside door at all, just let it drift in. They would cut a hatch in the roof of the porch, make a ladder from round sticks, and go in and out through the roof. That was the safest route to go.

Violet did everything for Marguerite. She was her nurse, cook, caretaker, and mother. She rubbed her back, combed her hair, and got her meals. Violet told Marguerite the inside room would be their bathroom. She provided one of the chamber pots and a dung pail.

"I feel like a child again," Marguerite said to Violet. "When we get home, I will make sure that Papa pays you double for all of this."

"Did you know that your father has paid me double for the work I have done for him ever since you were born?" asked Violet.

"No, I never knew that," said Marguerite.

"Well he has, and my pay is still continuing. That's the reason he sent me with you. He knew I would do all I could to take care of you and stand by you, no matter what happened."

Marguerite put her arms around Violet and held her as a child would hold her mother.

During Christmas, the women tried to make the best of everything. They had plenty of food and wood for the stove. For Christmas Day dinner, they had an eider duck baked with dumplings, and bakeapples for dessert.

It was not a very happy time for them, but "at least we are in a shelter, with a stove burning and food to eat," Violet told Marguerite.

By the end of December, Marguerite started having pains. She spent most of her time in bed, covered in heavy blankets.

Violet became more concerned as the time drew closer for the baby's arrival. She knew about Marguerite's mother, how she had died when Marguerite was born, even with a physician and midwife present.

"My, my," she would say to herself. "What will I do if there are complications beyond my control?"

But Marguerite was like her father, strong, stubborn and determined. Violet had heard him say many times that his wife was a very delicate person who was unable to bear children. "Maybe Marguerite can handle it," Violet kept saying to herself. But she couldn't keep from worrying.

Around the first week of January, Violet went up through the hatch in the porch and out onto the snow. The only thing that could be seen was the stovepipe and the top of the woodpile.

The snow had drifted so hard she could walk on it. She noticed tracks of wild animals, tracks that looked like those of a dog. She noticed that the animals did not come very close to the hut, but circled the area.

She knew there were no dogs around and the tracks were definitely not fox. They had to be the tracks of wolves. "This is in the north where wolves live so it must be wolves," she thought.

Violet walked up to the woods where she cut firewood and observed that wolf tracks were everywhere. Concerned it might worry Marguerite, she decided not to tell her until after the baby was born. Violet knew wherever she went from now on she would have to be very careful because of the wolves.

CHAPTER 13

The Baby

The exact date is not recorded, but historians write that sometime around the last week of January Marguerite had a baby that only lived for one day. It was also written she was brave and strong during the delivery and never once lost control. She kept her wits about her through it all.

During the years 1901 to 1943, L'Anse au Pigeon was a small thriving community with a midwife named Emily Jane Roberts. She had been trained by Sir Wilfred Grenfell, the famous medical doctor who came to the area in 1892.

This lady delivered all the babies that "came into the world at Lancy Pigeon," as she would say. In fact, this story of Marguerite was helped along by an eighty-year-old gentleman, Norm Tucker, who was born just a few hundred feet from the very spot where Marguerite had her baby hundreds of years before.

After Violet delivered Marguerite's baby girl, she couldn't sleep for many nights afterwards, especially after the baby died.

Marguerite too lay sleepless. She was haunted by the thought that her baby had died and might not have if only she were home in France. Violet had done the best she could and she would be eternally grateful for that. But for the rest of her life, she would always wonder if the baby would have lived if more medical help were available. It was a question that would remain forever unanswered.

Marguerite hadn't been out of the hut since the morning she shot the ducks. She hadn't seen the huge snowdrifts that surrounded the area. She hadn't seen the tracks of roaming wolves that sought to devour anything they could get their teeth into.

Violet knew the body of the one-day-old infant could not be left in the hut. The baby would have to be buried as soon as possible.

Marguerite was broken hearted when Violet told her that her baby had died. She wept uncontrollably for two days.

When Violet said she would have to bury the baby, Marguerite asked if the child could be placed in the grave with Pierre.

Violet knew that was impossible due to the frozen ground and the depth of snow. However, she told Marguerite it could be done, and she would do it.

Violet wrapped the baby in one of Marguerite's dresses and tied it tight. She said a prayer, and to the sound of Marguerite weeping inconsolably, she carried the tiny body outside.

She knew that Marguerite couldn't get out of bed. So she decided she would bury the baby somewhere in a snowdrift, and hope it would be gone by the time the snow melted. She asked God to forgive her because she would have to lie about the burial when she returned to the hut.

Violet went to the area where she had been cutting firewood. She dug a hole to place the baby in and covered it with snow. She said a prayer, waited for an hour, then came back to the hut.

Marguerite didn't ask any questions about the burial. She may have had an idea, though, what Violet had done.

Three weeks after Marguerite had the baby, she was back on her feet and feeling stronger.

The days were getting longer and the sun was beginning to show its power. March month was on the rise.

One afternoon around the first week of March, the two women finished their lunch and were just about finished washing dishes when they saw the stovepipes moving. They knew something was wrong.

They looked at each other and jumped to their feet.

Marguerite signaled to be quiet as she crept out into the porch and slowly lifted the hatch in the roof.

Her eyes stared into the eyes of a great white creature that was standing only a few feet away.

She knew immediately what it was. It was a huge polar bear. She had heard and read about them.

Violet was watching her and knew she had seen something out of the ordinary.

"My God, what is it?" she asked, as Marguerite quickly closed the hatch.

"Get the gun, Violet, get the gun."

"What is it?" Violet wanted to know.

"A huge polar bear is standing on the roof near the stovepipes," said Marguerite.

Violet rushed in and took the gun down from the wall and handed it to Marguerite, saying, "The flint isn't on it."

Marguerite primed the cup, put the flint on the gun, and crept back up the ladder. She opened the hatch all the way up, and then cocked the hammer.

The polar bear was very close, not more then twenty feet from her, standing on its hind legs and looking straight at her.

Marguerite rested her elbows on the roof as she took aim and fired. It was quite an explosion. Black smoke billowed up from the hatch.

The bear staggered and fell. It got up again and ran for a few feet before letting out a roar that almost shook L'Anse au Pigeon. It fell not far from the woodpile, dead in its tracks.

The women walked cautiously over to the huge animal. They had never seen anything like it before.

"It's a polar bear or a water bear," said Violet.

"Yes, I've read about these animals. They have the best coats of fur in the world," said Marguerite.

"I've heard that the meat is good to eat. If that's the case, we have enough fresh meat for a whole year," said Violet.

With difficulty, the women rolled the bear onto its back.

"I suppose we'll have to skin it the same as Pierre skinned the deer – split it down the stomach first, and skin it, then paunch it afterwards," said Violet.

"Yes, I think that's the way we'll do it," said Marguerite.

After the women had managed the difficult task of skinning the polar bear, they immediately took the skin to the hut and spread it on the floor, with the fur side down. They would have to clean the skin and sprinkle salt on it in order to cut the grease from it. They would have to put the skin as close to the stove as possible to dry it, and then work it soft. This would have to be done to preserve it till the warm weather came, and then they could put it out into the sun to dry. Violet knew all about this.

They went back to the carcass and paunched it.

The two hinds were approximately a hundred pounds each, all-solid meat. They dug a hole in the snow and placed the meat in it.

"We won't cover it over until tomorrow. It has to freeze first," said Violet.

"What if the wolves take the meat tonight?" asked Marguerite.

"No, they'll eat the paunch first. It will be frozen by tonight. We'll bury it tomorrow," said Violet.

They cut up a boiler full of the ribs and put them on the stove to cook.

They took the heart, liver and the head and put them in the porch to cook later on. Nothing was wasted.

That night they heard growling outside and knew the wolves were feasting off the remains of the polar bear.

The next morning, the women were up at dawn and out looking at the meat they had put in the hole. It wasn't touched, but it was frozen. The paunch had been carried away and eaten by the wolves.

One morning during the end of March, the women heard something while they were getting breakfast. Violet opened the hatch to take a look. When she opened the hatch, the noise was much louder. She got up on the roof and turned towards the ocean. As far as she could see, there was nothing but a field of Arctic ice.

"The sound is coming from the ice," she said as Marguerite joined her on the roof.

The women looked closely over the field of ice. Then they saw what was making the noise. It was young seals, white coats. (*Young harp seals approximately one month old.*)

The seals were close to the rocks, hundreds of them, as white as snow. The women just stood and stared at them, speechless.

As the spring came on and the snow started to melt, Violet grew worried about where she had hidden the baby's body. One evening, she told Marguerite she was going to go up on the hill behind their hut and have a look around.

Carrying a shovel, she climbed the hill and looked out over the ocean. As far as she could see in all directions there was a solid field of Arctic ice. She noticed in some places the ice was black with older harp seals.

She decided to walk down through the drove of timber that stretched below her, the place where she cut her firewood. It was where she had hidden the baby's body.

She came to the spot and discovered the body was gone, and had been for some time. She knew animals had taken it. As she walked back to the hut she felt guilty and wondered if she had done the right thing. She was afraid that her actions were going to haunt her, but what else could she have done?

As the snow started to melt and the Arctic ice moved off, there were large islands of ice in every direction.

One day, the women counted over a hundred icebergs as they sat on the hill above their hut.

They would sit and watch for hours to see if a ship of any kind would come into view. While they sat there, they would watch the mighty bergs founder and roll over like monsters alive in the ocean.

One day in late May, they saw four large ships come into view. They jumped and waved and yelled, but to no avail. The ships veered to the left and went on south.

Another day, they stood on the high mountain and saw five ships come into view from the east. They watched as the ships continued on through the Strait of Belle Isle, going towards Quebec.

By the first week in June, the snow was gone and the ice along the shoreline had melted.

Marguerite walked up around the inner pond to Pierre's grave. She stood on the edge of his grave and wept. She felt a sense of disbelief. She could not bring herself to believe that her beloved Pierre was under the soil she stood upon.

She looked around to see if there was a flower of some kind she could pick to put on his grave. There was nothing, just a few blades of green grass hugging a rock for warmth nearby. She bent down and picked the grass, and placed it on Pierre's grave. She decided later on she would make a wooden cross and erect it there.

Violet decided to take inventory of the remaining food supply. There was some dry salt fish left, but it was starting to smell bad and it was slimy. They had a full barrel of flour and some of the hard bread. The hard bread was moldy but edible if starvation set in. They had a fair amount of beans, peas and rice left. There was salt pickled fish and some deer meat in the flour barrel, but it was turning black.

The ducks, the polar bear meat, the salmon and the Arctic char were all gone. She noted this was the best food of all and it had quickly disappeared.

One evening, the women were trying to determine how they could attract a ship. Jumping and waving didn't work. They needed something more, something that would be seen from far away.

'I know what we can do,' said Violet. "Let's have everything ready to start a fire and make smoke. Once the people on a ship see the smoke they may come and investigate."

"How will we get a fire going in time for the people to see it?" asked Marguerite.

"What we'll do is find a lot of good, quick burning material and tie it up in a blanket and have it ready to light when we sight a ship. We will have one of the buckets ready to take the fire out of the stove and run out with it. You carry the bucket of fire and I will carry the blanket of dry kindling.

We can start a fire quickly that way," said Violet.

"That's a good idea," said Marguerite.

"Once we get a ship's attention, we can wave and call out to them," said Violet, as Marguerite nodded in agreement.

One afternoon during the first week in July, the women were up around the inner pond. They fished for trout in the pool while the tide was out and the pool was full. It had been foggy most of the day with very little visibility.

When they returned to the hut, they took off their wet clothes and changed into their long dark dresses.

They were sitting at the table wondering if they should fry some trout for the evening meal when they heard a sound that made them jump almost out of their skin.

"Did you hear that?" yelled Marguerite.

"Yes, yes, I heard it, it sounds like a ship's bell," Violet shouted as she bolted for the door.

The women almost got caught in the doorway going out.

They ran up the hill. From this vantage point, they could see a small rowboat off the harbour. They went berserk, jumping up and screaming and waving their arms. They looked like two people doing a war dance.

The rowboat stopped when it got so close, and then turned around and went back to the ship.

The women screamed and roared but to no avail. The ship took the rowboat aboard, hoisted its sails, and moved on.

The women couldn't help themselves. They sat down on the top of the hill and started crying. "We must have frightened them away," said Violet, as she covered her now wrinkled face.

The ship they saw was a French vessel looking for a good place to go fishing for the summer. It had just arrived from France and L'Anse au Pigeon was the first land they'd sighted.

The one thing that Violet didn't know and would never know was that she and Marguerite were living on an island three miles long by two miles wide, and only three hundred feet from the main island of Newfoundland at its western end.

When the French captain sent a party ashore to take a look at the small harbour to see if it was a good place to fish, the fishermen in the rowboat saw two figures jumping up and down, seeming to be dancing in some kind of demonic dance. They thought the place was full of demons and got frightened and turned back. The captain put a name on the island, calling it Quirpon Island,

"The Island of Demons." Word of the island spread far and wide among French fishermen.

It was a terrible evening for the women, worse even than the afternoon they were abandoned.

"I could look into the faces of the men, we were so close to them," said Marguerite, as she sat at the table with tears in her eyes.

"It looked like they were coming straight into the harbour until they saw us. One man pointed at us, then the other two stopped rowing and looked in our direction. That was when we started screeching to them. They turned around then and headed back to their ship," said Violet.

The women sat at the table and stared at the walls. Violet put her head on the table and cried.

After the women had eaten their supper and darkness had settled in for the night, their hut was filled with gloom and doom. They again talked about how they could attract a ship to pick them up.

"We have to do something different than we did this evening," said Violet.

"We didn't have time to light the fire and make a smoke," said Marguerite.

"I know," said Violet.

"Well, what else can we do?" asked Marguerite.

"I have an idea as to what we can do," said Violet.

"What can we do?"

"We can make a large French flag and tie it to a pole up on the island. Passing ships will surely see the flag and come in to investigate," said Violet.

"What can we use to make a flag?" asked Marguerite.

"You have many gowns in your trunk that we could use to make a flag. All we have to do is get the right colours," said Violet.

" I think there is something else we can do to attract men to pick us up," said Marguerite.

"What?" Violet asked.

"We should cut our hair. We must look like two witches to anyone coming here from France."

Violet agreed. That night, in the dull light of an oil lamp, a young French princess sat on the edge of a bunk that was covered by a caribou skin and had her hair cut short. She then cut her maid's hair.

The next morning, the women started looking for the right material to make a French flag. They found enough material in four of Marguerite's finest dresses to make a flag six feet long by five feet wide, with colours that matched the French flag.

Violet went up the side of the hill and cut a slender flagpole, twelve feet long. She brought it down and tied the flag to it. She stuck the flag up on the island, put rocks around it, and tied it with ropes to keep it in place.

There was now something that any passing ship could see.

The two women spent most of their time gathering food, fish, birds and marsh berries left over from the fall before.

There was so much fish they couldn't believe their eyes.

One day, they took the gun and went over to Degrat Cove to see if they could get some duck eggs. The water was low in the cove; at one place it was almost dry.

They decided to walk out on Degrat Island and have a look around. Along the edge of the grass, next to the water, there were thousands of eider duck nests. They were amazed. As they walked along, the nesting hens left their nests and flew all around them. The water around the island was almost covered with birds of varying size and color. The sound of the waterfowl almost deafened the women.

"This New World is a place that France should have," Violet said, as the birds flew overhead.

"If my uncle had kept his promise and claimed this land for France, it would have been the country's greatest glory," said Marguerite.

The women took off their coats and started gathering duck eggs. They decided to row over in the boat and get as many as they wanted the following day, if the weather was suitable.

Around the middle of July, the women started picking berries. The bakeapples were ripe enough to make jam.

Every day, they spent time watching for a ship to appear, but none came. They saw several far in the distance going through the Strait of Belle Isle, but they were too far away to even wave at.

One day, Marguerite was watching Violet as she came from the pool up near the brook. She was walking very slowly and had her hand to her chest. She appeared to be in pain. When she arrived at the hut, Marguerite asked her if she was feeling sick.

"Why do you ask?" said Violet.

"I saw you coming from the brook with your hand on your chest, and you looked as though you were in pain. Is there something wrong?"

"Oh, it's nothing to be concerned about. I'll be fine," Violet lied.

Marguerite dropped the subject.

In August, the women started picking bakeapples to store for the winter. Their hopes of getting back to France began to fade as the summer months rolled by.

They went to work cutting firewood and bringing it to the hut. They knew they needed wood and food in order to survive during the coming winter.

One morning, as they were having breakfast, they heard strange noises outside.

"What's that, Violet?" asked Marguerite, as she jumped from the table.

"I don't know," said Violet, who was equally startled.

They went to the door as the noise got louder. They cautiously opened the door and peered out. They slowly crept outside, looking fearfully around. The noise was coming from behind the hut. They didn't know what to expect.

"It sounds like a person calling," said Marguerite. "Hello, hello, who's there?" she called.

There was no reply so she called again, but still no answer. Marguerite walked behind the hut and looked around, but saw nothing. Violet could only shake her head, but she, like Marguerite, was certain they had heard someone or something.

The sound had not come from the ocean, it came from the land. Perhaps it was an Indian or an Eskimo.

However, it made no difference what they'd heard. Life had to go on, preparations had to be made for their survival, come hell or high water.

As the women worked with their bare hands, fighting for survival, Violet grew increasingly pale and it was obvious she was not feeling well. She tired easily and spent a lot of time lying down.

Marguerite tried to ask her what her problem was, but she would only say she had the flu. The younger woman knew the difference.

One day, with plenty of fish everywhere around the harbour, the women decided to put their net in the water. When they checked an hour later, it was full, so full of mostly salmon that it had sunk to the bottom.

It was quite a task getting the fish out. They cleaned as many as they could handle, then salted and packed the rest in one of the flour barrels.

One day, they saw a pack of wolves near the brook eating fish that had got trapped and died inside the sand bar when the tide went out. There must have been twenty or more of these ferocious animals, eating and fighting.

When the women saw the wolves they were concerned, because the creatures looked like they were ready to devour anything that came along.

"We won't be able to go to the brook for water any more, without taking the gun," said Violet.

"Even with the gun, it will be dangerous," said Marguerite.

Violet said they would leave the salmon in the barrel with the salt. She said before cooking it, they would have to water it for three days to get the salt out.

"We'll try and catch some codfish to dry in the sun too. Dried cod will last all winter," said Marguerite.

The women estimated they had picked and preserved as many berries as they had the previous year. To get them over the winter, they hoped with any luck they might shoot a caribou (deer) or two.

One evening just before dark, they heard the same noise as they had heard a week ago. This time it was coming from the other side of the harbour, not far from where Pierre had killed the walrus.

Earlier, they had seen four or five wolves on the beach in front of their hut, eating the remains of the cod they had cleaned in the afternoon.

Violet wanted to go and see if she could find out what or who was making the noise. Marguerite wouldn't let her go for fear of the wolves on the beach. The two peeked through the door, watching and wondering what would happen next.

Early in September, the wolves became very aggressive. At night, they would tear at the outside door trying to get in. The women heard them scratching around the top of the roof. At one point, they shook the stovepipe.

"We'll have to start shooting them," said Marguerite.

"Tomorrow morning we'll have the two guns ready and waiting for them. If we can kill some of them, it may scare the rest off," said Violet.

Marguerite agreed.

The women had a sleepless night, fearing that the wolves would come into their hut. At one point, they thought they would have to take a random shot outside to scare them away.

Early the next morning, the women crept cautiously outdoors carrying the two loaded guns. Marguerite was in the lead. The minute she was outside, she saw four or five wolves standing not far from the woodpile and staring at her as if they were expecting her. She immediately took aim and fired. She killed two and wounded four or five more.

Violet handed her the other gun. Marguerite walked to the woodpile and saw three more of the savage animals not far away. She took aim and fired, wounding all three.

After this encounter with the wolves, the women started gathering fire-wood again. Violet was having difficulty carrying wood because of the pain in her chest. Marguerite told her she was not to carry any more wood or use the axe.

"It's my turn to take care of you now, Violet," she said.

Violet knew something was seriously wrong. She could feel the pain slowly dragging her down. She worried about Marguerite. What if something happened, and she should die, what would happen to Marguerite? She was afraid to think about it.

Marguerite could see she was ill and tried to keep her from doing chores. In the mornings, Violet could barely get out of bed. She would cough and rub her chest. While she agreed not to do chores, she was not content with lying down and wanted to do something so she decided that her job would be to look out for passing ships.

Marguerite would pack her a small lunch and row her across the harbour if it was a clear morning. Violet would slowly make her way up the hill and sit for most of the day, wrapped in a heavy blanket, watching the ocean and praying for a miracle.

One evening in mid-October, just before the sun went down, Marguerite went to get Violet. She quickly walked up the hill to where Violet was sitting. The women sat quietly, talking about what they would do if a ship were spotted. They spoke of how good it would be to be back home again in France.

"Cherie, I want to hold your hand while I tell you something," said the now frail Violet. "There's something you have to know, something that is going to happen."

Marguerite held her breath. She knew what this motherly creature had to tell her would be something she didn't want to hear.

"Yes," she finally said, as fear gripped her heart. "What is it, Violet?"

The older woman gathered her strength. "I am not very well Marguerite, I think I'm going to die," she said. "I've been sick for more than three months and I'm getting worse every day. I have pain in my chest continually."

Marguerite burst into tears as she listened with disbelief to this woman who was the only mother she had ever known.

"Nothing is going to happen to you, Violet," she said. "It's just that you are not feeling well. The pressure of being stuck here for so long has gotten to you, but we could be rescued any day now. You just wait and see."

"No, I will never see my homeland of France again. Time is running out for me. The ships have stopped going to France for another year. The cold windy weather is coming on. All the fishing ships laden with cod have gone back home. We are the only two left here in the New World for another winter." Violet spoke gently to the weeping young woman who sat next to her holding her hand.

She had raised Marguerite from a baby to a woman who was now a seasoned survivor, and a fighter. Violet knew it was time to tell her about her illness, how she knew she would soon die, and how Marguerite would then be alone to try and survive in the wilds of the New World, battling the elements of nature: wolves, polar bears and the strange sounds that echoed and re-echoed throughout the night.

"If I die, I want you to bury me somewhere on the edge of this hill in sight of Pierre's grave. I loved him like a son. Try and put a small cross on my grave if you can. When you get back to France, tell your father that I love him and my portion of his will goes to you. He will understand."

With tears in her eyes, Marguerite promised she would do all that Violet requested.

On trembling legs, Violet stood and stared out over the broad Atlantic, where there was nothing to see but a vast expanse of water.

"Damn you, Jean Francois de la Roberval," she said as she angrily shook her fist at the sky. "May you forever perish like a dog on the streets of France for what you've done to us, and may your bones burn in eternal hell."

With those words still echoing in the air, the women walked towards the rowboat, Violet supported by Marguerite.

That evening, Marguerite took inventory of the food that was left. Most of the salt was gone, but there was a half-barrel of flour and a half bag of hard bread, as well as a good portion of beans and peas. There were enough berries and salt salmon. The dry salt fish and trout were in good supply. She hoped she would kill a caribou during the fall or winter. If she had to, she would kill a seal or two.

Marguerite sadly knew Violet wouldn't last much longer. But, even though she slept for very short periods, the older woman still insisted on going up on the hills and watching for a ship every clear morning.

It was obvious that Violet was having nightmares. At times, she would scream and pull her hair while sleeping. One night she started calling out to a baby, saying the wolves were coming.

"Run, baby, run," she shouted. "They're coming, they're coming. Run baby run."

Marguerite was certain Violet was calling her dead baby girl. She felt sure that Violet was having nightmares about the baby and couldn't help wondering what it was all about.

Violet would wake up bathed in sweat and tell Marguerite she was having nightmares. Several times, Violet tried to tell Marguerite what had happened to her baby's body, but her courage always failed her. She knew the truth could break Marguerite's heart and that she would likely hate her forever. But the thought of what had happened haunted Violet night and day.

CHAPTER 14

More Tragedy

One morning, Marguerite sat at the table while Violet lay resting in bed. Suddenly, they heard the loud calling sound again; it seemed closer than before.

Without saying anything, Marguerite took the gun, which was already loaded, put the flint in place and went outside.

She slowly and quietly opened the door and edged her way along by the woodpile. The sound was coming from the direction of the inner pond. She tuned her ear to the sound and keenly zeroed in on it. She heard it again. She thought she saw movement, and then she saw it, blending in with the surroundings, a creature with a face almost like a human. The creature was perched on a rock and looking at her, no more than a hundred feet away. She had never seen anything like it before.

She cocked the hammer, took aim, and fired. The creature fell over, screeching and batting its wings on the ground.

Marguerite carried the dead creature back to the hut.

Violet was sitting at the table when Marguerite came in, holding up whatever it was she was sure had been calling to them for days.

"Look at this," she said, holding it out for Violet to see. "A body like a bird and a face like a human."

Violet took one look. "A barn owl, it's a barn owl," she said.

"A barn owl? Do you think it has been calling us?"

"Yes, that's it. I've heard of barn owls before, but I never thought they would be here in the New World," said Violet. "They're good to eat, though, just like chicken. We'll cook it for supper."

"How do I prepare it?" asked Marguerite.

"First you have to skin it, then remove the insides and wash it in salt water before you put it in the frying pan. Add a drop of seal oil so it won't stick to the pan."

"It will be a dish fit for a queen," smiled Marguerite, as she put away the gun and proceeded to get breakfast.

As they ate their meal of bread and boiled fish, Marguerite mused aloud about the tracks of people they'd seen when they first arrived.

"I wonder what happened to the natives who were here before we came. We have never seen a sign of them since. I wonder if they got scared and left?"

"I don't think they got scared. They're just avoiding us, although they could be keeping an eye on us," said Violet.

"One of those days I am going to go down around Degrat Cove and see if I can locate a few of them," said Marguerite.

Violet started to cough. She was pale as she lay back down on the bunk.

"I wonder what day of the week it is?" she asked.

"It's Friday, according to your diary," said Marguerite.

"There is something I have to tell you, cherie," said Violet.

"Yes, what is it?" said Marguerite, as she looked sadly at the fading woman.

"If I die, you are going to be alone. You will have to keep your nerve up. Sometimes, when people are alone, they have a tendency to see and hear things. Some say they see ghosts and spirits, others say they see devils and demons. If that ever happens to you and you can't control it, take my Bible and place it on the table and keep it there, then make a wooden cross and nail it on the roof of the hut. Nothing will come near it.

"And, cherie, please bring my diary back to your father and let him be the first to read it. I wrote it for him, at his request."

Violet said nothing else as she closed her eyes.

Marguerite had the outside porch filled with firewood, and a large pile outside. She also had firewood stuck up near the hut just in case she ran short. Her intention was to use the wood outside first, as long as she could manage the snow.

Just before noon, Violet got out of bed and washed herself. Marguerite prepared her meal, and told her it was a lovely fall day.

"I'm going to sit on the hill again this afternoon, Marguerite," said Violet.

"You had best stay here and rest. I'll go over on the hill and have a look around," said Marguerite.

Violet insisted on going, but Marguerite refused to let her go, saying that tomorrow would be a good day and it was better to wait. Violet finally agreed.

"The chilly weather is starting to set in," she said. "Soon, snow will he falling. Last year, the ground was covered with snow by the middle of November."

Marguerite dreaded spending another winter in this God forsaken land. The thought of it almost drove her crazy. But what could she do?

It was now late October and Violet was very sick. A couple of times during the night, Marguerite thought Violet had passed away. However, the next morning she was feeling better and insisted on going across the harbour and up on the hills to look for a ship that might be going to France. Marguerite could not discourage her. She said she had to go.

Marguerite helped Violet dress and gave her water and bread with a little blackberry jam. She helped her walk to the rowboat and climb aboard. Marguerite rowed across the harbour and landed on the small sandy beach. It took some time to get Violet out of the boat and up to the top of the hill, to the lookout.

Marguerite wrapped her in a blanket and went back to the boat to get the gun. She told Violet she was going over around Degrat Cove and up on the high hill to the west. Violet cautioned her to be careful.

Marguerite was gone for a couple of hours. As she walked back, planning to take Violet to the hut for lunch, she saw the older woman lying down. She watched her for a few minutes and saw no movement.

Thinking she was asleep, she called, "Violet, wake up. We're going back to the hut."

There was no answer, no movement. Marguerite stood and stared. She called again, but there was no answer.

"My God, my God, Violet, answer me," she implored. But Marguerite knew that her adopted mother was gone, passed away, forever.

"Can't you say just one more word, Violet, just one more word?" she cried, but Violet was silent. Marguerite would never hear her speak again.

Sorrow and grief are not really the right words to explain the feelings deep in Marguerite's heart as she looked into Violet's face that evening. She put her arms around Violet and felt her warm face for the last time. Soon, the coldness of death would turn her warm body into nothing more than sand on the seashore.

Marguerite covered Violet's face with the corner of the blanket, then, steadying herself, she stood up.

What would she do now? All alone, stuck on a rocky island on the edge of the Labrador Sea with winter quickly closing in.

The Labrador Sea is one of the most unforgiving waterways on earth. It has the coldest water temperature and is strewn with icebergs and massive ice flows, sometimes for ten months of the year. It has no mercy, and its violent nature can never be tamed.

Marguerite sat on a rock near Violet and looked towards the harbour. She didn't hate this place, because it wasn't to blame.

But every time she thought about her uncle and what he had done, she felt hatred towards him and everything that he stood for.

She thought about Pierre and how she had loved him. She thought about her baby girl who had only lived for one day, and now Violet, the only mother she had ever known, was gone from her. It was her turn next, she was the only one left. When she was gone, the plan of her hated uncle would be complete.

She stood up, dried her tears, and swore that she would survive and get back to France to seek revenge.

With determination on her face, Marguerite began the task of burying her adoptive mother.

Leaving her body at the lookout, she walked to the place where Violet had said she wanted to be buried. It wasn't very far from where she had died. Standing there, Marguerite could see Pierre's grave and where Violet said she had buried her baby.

"Violet must have put quite a lot of thought into selecting this gravesite," she said to herself.

Marguerite cried all the way back to the hut. As she rowed, the sound of the oars seemed to say, "You are alone now, Marguerite. What will you do?"

Going into the hut, she looked around. All was silent. From now on the only sounds in the hut would come from her. As she gazed around, she could almost see Violet sitting at the table. The thought that she would never sit there again almost drove her crazy, and she walked outside to escape such thoughts. She remembered the Bible that Violet had in her trunk and how she wanted it read at her burial. She went inside to get it and found that Violet had marked the page she wanted her to read.

After wrapping the Bible in a towel, she put it aboard the boat together with tools for digging a grave. Her plan was to wrap Violet's body in a blanket, put her prayer beads in her hands, read the Bible and say a prayer, but how could she do it?

She rowed across the harbour and tied the boat to a rock that had the name '*Valentine*' painted on it.

She took the tools and the Bible to the gravesite. Going to Violet, she wrapped her body in a blanket. She somehow managed to carry the body to the gravesite overlooking the harbour.

She carefully laid the body down and started to dig the grave, cutting sod on the edge of the bog and rolling it back. The digging was easy because the boggy area was free of rock and roots.

When the grave was dug, she uncovered the body and placed Violet's rosary beads in her folded hands. She kissed her dear adopted mother for the last time and said au revoir, then carefully wrapped her body again. She placed Violet's body in the shallow grave and tucked the blanket tightly around her.

As a light warm westerly wind blew gently across her face, Marguerite opened the Bible to the page Violet had marked and began to read:

"Yea though I walk through the valley of the shadow of death, I will fear no evil for thou art with me, thy rod and thy staff thou comfort me."

After she'd finished reading, she picked up a handful of soil and said, "Ashes to ashes, dust to dust, from dust you came and to dust you must return."

Tears ran down her cheeks as she sprinkled the soil over Violet's body. Standing all alone on the hillside of L'Anse au Pigeon, with no one to hold or comfort her, or offer pity, Marguerite cried and sobbed with a broken heart.

On her way back to the boat, she put down the shovel and pick, and walked over to Pierre's grave with the Bible under her arm. She was weeping when she arrived at the cross that marked her lover's shallow grave. She laid the Bible on the grave and covered her face with her hands as she knelt on the cold earth, sobbing her heart out as tears ran through her fingers.

As she knelt there with her hands covering her face, it was as though a voice said, 'Open your eyes, Marguerite.' She opened her eyes and peeked through her fingers. She closed her eyes and thought for a few seconds and then opened them once again.

"I see something shining," she said to herself as she looked at her hands. "My God," she said aloud. "It's the ring."

Marguerite stood up. As she stared at the ring on her finger she forgot where she was for a moment. "This damn ring, it has been a curse to me," she said. "Ever since I put it on, all I've had is bad luck. Now the devil can have it."

With those words, she took the ring from her finger and threw it towards the pond and into the black mud that lined the shoreline. "I hate you, ring," she said as she picked up the Bible and walked to the boat.

CHAPTER 15

Marguerite Alone

The November winds blow very cold along the rugged coastline of the Great Northern Peninsula of Newfoundland.

There have been many songs written and stories told about the men and women who have perished in conditions much more favourable than a young French woman had to endure on the extreme tip of the Appalachian Mountain range that runs from Florida to Cape Bauld.

Marguerite landed the rowboat on the beach near the hut, then looked back over her shoulder and out at the wide ocean. The hills that surrounded the harbour looked dismal, with trees bent and stunted from the continuous strong northwesterly winds and shrouded in a cloak of gray.

Marguerite sized up her situation and knew the coming spring would produce a rugged, half starved individual full of hatred and revenge. If she survived, she would have to strive to overcome these feelings.

She pulled the boat upon the shore and tied it to the hut. She dreaded to go inside the door. Steeling herself, she took the pick, shovel, and the Bible from the boat and carried them in.

"Where do I begin now?" she said aloud, knowing hers were the only words she would hear from now on.

Taking the cover off the tub that was filled with walrus oil, she estimated there was one gallon left.

"I will need more of this to last the winter," she said, deciding that if a seal happened to come within shooting distance she would have to kill it in order to get more fat to make oil for the lamp.

After getting settled in the hut, she told herself that somehow she would have to survive, no matter what happened.

She thought about Pierre and Violet and the baby she never got to hold or cuddle. She made up her mind not to cry. Her aim was to survive until spring when perhaps a ship would pick her up.

As she thought about her surroundings, she wondered what she could do to pass the time. There wasn't very much. Violet had knit all the wool she could get her hands on; she'd even unraveled socks three times and re-knit them.

She remembered Violet telling her she had intended to make a coat for each of them out of animal skins. Violet had worked on the skins during the spring and summer and had made them as soft as velvet, especially the polar bear skin. Marguerite thought if she could shape the arms, maybe she could carry on and make herself a warm fur coat.

In early December, the frost and snow came and stayed on the ground. It was a horrible feeling to realize she would likely encounter polar bears and wolves over the long winter months. She would have to start bringing extra wood into the hut because it could be risky going outside. She could block the door where the wood was stored and start using the hatch in the roof again. That would be her safest step.

Marguerite started cutting wood in short lengths for the stove and stacking it indoors. She stacked some in the front of the hut where Violet used to sleep. She was sure she had plenty for the winter.

Sometime around the first week in December, a terrible storm started, bringing with it wind and snow. Mountainous seas rolled in. Marguerite could do nothing, just sit and listen. She made a few attempts to look outside but it was impossible. Spray from the waves pounding on the shore was covering the hut, leaving a sheet of ice over everything. Finally, there came a day when she managed to look out and see waves rolling in the harbour. Debris from the ocean bottom was strewn around everywhere. The waves came up to her door and she considered herself fortunate that Pierre and Violet had moved the hut further back.

The storm continued for three days.

During the storm, with nothing to keep her mind off the weather, Marguerite started playing the violin. She knew how to hold the violin and could remember the chords Pierre had taught her. Putting them together would be her biggest task.

She kept the fire going until she went to bed and then tucked the bedclothes tightly around her. If it was very cold, she covered herself with caribou skins.

When the storm subsided, Marguerite went up on the small hill further out the harbour and looked at the ocean. She saw flocks of eider ducks in the air and in the water feeding. She decided if they came in the harbour she would have a shot at them.

Heavy slob ice was beginning to form on the ocean; she could see it in the distance. Early one morning, she got out of bed and opened the hatch. When she peered out, she saw seals on the rocks in the exact place where Pierre had shot the walrus. She watched the seals for some time, wanting to make sure they weren't walruses.

Getting the loaded gun, she put the flint in place and then quietly got up through the hatch. She was uneasy about her shoulder when firing the gun, but she had no choice if she was going to obtain more fat to make oil for the lamp.

Taking careful aim, she fired. The black smoke kept her from seeing if she had hit or missed. When the smoke cleared, she could see she had hit all three of the seals. Two were still on the rocks, while one was in the water, floundering and bleeding.

She couldn't get the boat in the water due to the build up of ice, so she had to walk around the pond to get to the seals.

With her knife, rope and gun in hand, she walked around the harbour to find she had killed one seal, but the other two wounded seals had escaped. She cut the fat from the seal carcass and carried it to the hut where she boiled it into oil, pleased she would now have enough oil to keep her lamp lit for the winter. She also brought most of the seal meat to the hut and buried it in snow to keep it from spoiling.

Marguerite stayed indoors most of December. Every time she went out she felt the cold pierce her skin like a knife. What she found most disturbing, however, was the howling of the wolves at night, every night. One morning, she saw several caribou not far from the hut, but was afraid to go after them because of wolves.

Sometime during the end of December, on a stormy evening with high wind and blowing snow, she thought she heard someone calling. She knew the sound hadn't come from a ship because there was a solid jam of Arctic ice packed close to the land, and no ships were on the ocean around Newfoundland this time of the year.

With no sea heaving now due to the pack ice, Marguerite didn't know what to think of the sounds coming from the outside.

"It must be another owl hooting," she said to herself.

As she went up into the hatch, vowing to shoot the owl just to stop the calling, the sound stopped.

She opened the hatch and peeked out. All was quiet.

Marguerite looked over towards the rocky cliffs on the other side of the harbour. She thought she saw something moving and she stood watching, staring through the drifts.

It was twilight, and she heard the sound again, coming from the same direction. Then she thought she saw someone moving and waving. It looked like a person sitting on a rock, holding something in his or her arms.

She stood up on the roof and looked across. She cupped her mouth with her hands and called, "Hello, is anyone there?" There was no answer. She called a second time, but there was no response. She stared in the direction where she thought she'd seen something, but could see nothing.

Further up, near the inner pond area, she saw what looked like wolves, and that so frightened her she went into the hut.

She sat at the table in wonderment, thinking about what she had seen, or thought she had seen. It looked like a woman with a baby wrapped in her arms. She was puzzled about it all.

That night, Marguerite lay awake, wondering if she'd seen the ghost of Violet carrying her baby. The thought frightened her. How could she be so foolish as to even think such a thing?

All night, the wind blew with heavy drifting as Marguerite huddled close to the stove, wrapped in a caribou skin. She could feel the cold wind coming in around the door as the hut shook. Marguerite thought how lucky she was to have a fire. Without it, she wouldn't have lasted long.

The iron pipe going up from the stove shook as if there was a giant hand moving it back and forth. She hoped and prayed that the ship's sail over the roof would stay in place. If it ripped off, the roof would have less protection.

This was the biggest storm she had experienced since she arrived in the New World. The wind was in a different direction, though, coming off the land. She had no fear of the sea heaving and washing her away.

She kept the fire going all night, and the seal oil lamp never went out. She needed it in case she had to re-light the fire.

The next morning, the wind was gone and so was the ice that was blocking the harbour, but it was as cold as cold could be. The ocean was a dark blue with streaks of ice slowly going by and carried by the tide. A frosty vapour rose from the ocean.

Marguerite decided to have her breakfast. The iron kettle on the stove sent steam to the ceiling as she mixed flour and water with a little salt.

She had boiled fish left over from the evening before in a pot on the stove. She put the frying pan on the stove, heated a little seal oil, added her dough, and watched as it sizzled in the pan and slowly turned a golden brown. She turned the pancake over and let it cook on the other side. She ate her pancake with a cup of hot water, after she'd first bowed her head and thanked the good Lord for what she had.

After breakfast, she decided to go outside. She felt a need to get out of the hut and get her mind off things inside. She filled the stove with wood and closed it off, then put on her warmest clothes and climbed out through the hatch with her gun in her hand.

It was a frosty morning. The wind overnight had blown most of the snow away from the hut area.

She started walking along the shoreline to the inner pond. The tide was low and the pond was frozen. She saw wolf tracks everywhere. The wolves were patrolling the shoreline in search of anything that came ashore, particularly dead seals and birds.

She walked to Pierre's grave and said a prayer for him and her baby. She then decided to have a look at the place where she thought she'd seen someone the evening before. There was no sign of anyone or anything there. She paused at Violet's grave to say a prayer before walking up to the lookout where Violet had spent many hours looking for ships.

Marguerite decided to walk over towards Degrat Cove and have a look around. On the way, she saw someone upon one of the high hills overlooking Degrat.

Whoever it was, was looking in her direction.

Without thinking, she called out.

Her heart started to pound as she stood there.

She knew she was staring at someone, either a native or an apparition.

The person waved to her, then walked away, down over the hill in the other direction.

"Someone is here beside me," she said to herself. "All I have to do now is make contact. But how can I do that?"

Her heart felt lighter, knowing there was someone else in the New World, someone besides herself, and not far away.

She walked back to Violet's lookout and wondered if someone had been watching Violet. Maybe someone had, she thought, but if they had, why hadn't they approached her?

Marguerite noticed the heavy ice field was getting closer to shore. It was a heavy field of ice with icebergs in it.

She made her way back to the hut and checked on her fire. "If only I can make contact with whoever it is I saw on the hill, whether it's a native or a non-native, I don't care just as long as it is a living human being," she said to herself.

She started to make plans about how she would contact the person. There was someone out there and they were on the move just like her, either hunting or scouting the country and looking for something. Her thoughts raced, searching for answers, searching for a way.

Marguerite picked up the violin and ran the bow across the strings, using the chords that Pierre had taught her. Much to her surprise, she heard the makings of a tune.

This young princess, who had spent most of her life living in an elaborate castle on the outskirts of Paris, now stood on a ladder made of round sticks, with her head and shoulders up through a hatch in a hut that was made from an overturned boat. This princess, cast away in a rocky cove at the edge of the cruel Labrador Sea, was far away from home and civilization, and longing to make contact with one of the natives in her New World.

During the first two weeks in January, the weather turned severe. Every day, snow drifted across the barren hills and around the little harbour of L'Anse au Pigeon.

Unable to venture outside for fear of freezing, Marguerite stayed indoors and kept a very low fire going. She cut up one of the caribou skins and made a pair of pants for herself from the hide. They weren't the finest pair of pants ever made, but they fit.

She spent time practicing on the violin, using the few chords she knew. She was beginning to develop a few tunes which entertained her during the long evenings.

The winter she spent alone in L'Anse au Pigeon was cold and stormy. It seemed like every time the wind blew, it turned into a major blizzard.

One stormy evening, she heard what sounded like someone screaming above the moaning wind. She went up the ladder and lifted the hatch up far enough to peep out. The harbour was partly frozen over, especially the part near the hut. She lifted the hatch and went further up so that she could see all around.

The screeching sound was coming from behind the hut and high up on the hill in back. She looked closely and saw something move on the hill. She stared again in disbelief. It looked like a person wearing a long heavy coat. Marguerite was sure it was a person standing there. She waved, but it didn't move. She knew it hadn't always been there, as she had looked in that direction a thousand times before.

She called out "Hello, hello" but there was no response.

The screeching had stopped the second she opened the hatch.

"It must be an owl or a large bird," she told herself. Then she watched as the person walked along the hill for a few steps before disappearing behind some boulders.

She went down and closed the hatch. For the first time, she felt really frightened, knowing that what she saw was a person, and that person would only screech and stare, and was coming closer every time.

Marguerite sat quietly as the storm outside increased in fury. Her mind was in turmoil. Outside, something or someone was lurking in the darkness.

"What could it be?" she asked herself. "Will they harm me, or are they trying to frighten me?"

Marguerite wasn't sure. Then she remembered Violet's words: "If you ever get tormented with ghosts or demons, put the Bible on the table, make a wooden cross, and nail it to the roof of the hut."

Marguerite got Violet's Bible from the trunk, opened it, and placed it on the table. She put the lamp on the table and stared at the burning stove that flickered its light around the hut. That was the only moving company she had as she found two pieces of wood out in the porch and started making a wooden cross.

During the night, the storm raged on and the stovepipe shook so much that she decided to let the fire burn itself out for fear of catching the hut on fire.

Early the next morning, Marguerite got the fire going. The wind had subsided, but the hut was freezing.

Before going to bed, she had made a crude cross she hoped would keep away whoever or whatever was watching the hut. After breakfast, she went outside and nailed the cross to the end of the hut facing the frozen harbour. It was bitterly cold with heaps of snow and snowdrifts everywhere. The hills as far as she could see were shrouded in a white blanket.

Something strange was happening. Every time she saw a person, or what resembled a person, a terrible storm was sure to follow. Last night had been too stormy for anyone to be roaming the hills. Marguerite hoped the cross would take care of whatever was going on. Violet had said it would and she believed her.

As she looked around the harbour, Marguerite saw heavy ice fields in the distance. She also saw many thousands of eider ducks feeding on the shoals and around the shoreline. She wondered where they went when a storm like last night's swept over them. She was sure that many died in such a storm.

Marguerite decided to take the gun and go up on the hill behind the hut and have a look around. She was curious to find out if there had been a real person up there last evening.

"If there are tracks, it was a real person. If no tracks can be found, then it must be one of the demons Violet talked about," she said to herself.

She pulled on her caribou skin pants, picked up her loaded gun, and walked up on the high hill. She searched the area where she thought she'd seen a person, but there were no tracks anywhere.

While she was up on the hill, she had a good view of the entire area. It was a beautiful sight to behold. As far as she could see, there were fields of heavy ice that were covered with black spots. She knew at first glance it was seals. "There must be millions of them out there," she said to herself.

As she watched, she saw two large polar bears amongst the seals. She feared she could have trouble with them because they lived on the land, and she was in their territory.

But even though she feared the huge animals because they were very powerful beasts of prey, she hoped they would come close to the hut so she could kill one of them. Their meat last year had been very tasty, and another bearskin would help make her bed softer. "You are my protection, old fellow," she muttered as she patted the stock of her gun.

As she descended the high hill, she noticed the cross on the roof of the hut and laughed out loud. "It looks like a church," she said. "All I need now is a steeple — and what I wouldn't give for a congregation."

Marguerite's food was getting low. She still had beans and peas but no great amount of either. She used her scanty supply of flour to make pancakes because there was no yeast cake left to make bread. She had plenty of berries and fish left, but her cupboards were getting increasingly bare. She would have to go on rations, and it was still the first week in February.

One morning in mid-February, Marguerite heard a commotion out near the front of the hut. She got the gun and opened the hatch. In front of her, she saw a pack of wolves surrounding the hole where she had dumped the waste pail and some bones from the seal meat.

Putting the flint in place, she primed the gun with powder and cocked the hammer. Taking aim at close range, she fired. There was an awful roar. As the wolves ran for the hills, she could see that two lay dead in the snow.

Marguerite walked over to the dead animals, noticing their large teeth and the scars around their heads. She dragged their bodies to the edge of the ice. She was afraid to eat the wolves, so she threw their bodies into the ocean. Returning to the hut, she reloaded the gun for future use.

The snow by now was up over the hut, with only the stovepipe and the cross visible. During the afternoon, she decided to take a walk upon what is now called "the middle hill." The snow had drifted hard, which made for good walking. She took her shotgun with her as protection from wolves and polar bears. As she walked, she looked for signs of human habitation. There were many animal tracks, but no others.

When Marguerite reached the top of the middle hill, she could see in every direction and she made a surprising discovery. She was on an island. She looked to the northwest and saw a large harbour. *This was the place that French explorer Jacques Cartier named Quirpon and where he had anchored his fleet and permitted his sailors' time to go ashore and stretch their legs after the long ocean voyage from France to North America. Cartier named one of the islands that made up the harbour after him.*

As Marguerite looked to the northeast and nine miles in the distance, she saw a large island shrouded in its snowy wonder. Surrounded by high towering cliffs, the island was named Belle Isle by the Portuguese. Historians say that Belle Isle is the northernmost end of the great North American mountain range called the Appalachians, which stretch from Florida to Belle Isle. Further to the north, she could see a large landmass we know today as Labrador. Marguerite would never know the names of those places; they would be visual memories she carried for the rest of her life.

Marguerite could hardly believe what she was seeing. The entire ocean as far as the eye could see was covered with heavy Arctic ice. For a few minutes, she forgot about her problems and gazed at the splendour before her. Great icebergs towered in the afternoon sun as Arctic ice flows moved with the tide.

She saw huge flocks of eider ducks and suspected they were looking for open water to land upon and feed. They were looking, just like her, but they were home. Her home was on the other side of the world. As she looked at the deep blue sky, her mind went back to France and she spoke aloud, "I wonder if I will ever get back home again, or will I die here in the wilderness, just like Pierre, my baby and Violet?"

With those words, she put her hands over her face and wept.

CHAPTER 16

Following The Admiral

Admiral de Roberval's flagship, *Valentine*, commanded by Captain Fonteneau, hoisted its canvas and started to move from its position off the harbour of L'Anse au Pigeon. The flagship was in sight of the *Anne,* which was coming from the southwest and expected to catch up with them within an hour.

Captain Fonteneau was not a happy man. He told Major Jacques he had seen it all now and was just about to his limit with Admiral Roberval.

"It's only my loyalty to France that keeps me from disobeying orders, especially after what we did to three of our people. Imagine abandoning a young princess, a commissioned officer of the French army, and a French lady, dumping them off among the wolves, bears, and the rocky barrens of a desolated island, not knowing if the natives will scalp them on the first day. What are we coming to, Major Jacques?" asked the angry captain.

"I'm not sure what I think about it all. The biggest problem I have is how I will be able to justify this act when I report to my commanding officer back in France," said Major Jacques.

"Everyone aboard this ship is upset about what happened," said the captain.

"The next few days will be critical ones for all of us," said Major Jacques. "There are so many things that I can't explain to my troops yet. All I can do is tell them to be careful what they say."

"When we get up the St Lawrence River to Charlesbourg and get in contact with Cartier, he may do something about it. He's not a very good friend of Roberval either," said Captain Fonteneau.

"I talked to another officer and he's got the same feeling as me, that we will never see Lieutenant Pierre de Val again," said Major Jacques.

"I can tell you with certainty that this ship will not come back for the three people we just put ashore. The simple fact is that if Marguerite makes it back to France after being abandoned, her father will have the admiral hung from the gallows," said Captain Fonteneau, his words surprising Major Jacques.

The major swore as he left the captain's stateroom. He was certain his lieutenant would die in the wilderness of North America.

Just before dark that evening the three ships rendezvoused somewhere in the Strait of Belle Isle, and the admiral was transferred back to the *Valentine*.

Roberval was no fool. He could sense when trouble was brewing. When he arrived back on his ship, he had his plan made. He called for Captain Fonteneau and Major Jacques to come to his quarters.

"Gentlemen," he began, "it looks like we are going to have trouble aboard the *Lechefraye*. I want to make you aware that on board that ship I have more than one hundred seasoned criminals selected from jails in France. Most of them were waiting to go to the gallows, the rest are common criminals. I am taking them to Cartier's fort at Charlesbourg-Royal. They are going to work there as labourers." The admiral paused and cleared his throat. "It appears that some of the criminals are acting up and the captain is very concerned. I want you both to help put a stop to any uprising that may occur."

Major Jacques knew immediately what the admiral had in mind. Roberval was afraid of the army troops he had aboard his ship and wanted them split up among the other ships.

"I intend to have you take about thirty of your troops and put them aboard the *Lechefraye* tomorrow morning to guard the prisoners and keep them in line," said the admiral as he turned to Major Jacques. "You will have full authority to kill any of them without trial if they give you any trouble. You and your men will be billeted below deck where there's a kitchen and supplies are already waiting."

Major Jacques didn't like it. He knew what the conditions were like aboard that ship. She had a crew of mostly half-crazy drunken sailors who had fought in most of France's naval battles over the past twenty years.

But the men he himself had picked to come with him on this expedition were some of the toughest men in the French army. His men would not be pushed around and he suspected that was the reason Roberval wanted to transport them to another ship.

"Will this be a permanent move, Admiral?" asked Jacques.

"No, it's only until we get to Charlesbourg-Royal and put the criminals ashore. They will be left there for Cartier," said the admiral. "When we leave, we will be taking some criminals aboard who have served their time and are ready to go home to France."

"What about the Indian guides we are supposed to pick up and bring to Newfoundland. Where do we go to get them," asked Major Jacques.

"We intend to get them somewhere around the Saguenay River, in the area we call the land of the barbarians," said Roberval.

"When we go aboard the *Lechefraye,* do you want us to go in full battle order with our weapons?" asked Major Jacques.

"No, a show of strength will do," said the admiral.

All that night Major Jacques and half his troops were busy as they prepared to move to the *Lechefraye.* There were a lot of angry mutterings. Some of the soldiers said they should refuse the admiral's orders because they were leaving Lieutenant Pierre de Val on an island with no intention of retrieving him.

Major Jacques refused to listen. He told his troops the admiral was the supreme commander and if he gave an order, it would be carried out.

The next morning, the ships went into a deep bay and tied up side by side as the troops were transferred.

Admiral Roberval and the captains of his two other ships planned to make their raids on the English colonists in Newfoundland sometime in the fall, if all went well. These plans were kept a secret from Captain Fonteneau. He only knew about the plan for the prisoners and the day-to-day operation of the *Valentine.*

Major Jacques knew nothing about the plan to attack the colonists overland from Placentia and through to St John's, sometime between September and November.

Most of the summer was spent around Charlesbourg-Royal where Jacques Cartier had built a fort and where Roberval tried to establish a colony. Roberval sent some of his men on an expedition further up the St. Lawrence River on a quest for gold. He put the rest of his men to work, using the prisoners as slave labourers.

The historian Thevet wrote that Roberval showed no mercy to those wretched souls. He was very cruel in his dealings with them, so cruel that he had to suppress several uprisings, and he did that in a very cruel manner. It wasn't uncommon for him to beat a man to death in front of everyone else. He would make prisoners work without food or water for long periods of time. If anyone fainted, he would be beaten severely.

One day, Roberval hung six men as a warning to others.

His favorite punishment for those who stole was to chain their hands and feet and put them on a small island not far away.

It appeared that whatever Admiral Roberval did it was of a cruel nature.

During this period of time, merchant ships from Britain and Spain and other countries were traveling to and from North and South America. The ships were reported to be filled with treasure when they were bound for their home countries in Europe.

The merchant ships faced danger from pirates operating around the Spanish Main and the northeast coast of North America. Warships belonging to nations patrolling the high seas did not usually attack merchant ships. However, Admiral Roberval had heard about the reported treasures aboard these merchant ships and he decided to attack them. If any treasure were found, it would belong to him.

In August, Roberval left the upper St. Lawrence River, on his way to attack the English colonists around the Avalon Peninsula of Newfoundland. It was, however, too early in the season to carry out his plan because English fishermen in Newfoundland were on the ocean just starting to fish and might see them and give a warning. There were several British men-of-war on hand to protect the fishermen, as well as the ships that were collecting dried cod destined for England.

It was obvious that Admiral Roberval did not want to attack the powerful British navy. He would rather fight unarmed fishermen, old men, women and small children.

While he was waiting for the right time to sail, he decided to attack the merchant ships around the east coast and see if he could acquire some of the treasures reported to be on board these vessels.

On an earlier trip to the New World, Jacques Cartier had slipped away from Roberval one dark night and returned to France. Cartier believed his ships were filled with gold and diamonds he had found in the wilderness of Upper Canada.

Cartier's valuable treasure turned out to be fool's gold.

Roberval figured if he could now attack the merchant ships and get their gold and treasure it would put him in great favour with King Francois and he would be permitted to sail anywhere he liked with the French navy.

During the late summer and early fall, he attacked and robbed several of these merchant ships and took their cargo. He killed everyone aboard and sank the ships, destroying all evidence as he acquired treasure for the king.

He was reported being seen attacking British ships in the Caribbean, which caused a diplomatic crisis to occur. The English ambassador went to King Francois and complained about Roberval's looting and sinking of English merchant ships off the coast of America.

Roberval went south as far as the Caribbean and north as far as Labrador. Although he came within a few miles of the island where he had abandoned Marguerite and her companions in June, he sailed on by and refused to even glance in that direction, even though Captain Fonteneau and Major Jacques pleaded with him to pick them up.

In October, Roberval returned to Charlesbourg-Royal and stayed for two weeks.

While they were waiting for a favourable date to sail to Newfoundland, Roberval sent several boats on an expedition further up the St. Lawrence River in search of gold and precious stones. This expedition consisted of seventy or eighty men. Several of the boats ran into trouble and overturned, causing many lives to be lost. This trip caused a delay in Roberval leaving Charlesbourg-Royal and resulted in his ships getting frozen in ice. Great hardship was in store for Roberval's men during the long, cold Canadian winter. The colony was affected by much disease and famine. During the winter, several uprisings occurred which Roberval had to forcibly suppress, causing more loss of lives.

In June of the next spring, a ship arrived with orders for Admiral de Roberval to return to France for a new assignment to the North African colonies.

This was not good news for Roberval, who was still eager to attack the English in Newfoundland. But, in obedience to the king, he left the New World to return to France.

He had, however, no intention of going back to the northern tip of Newfoundland and picking up the three passengers he had put ashore over a year ago, and he said so in no uncertain terms.

Roberval set his course through the Cabot Strait and around the south coast of Newfoundland, heading out into the Atlantic Ocean. The *Valentine* and the other two ships under his command had a rough voyage back to France.

On his return, Roberval wrote a report in which he expressed his disappointment at not having the opportunity to attack the English in Newfoundland. There was no mention of Marguerite and her companions in his report.

Meantime, Major Jacques had made up his mind that he would go to the highest military officials in France and report what Roberval had done to three citizens of France.

Jacques had many conversations with Captain Fonteneau about the matter. The captain agreed that he would report the incident as well. It appeared both officers were prepared to put their careers on the line if necessary.

Roberval couldn't wait to get rid of the army personnel he had aboard, in particular Major Jacques. When the ships were in sight of St. Malo, Roberval gave orders to the major to prepare his troops for immediate disembarkation the minute the *Valentine's* lines were cast ashore.

Major Jacques was pleased to be back in France and finished with the worst assignment of his military career. He had not written his report about the castaways while aboard ship for fear of the admiral having his men do a search and finding it. If truth be told, he feared for his life at all times.

He was aware that Roberval did not like him. The admiral had told several officers that the army major was treading on dangerous ground, but he was not prepared to do anything about it because the soldiers would defend their commanding officer.

But now Jacques was off the *Valentine* with his troops and ready to make a full report about what had happened to his lieutenant. Major Jacques wrote his report, then met with his commanding officer and his staff. He discussed in full detail what had happened to Lieutenant Pierre de Val in a room filled with very angry men.

The major's commanding officer ordered him not to say anything more about the matter. He said he would take it further.

"It's not me you have to worry about spreading the word regarding this incident, Sir," said Major Jacques. "It's everyone aboard the *Valentine*, even the admiral's men. Everyone was angry."

"They won't spread the word because Admiral Roberval and the *Valentine* leave tomorrow morning for the coast of North Africa, on a two year voyage," said the commanding officer.

That was not good news for Major Jacques. He hoped if someone could get the story to the proper people in time, there might be a chance Captain Fonteneau would go back to where the three were abandoned and rescue them.

But now the captain was leaving on a two-year voyage with all of his crew. Jacques knew it would now be up to him to do something about solving the problem.

Major Jacques realized he had to obey orders or suffer the consequences. He also knew there were always ways around doing things. He knew where Pierre de Val's father lived and how to get in touch with him. He decided to draft a letter to the tailor in Lille, and outline what the admiral had done to his son, as well as to Marguerite and Violet. He would ask Pierre's father to contact Baron Roberval and tell him how his daughter had been thrown out with nothing, among the wild animals of North America, over a year ago. He ended his letter by saying he was under orders to be silent.

CHAPTER 17
Marguerite's Troubles

It is now the first of March. The days are getting longer and the sun is starting to give a little heat.

Marguerite is having trouble trying to keep her wits about her. Life is getting harder and except for some salt fish and flour almost all her food is gone. Her clothes are little more then rags.

She cut up most of the dresses she had to make undergarments and flags. She keeps two flags flying in case a ship comes into view.

Late one foggy evening around the last of March, as fog and drizzle settled in around the harbour, Marguerite was startled by what sounded like someone calling her. She rushed up through the hatch and listened. She heard the sound several times. It sounded as if it was coming from across the harbour. She stared through the light mist and focused her eyes on something moving near the base of the hill. Then she saw a person standing there, holding something wrapped in her arms. She immediately recognized the person as Violet. First she was scared, then she called to her, "Is that you, Violet, is that my baby in your arms?" She watched as the person, whose face was partly covered, stared at her in silence. "Can you say something, Violet? Can you come here and bring my baby?" Marguerite called to the ghostly figure.

She went outside the hut and looked again at the place where the ghost was standing. It was gone. The minute she took her eyes off the ghost, it disappeared.

Marguerite knew it was the ghost of Violet carrying the baby, her baby, who had lived only one day. But why was Violet always carrying the baby? There must be something more that Violet hadn't told her. She remembered that Violet had wanted to tell her something important before she died. Maybe it was something concerning the baby.

Marguerite realized every time she saw or heard something like this there would be a storm coming, and come it did.

That night, wind and rain swept in from the ocean at a terrific force, bringing sleet and snow that battered everything.

The hut started leaking. Marguerite put buckets and pots under the leaks to catch the water. She felt the wind as it came in   around the cracks in the door and her small oil light flickered in the draft. She spent all night trying to keep warm and dry.

During the night she heard what seemed to be children crying. Next morning she looked outside, hoping to find out what was making the noise. The weather wasn't good; it was still blowing a gale. The harbour was packed full of rough Arctic ice, crunching and heaving in the giant swells that smashed against the granite cliffs.

Then she saw what was making the noise. It was young seals being tossed and crunched by the rolling ice. The harbour was full of young seals. They were everywhere, even up on the land. There were seals crawling around the salt pond area. They were snow white.

While talking to Norm Tucker, one of the old timers who grew up in L'Anse au Pigeon, I was told it was a common sight to see and hear young harp seals in the harbour every spring, The seals came within a few feet of the large house near the shore.

As Marguerite watched the pounding ice, she saw many dead young seals floating in the ice along the shore.

She knew the young seals were harmless, but due to the harsh weather she couldn't rescue them. She watched helplessly as one by one they were crushed to death, and the crying was continued by those still living.

The author was at L'Anse au Pigeon in early summer and saw several carcasses of young seals along the beaches. The seals were killed when they were caught in a storm near the shore and smashed against the rocks.

After the storm calmed down, Marguerite walked around the saltwater pond and out to the young seals. She discovered they weren't afraid of her. She could smoothe them down and even take them up in her arms if she wanted. It seemed as though the seals were all talking to her and for a moment she didn't feel alone anymore. She was amazed how silky the fur was on these young animals, and how warm they were in such cold temperatures. She saw hundreds more seals, dead around the shoreline and floating in the water. Most had just died.

Knowing that survival was her top priority, Marguerite realized these dead animals could be her source of food until the fish arrived.

She wondered if she could make clothes from the furry skins? If Violet was alive, she would know what to do. Marguerite made up her mind to try and make clothes herself. She needed them if she was going to survive.

She pulled six of the dead animals ashore and paunched them. The fat next to the skin would be rendered to make oil for cooking her food and for lighting her lamp. She knew the meat was excellent for eating as long as it was fresh. To keep it fresh, she would bury it in the snow.

April month proved to be very cold and windy. She stayed indoors most of the time. Her firewood was getting scarce. And there were holes in the iron stovepipe, it was beginning to rust badly. This worried her because if the pipe crumbled she would not be able to have fire in the hut. She hoped her wood would last until the warm weather came.

Marguerite was now becoming quite accomplished on the violin, playing several tunes, some that she had created herself.

She hoped by June month a ship would come. She wasn't concerned about its origin as long as it was a ship. She would even welcome a pirate ship as long as it took her aboard.

She wondered what would happen if a ship came and rescued her. Would she be able to take her trunks with her? Would they just take her off the beach and sail for France or wherever they were going? She wasn't concerned as long as she got rescued and went on her way to civilization. However she would like to take some of her personal belongings, especially Pierre's violin and Violet's Bible and diary.

Marguerite knew she could not survive another winter here. She would have no food except for what she could obtain herself. And the stovepipe would be burnt out. That was her biggest concern. If that happened, it would be the end, she would freeze to death.

She thought about these things continuously. She was living on mostly seal meat. She would wrap coarse salt in a cloth and crush it into powder then sprinkle it on her food.

She had some berries left, and even though they were getting very sour she had no choice but to eat them with the little pancakes she made, cooked in seal oil.

From the calendar Violet had made, she could tell it was now the first of May. She felt the warmth of the sun and watched each day as the snow gradually melted. It was good to get some fresh water from the river, instead of drinking water from melted snow as she'd done all winter.

She dug the snow away from the door of the hut and started using it again. This was a relief, not having to climb up and down a ladder in order to get in and out of the hut over snow banks.

Marguerite was anxiously waiting for the ice in and around the salt pond to melt. When the ice disappeared trout came in by the thousands, swimming up the river. The fish would get trapped in the large pool outside. Every time the tide went out, it was just a matter of taking all she wanted.

She was eager to get the boat in the water and put the net out for salmon. This would happen as soon as the heavy Arctic ice moved off from the land and out of the harbour.

With her hopes built on getting fresh fish, she felt a little more secure. She would soon have things to occupy her time during the long evenings.

She saw wolves late in the evenings roving the high hills. They were waiting to patrol the hut area during the night, and she would hear their howls and see their tracks in the morning. She wasn't as concerned about them now because she was getting use to them. In fact, she would sit and watch them for hours, they were company for her.

One cold crispy morning, Marguerite decided to walk in around the salt pond and see if any trout had arrived. It was slippery along the edge of the ice near the shoreline. Frost covered everything.

As she walked along, she suddenly slipped and fell. She slid off the edge of the ice and landed on the rocky beach about six feet below. She landed on her knee and ankle.

The pain in her leg was more than she could bear.

She knew by the pain she had a lot of damage done to her leg. She thought she might have broken her leg.

With great difficulty, she picked herself up and sat on a rock. She felt her kneecap and it appeared to be dislocated. Her ankle felt as though it was broken. "I will have to get back to the hut somehow," she moaned, holding onto the edge of the shore ice and hopping along on one leg.

She was about two hundred yards from the hut, but it took her nearly an hour to get there. She dragged herself along to the door and fell inside. She started crying uncontrollably with the pain and saying, "My oh my, what am I going to do now? How am I going to manage?"

She somehow got into the kitchen area and climbed onto the bed. After she painfully removed her boot she discovered that her ankle wasn't broken. It was, however, badly cut and bruised, and the lower part of her foot was also bruised.

Her knee was hurting the most, but although it was swollen there didn't appear to be any broken bones. Limping outside with the help of a stick, she got a jug full of snow, wrapped it in a cloth, and put it on her knee. That stopped the swelling and eased the pain.

Marguerite wouldn't be able to move around for at least two weeks. By then, most of the ice and snow would be melted.

While nursing her sore leg, she decided to make a pair of boots from the polar bear skin that she used as a rug to sleep on. Violet had talked about making skin boots shortly before she died, but had never said anything about how to make them. Marguerite knew the hair would have to come off the hide. If it were left on, it would collect mud and dirt, and if the boots got wet they would be too heavy for walking. The young princess made several attempts to make skin boots but gave up. She settled for a large piece of skin that she wrapped around her foot and tied tight below the knee. She would wear these boots when the snow went.

In two weeks, Marguerite's knee and ankle were better. By then, the sea trout and Arctic char were plentiful in the pool at the saltwater pond. She launched the boat and went in near the pool. She caught about a dozen fish, then went back to the hut and cleaned them. She had only a half bag of salt left for curing fish, so she decided against salting any of the fish she'd caught. She made pickle from a little salt and put some of the char to soak in the salty brine. This would cure them enough to dry in the sun.

From now on, Marguerite would catch just enough fish to eat. She would wait till later, maybe in August, to use the last of her salt, just in case she was caught here for another winter.

Every day, after the snow melted, she went to where Pierre and her baby and Violet were buried, wearing her homemade boots. She had the skin sewn together with fish line, making them secure on her feet.

When the flowers started to bloom, she placed some on the graves of her loved ones, and said a prayer for them.

One day in early August, she decided to walk up to the end of the island and have a look around, just to see what was there. By now, her nerve was getting much better for exploring the area.

She loaded the gun and took extra shot and powder in case it was needed.

She walked up through the valley in the centre of the island and passed several places where the trees were tall. She saw wolf and fox tracks everywhere. There were many ducks in the ponds. She could have shot them if she needed.

There were footprints of people in the mud as she got further up through the valley. Perhaps it was natives, she thought.

In the distance she could see a high hill with a large pile of rocks stacked up. She walked up to have a look.

When she got to the base of the hill she saw rocks arranged in such a fashion that it looked as though someone had placed them there.

She climbed the hill and examined the rock pile. She was certain it was put there by people. The rocks had not fallen there. The rocks were packed around to form a circle and stacked over six feet high.

From where she stood, she could see very clearly out to sea and all around the inner harbour. She could even see the entrance coming in through the southern direction.

It is to be noted that historians writing about this particular area have stated the Vikings and Basques visited the area. These people were famous for erecting distinguishing landmarks they would recognize while traveling on the highest hills. Some used the landmarks to stake a claim on the land, others buried their dead by the rock piles. In the early part of the century the Newfoundland government erected a light on the hill to guide ships coming into Quirpon Harbour. Transport Canada still maintains the light.

Marguerite looked at the rocks and imagined people bringing them up from the shoreline to make a rock pile big enough to be seen for miles around. "But who could it be?" she wondered, as she leaned against the rocks and looked in all directions. She was convinced that ships going and coming from the New World used this place as a point of navigation.

After having a good look around, Marguerite hurried back to the hut to continue her ever-hopeful watch for ships. When she arrived back, she was surprised to find what appeared to be a gift outside the door. Carefully arranged in a small birch bark container there were two pale greenish blue eggs. They must be sea bird eggs, she thought, taken from the high cliffs. But who had put them there?

Marguerite boiled the eggs and ate them with great enjoyment, even as she continued to ponder over who had given them to her.

Over the next weeks, more of the eggs were left outside her door. One day, she happened to be near the door when she heard a gentle rustle outside and when she looked out she saw a little girl with long dark hair plaited with feathers holding two eggs in her hands. The child looked to be eight or nine years old.

Marguerite opened the door and smiled at the little girl and she shyly smiled back. Marguerite saw she had big brown eyes and was wearing a short gown made from an animal skin.

The little girl held out the eggs to Marguerite who took them and motioned for her to wait. Rushing to her trunk, she took out a bead necklace and gave it to the child who immediately put it on. She and Marguerite smiled at each other again. The little girl then skipped away, disappearing up over the hill.

Many times, Marguerite wanted to follow the little girl, to see where she was living and meet her people. But something always held her back. She realized it was fear. All the stories she'd heard about how natives in the New World had scalped people and taken women and used them in unmentionable ways came back to her. What would happen to her if she followed the little girl and met natives like that? As much as she longed for human contact, she was much too afraid to follow the child.

Over the summer, the little girl came a few more times, each time bearing a small gift, more eggs, a feather, a smooth beach rock. Marguerite eagerly watched and waited for her to appear and presented her with gifts in return, a pewter cup, a button, a French coin.

It was quite a summer for Marguerite as she tried to survive the best way she knew how in L'Anse au Pigeon.

Around the middle of June, she saw several ships come into view and go up through the Strait of Belle Isle. She lit fires, making heavy smoke, and waved the French flag. But the ships were all too far away to see her or the smoke that rose in the air.

Marguerite knew of no other way to attract the ships, only to make smoke, wave the flag, and pray they would come closer.

Every morning she saw wolves around the salt pond and in the cove on the other side of the harbour, eating the decaying carcasses of the young seals and the dead fish that got trapped when the tide went out.

In the middle of July, the wild berries started to ripen enough to make jam. She picked half-ripened bakeapples and boiled them in water, then made pancakes out of the ration of flour she had left. She fried the pancakes in seal oil and put the bakeapple jam over them. This made a meal for her, a change from fish and seal meat.

She cooked her meals at night because all day long she would sit at the lookout watching for ships, hoping they would see her signal.

One morning she put out the net to catch codfish and salmon. She needed something different to eat. She just barely had the net in the water when she saw salmon and Arctic char entering it. Within a short time, she found she had a good catch of fish.

"This must be the best place in the world to catch fish," she smiled to herself as she hauled in her net.

It is suggested you read "The Curse Of The Red Cross Ring" about fishing skipper Az Roberts who lived and fished at L'Anse au Pigeon during the period 1901 to 1943. Go to Google and log on Earl B. Pilgrim.com to get an outline of how plentiful the fish were in this area.

One morning, Marguerite saw an old doe caribou and her young calf feeding on the hillside not far from the salt pond. She decided to kill the calf rather than the large doe. She got the shotgun and went after the animal, stalking it very carefully. It took her an hour to get close enough to shoot and kill the young calf. It weighed about forty pounds and she managed to bring it to the shore of the salt pond and put it aboard the boat. Back at the hut, she paunched and skinned the calf. The meat was the best she had ever eaten. It lasted her for more than two weeks.

CHAPTER 18
Commodore Pierre de Mont

Around the same time that Marguerite was put ashore on Quirpon Island, a Frenchman by the name of Pierre de Mont was coming to the island area to get water for his fishing boats. De Mont had several ships under his command fishing around the Bay of Fundy. Whenever one of his ships was loaded with salt fish he would send it to the Quirpon Harbour area to wait for the rest to catch up.

Every one of his fishing captains had orders to make sure there was enough fresh water aboard to make the journey across the Atlantic. When they arrived in the Quirpon Island area, their orders were to fill their water barrels. Because there are few brooks in the area, ships needing water sometimes had to search the small harbours and coves in order to find enough water to fill their casks.

De Mont was not a clever navigator like some of the old explorers around at that time. He always preferred crossing the Atlantic Ocean via the old traditional route, by using the tip of the Northern Peninsula at Quirpon Island, a direct easterly bearing to the west coast of Ireland.

Years later, his namesake, Pierre de Mont, crossed the Atlantic the same way. The latter Pierre de Mont, who established a colony on the Bay of Fundy in Acadia (Nova Scotia) in 1603, was an associate of Samuel de Champlain, who founded Quebec in 1608.

Marguerite knew nothing about the French fishing fleets stopping off in Quirpon Harbour. Her hope was that some ship might come in sight of the harbour of L'Anse au Pigeon and she would be able to attract their attention and be rescued. She never dreamt that French ships returning home were congregating just a few miles away from her.

Marguerite spent all the summer gathering berries and drying fish and praying she would not have to spend another winter in the Pigeon. July came and went, and although she saw many ships none came close enough to see her signals.

She was living on bakeapples, blackberries and fish of different kinds. Most all of her oil was gone and the last of the flour was used. She had a little hard bread left. She saw several caribou but was disappointed at not being able to get a shot at them.

Marguerite sat and thought about how she was going to be able to spend another winter in this place without supplies. She had no choice but to start getting ready. She couldn't lie down and die, she would have to go on fighting.

When she was not gathering food or cutting wood, she was watching the ocean.

Her clothing was in terrible shape. The only cloth that had any colour left was the flag, and she made sure that the blue, white and red colours of France could always be sighted by ships that might be passing.

It was around midday, during the middle of August, as she was cutting firewood near the hut, that she was startled by a sound. It had been a chilly morning. She wore her long heavy coat. Her hair was down to her shoulders and cut straight across with the heavy scissors Violet had used for cutting cloth. She wore a pair of caribou skin pants held up by rope. The shirt she wore was tattered. On her feet she had the skin boots she had made. They were lashed together with strands of rope.

When she heard the sound, she put down her axe and ran further out the cove to have a look.

She heard the sound again but couldn't focus in on the direction it was coming from. It sounded as though someone was striking wood with an axe. She stood still and listened.

Then she saw it. It was the spars of a ship with the sails up. The ship was on the other side of the rocky point sailing slowly along and about to come into view. She dropped her axe and ran for the high hill where the flag was flying. Several times she almost fell but she gained her step. When she got to the top of the hill, the ship was in full view, and much to her amazement it was turning towards her.

"Mon Dieu. Mon Dieu. My good Lord. It's coming for me, yes it's coming for me," she yelled.

Several ships had come into Quirpon Harbour that day and anchored near Jacques Cartier Island waiting for the rest of the fishing fleet to catch up. All of the ships were looking for water, but it was a dry summer and most of the brooks had dried up.

One captain decided to go searching for water around the island rather than sit idle.

French sailors were aware that Quirpon Island was the Isle of Demons. It was said to be peopled by so many demons that normally sailors wouldn't go ashore unless they had crucifixes in their hands. But in this case, where they needed water, they had no other choice but to put their fear aside.

The captain pulled up anchor and headed out around the island. As he came around Cape Bauld and Columbus Point, he knew from an old chart made by the Dutch years before that there was a small harbour there called L'Anse au Pigeon. He decided that was where he would look for water.

As he came around the point he noticed the wind was partly in his favour. The crew sounded the water and it was fine to venture in closer to the harbour. When he got within five hundred feet of the harbour entrance, he let down his anchor.

After the sails were reefed, he ordered his men to launch a rowboat and go in the harbour to see if they could find a brook to get fresh water.

Two men manned the oars and one took the tiller as they started heading for the harbour of L'Anse au Pigeon.

Marguerite froze in her tracks as she stood beneath the French flag staring at what was unfolding before her eyes.

"My God, my God," she whispered. "Am I going to be rescued?"

The small boat was getting closer. The men in it were now within hailing distance. She couldn't stand it any longer. She began to yell and scream. She didn't know what she was saying as she yelled to them and raced for the water's edge, certain the boat was going to land.

The men rowing the boat were aware that this was the dreaded Isle of Demons. Last year, one of their ships had sent in a water crew that had been chased away by demons. Now, here was one of those demons coming straight at them and ready to jump aboard.

"Stop men stop, for God's sake. Head back to the ship before we get torn to shreds by that wild creature," shouted the man at the tiller.

The men immediately turned the boat around and headed back to the ship.

Marguerite screamed and roared and jumped. "Come back, come back," she cried, but the frightened men never heard her.

Onboard the ship, the captain and some of his crew were watching the men row ashore.

The captain thought he saw something waving in the wind. "Hey, a flag. I think that's a French flag flying in there. Yes it is. And I can see a person on the beach," he said.

He watched as his men stopped rowing towards the shore and turned and began heading back to the ship.

"We saw demons! A demon was ready to grab us if we landed," one of the men shouted in great excitement as the rowboat drew near the ship.

"You ninnies. Get back there and see who it is," the captain yelled.

"Not me, Captain, you can go yourself," said the man at the tiller and he got out of the rowboat and climbed aboard the ship.

"If that's a demon on the shore then it's a French demon because it has a French flag flying," said the captain as he got aboard the rowboat and took the tiller. He ordered the men to row back to the harbour and to the person they had called a demon.

As the rowboat turned and went out of the harbour, Marguerite wept uncontrollably. She tried to scream but couldn't. She became hysterical, not knowing what to do. She kept waving and calling but to no avail as the men rowed frantically away from her. Feeling desperate, she took off her coat and began waving it and calling, "Help me, help me," but the men kept rowing.

Her hopes rose when she saw the rowboat heading back her way. "They are coming back again. Yes, they are coming back again," she said, afraid to believe her eyes.

Her heart was pounding hard inside her chest as sweat rolled down her face, but she knew she would have to be careful and not frighten the men away. She didn't know what to do. She was almost beside herself.

As the boat got closer, the man at the tiller ordered the two rowers to stop. "Who are you? Do you have a name?" he called to Marguerite.

"Yes," she said, her voice trembling as she spoke. "I am Princess Marguerite de la Roberval, Baroness of France. Admiral Jean Francois de la Roberval put me ashore here over two years ago. Please help me, Sir, please help me Sir, please help me," she pleaded in a quivering voice.

The captain was silent as he ordered his men to land the boat on the beach.

He told Marguerite to sit down and relax; he could see her pounding chest.

"Mademoiselle, you are now rescued," he said.

Marguerite's legs shook as she stood on the beach. The captain got out of the boat and walked towards her. His boss, Commodore de Mont, had told him to be on the lookout for a young Frenchwoman stranded somewhere around here. The captain himself had heard the stories making the rounds in every café in France, about what Admiral Roberval had done with the princess and her maid and the lieutenant. It was said they had been put ashore off the Quebec north shore on Harrington Island. But now, here he was, face to face with the woman whom all of France was talking about and every fisherman was keeping an eye out for. No one had dreamt the princess might be on Quirpon Island, the dreaded Isle of Demons.

As the captain walked towards her, he couldn't believe what he was seeing. Her face was brown from the sun and very beautiful, but the ragged clothes she wore told the whole story.

For a moment Marguerite stood as though frozen, not even hearing the captain's words. She began to shake. She couldn't believe it. There were three real live Frenchmen in front of her, and a ship in full view.

The captain intended to shake her hand, but Marguerite embraced him as though he were her father. She was weeping openly. The captain was an elderly man and he could not hold back his tears as he patted her back and told her not to cry.

"Everything will be all right for you now, My Lady, we will take you back home to France," he said.

The men accompanying the captain had tears in their eyes too. They had all heard the story of the princess.

After Marguerite had regained her composure, she shook hands with the two oarsmen and told them how glad she was to see them.

When she stepped back from the captain, he got a better look at her clothing. The caribou skin pants she wore hung around her legs with jagged edges and were held up by strands of rope, her footwear was round pieces of skin gathered around the edges and pulled together and also tied with strands of rope.

The shirt she wore was patch on top of patch, one that Violet had thrown away, worn out. Marguerite was a sad looking sight, even for these French fishermen who had never seen much in the way of riches in their whole lifetime.

"Where have you been living for two years?" the captain asked her.

Marguerite pointed to the hut. The three men turned and looked, all they could see was what looked like a hovel in the ground. The men stared at her in amazement.

"Will you please wait for me to get my bag? I will only be a minute," she said to the captain.

"Yes, we will wait for you. We'll wait for as long as it takes you to get ready," he told her. Then he asked, "Is there a brook or stream nearby? We want to fill our water barrels before crossing the Atlantic."

"Yes," she said, pointing to the salt pond. "There's a large stream that runs into the salt pond."

The captain told her to gather her things together. He said he was going back to the ship for more men and the water barrels.

Marguerite was afraid to be left, she said she wanted to go with him, she said she did not want to be alone anymore. The captain looked at her with pity in his eyes and said he would stay with her.

He told the two men with him to tell the mate to send in two barrels for water and a dozen men to fill them, right away.

After the men had left, Marguerite asked the captain to come to the hut. As they walked up to it, the captain saw the wooden cross nailed to the roof. He crossed himself when he saw it.

When Marguerite opened the door and he stepped inside the hut he was amazed how clean it was. The ship's sail on the floor was swept clean and washed. He smiled as he noticed the birch broom propped upright near the stove.

Marguerite sat down on the trunk, thinking she must look a sad sight to this French fishing captain. He asked her what she had been eating lately.

"In the last two months I have been eating fish and berries and mixing the little flour I have left with water," she answered. "And a dear little girl has been bringing me seabird eggs."

"A little girl?" the captain raised his eyebrows. "Do you mean a native?"

"I don't know who she is," said Marguerite. "But she's a dear pretty little thing who has been very kind and thoughtful."

"Weren't there three people put ashore by Admiral de Roberval?" asked the captain.

"Yes," she replied. "Both of them died. They are buried over there." She pointed to the other side of the harbour.

The captain asked if she had any other clothes other than what she was wearing.

"Yes," she said. "I have clothes in a trunk that I kept just in case I got rescued. Violet packed the clothes away before she died and told me not to wear them. She said some day a ship would pick me up, and sure enough you are here."

"When the men arrive with the water barrels you can start getting yourself ready while we fill them up. As soon as you are ready, I will take you out to the ship," said the captain.

It didn't take long for a larger boat to be launched and on its way in with the water barrels aboard along with a dozen men.

Every man on board the boat was standing on deck and looking ashore after hearing about the goings on in L'Anse au Pigeon harbour. The captain told the men to go ashore on the other side of the harbour. He didn't want them hanging around the hut until after Marguerite had left.

"The princess is getting her things ready to be taken out to the ship You men can go on to the brook and see about getting the water. We will have to wait for the tide to come in to get the boats inside. That'll be about an hour."

The men did as they were told.

Marguerite opened Violet's trunk and saw clothes suitable for wearing on board the ship. At the very bottom of the trunk, she found a package with her name on it. When she opened it, she discovered the same clothes she had worn when she went aboard the ship at St. Malo over two years ago. Her boots were rolled in the clothes.

She saw Violet's purse and in it she found a large sum of money and a letter addressed to her father marked 'confidential.' She also found the personal diary Violet had written for her father.

The clothes that Violet had worn when she left France were in the trunk and Marguerite decided to take them back with her, along with all of Violet's personal belongings.

Marguerite packed everything she wanted to take in one trunk, including Pierre's violin and his army uniform. She would take them to the city of Lille and give them to his father.

She tried to fix her hair the best she could, trimming the ragged ends with the scissors and making it even on both sides.

In just over an hour, the captain called and asked if she was ready.

"Yes," she replied. "For two years and three months I have been ready to leave, and now finally I can go."

"I will have the men take your things out of the hut and place them in the boat. We will take them aboard the ship."

Those were the best words Marguerite had ever heard in her life. She could hardly believe she was leaving this New World forever.

When Marguerite walked out of the hut that afternoon dressed in one of her gowns, the captain could not believe the change.

"Well, well! And how do you do, Your Highness?" he said with a wide grin when he saw her.

"I am overwhelmed with gratitude, Captain. You are the finest person I have ever met. My father will reward you and your men very generously when we get back to France."

The captain told her she was beautiful, and said he hoped she would have a pleasant trip home.

Two of the men took her trunk and the rest of the things she wanted to take and put it all in the rowboat.

"Would it be possible for me to go and have a last visit to the graves of the three I love?" she asked the captain.

"Certainly," he replied, wondering who the third person was. "If you need me, I can accompany you."

"Please, I would appreciate it," she said.

Marguerite and the captain went to the graves of Pierre and Violet for the last time. As she stood by Pierre's grave, the grave she believed contained the remains of their baby, the baby she hadn't given a name to before it died, she now named her Violet Marguerite de Roberval. She told the captain about the baby she'd had for Pierre and how the infant girl had died the next day. The old man could not control his grief as he wept with her.

With heavy hearts, they walked up the hill to Violet's grave. Marguerite told him this was the only mother she had ever known. She said Violet had nursed her when she was an infant and had nurtured and cared for her after they were put ashore, but now her remains lay in a shallow grave overlooking the harbour of L'Anse au Pigeon. She picked a few purple flowers that hugged the ground near some boulders and placed them on Violet's grave, at the same time blessing herself and saying a prayer.

The captain removed his hat. With tears running down his face, he asked God to protect the bones of the departed as they would rest forever in the rocky soil of North America. Marguerite quickly turned to him and said, "Captain, don't pray for their bones and soul. They are fine. But pray that a curse will fall on my uncle, Admiral de la Roberval that he may some day die like a dog on a street in France. That was Violet's last wish."

For a moment, Marguerite looked down on the flat plains below. In the distance, she could see the mound of earth that covered Pierre. All of a sudden, she thought about the ring she had thrown away not far from Pierre's grave. She was convinced the ring had been a curse from the very start of her journey. Now, she hoped it would be a curse to whoever would wear it. She wished with all her heart the ring would never be found.

She looked out over the salt pond at the men pulling the boat filled with water barrels and knew it was time to leave. She turned again and looked for the last time at Violet's mossy grave. With tearful eyes, she said a final goodbye to Pierre and Violet and her baby girl. She and the captain then slowly walked to the shoreline.

Marguerite bid a teary farewell to the hut that had been her home for more than two years. It had given her shelter and protection, but before she left, she asked the captain if he would have his men burn the hut.

"I don't want anything left standing in the New World that would be a memorial to the suffering we went through at the hands of Admiral de Roberval," she said.

The captain promised he would do as she asked.

Just before stepping into the boat that would take her out to the fishing schooner, Marguerite turned and waved, hoping that maybe the little native girl was somewhere watching.

Marguerite and the captain were alone as they rowed to the fishing schooner. On the way, he informed her that she would not be going across the Atlantic on his vessel.

"My boat is too deep in the water to give you a safe passage, and besides, we don't have a suitable place for you to sleep so we will put you aboard the company supply ship with Commodore Pierre de Mont, the owner of all our fishing boats. We have to wait for him before we leave, but he will be here tonight if the wind is favourable. You will have a pleasant trip aboard his ship. He has spoken about you a hundred times, wondering where you were put ashore," said the captain.

Marguerite smiled. She had no concerns about anything now that she was rescued and on her way back to France.

She thanked the captain again and reached over to give him a hug.

After the water barrels were put aboard, the captain sent some men ashore again to set fire to the hut. Marguerite watched it burn with tears running down her face. She thought of how the hut had protected her from wind, rain and snow, been a refuge from roving hungry wolves, and was where she had prepared her meals, played the violin, read Violet's Bible and prayed. She had spent many nights with Pierre under its roof and it was where he had suffered and died. She could not hold back her tears as she watched it go up in flames.

As the fishing schooner sailed around Pigeon Point, the last thing Marguerite saw was black smoke rising from the burning hut and the green grass that covered the graves of her loved ones. As tears fell from her eyes, she felt the fatherly arms of the captain go around her. She didn't know it, but she would never see L'Anse au Pigeon again.

CHAPTER 19

A Meeting With The Baron

Baron Charles de la Roberval was at his castle not far from the city of Paris. He was having a business meeting with some directors of his company when he received word that an ex-army officer named Major Jacques wanted to see him. The butler told the baron the gentleman said it was very important and could not wait. The baron sent word that although he was busy, he would adjourn his meeting for a few minutes and see him. He thought the matter was likely of little importance, but he always found the military interesting.

Major Jacques was escorted to the room where the baron sat at a table with several of the board members attending the meeting.

The major immediately recognized the baron. He saw a strong resemblance to Marguerite in his facial features.

"Good day, Baron de Roberval. I'm sorry for barging into your meeting this way, I apologize," he said as he held out his hand.

The baron shook hands and raised an eyebrow, wondering how it was this army major recognized him. "That's fine, Major," he said, smiling. "It must be a matter of utmost importance."

"I am ex-Major George Jacques, formally of the French infantry. I took early retirement two months ago, but if you want to address me as 'Major' that's okay with me," said Jacques.

"So, what can I do for you, Major?" asked the baron politely, as he took a sip of wine, appearing to be not very interested.

"There's not much you can do for me at this time. But there is a matter I think you should know about that is very important to you," said the well-spoken Jacques.

For the first time, the baron and his associates paid attention and really looked at the man in front of them.

"Yes, what is it, Major?" the baron asked curtly.

Jacques looked at the baron and his group for a moment, and then replied, "Maybe you should finish your meeting then hear what I have to tell you. I can return later this afternoon."

Baron Roberval sat up straight. He sensed something of grave importance in the voice of this ex-army officer. The baron turned to the men sitting with him and said, "We have finished our meeting now, haven't we, gentlemen?"

"Yes Sir, I think we have," answered one of his colleagues.

"Would you prefer a private meeting with me, Major?" the baron asked.

"I suppose it makes no difference. What I have to tell you will soon become such a public matter that every household in France will know about it," said Jacques.

He now had the attention of the baron and the four men sitting with him.

"Go ahead, Major, tell us what's on your mind," said the baron.

"Three months ago I came back from North America after commanding a fighting force to New France," Jacques began. "However, this is not what I want to talk to you about. What I want to tell you is of a more serious and urgent matter."

Baron Roberval's eyes opened wide as he stared into Jacques's face. He was afraid to hope he might have word of Marguerite. A lump formed in his throat and almost kept him from speaking.

"Major Jacques, I'd like for you to have a seat, please," he managed to get out. When Jacques was seated, the baron asked him to continue.

"I went aboard His Majesty's ship *Valentine* over a year ago at St. Malo bound for North America. The ship was under the command of Admiral de Roberval." Jacques paused for a moment, "On board, as you know, were your daughter, Marguerite, and Madame Violet."

Before Jacques could continue, the baron quickly cut in.

"Do you have any news of my daughter and Violet?" he asked anxiously.

"The answer is yes and no. That's the only way I can answer your question. This is what I came to talk to you about," said Jacques.

"What do you mean, Major? Is my daughter all right?"

"If you will permit me, Sir, I will tell you the whole story," said Jacques. The baron motioned for him to continue.

"We left St. Malo and were about a week at sea when I was called to the bridge by the captain of the *Valentine*. He told me he had just come from a meeting with a very angry admiral. He said Admiral Roberval had ordered me to go immediately and arrest one of my soldiers, a young lieutenant by the name of Pierre de Val who came from the city of Lille. I asked the reason and the captain said the admiral had received a complaint from one of his officers that de Val was having an affair with Marguerite. The admiral's orders were that the lieutenant be brought upon deck as soon as it was dark and thrown overboard, also Marguerite and Madame Violet. I told the captain I would do as the admiral ordered as far as arresting the lieutenant; as for throwing him into the ocean, however, I feared a mutiny from the ninety-armed soldiers I had below deck. The captain went to the admiral and delivered my message. When he came back he had new orders. The lieutenant was to be arrested and held in stocks until we reached the first land we saw, and then he would be burned at the stake. I did as I was told and arrested the lieutenant. I had no other choice."

At this point the baron held up his hand and stopped Jacques.

"Just a moment, Major," he said. "I would rather have a private conversation with you than hear the rest of what you have to tell me in public."

Jacques agreed and the baron asked the other men to leave the room for a while. After they gone out and shut the door, the baron asked Jacques to continue.

"I went below, arrested the lieutenant and put him in stocks. The rest of the soldiers under my command and some of the sailors wanted to take over the ship; however, we would not allow this to take place. The next morning, the captain called me to the bridge again and informed me of the new orders from the admiral. The admiral said Pierre de Val Cormier, your daughter, Marguerite, and Madame Violet would be put ashore and left on the first land we sighted in North America. I asked the captain what proof the admiral had that the lieutenant was having an affair with Marguerite. He said a naval officer, whom the admiral trusted, suspected it. I requested to see the admiral and talk to him about the matter but my request was denied.

"The captain of the *Valentine* was more upset about this matter than I was, but he was afraid to comment on it to anyone but me, for fear of being thrown overboard himself if the admiral found out. The admiral ordered the captain not to tell anyone the location where the three would be put ashore, and not to write the true location in his log. While on the journey across the Atlantic, the two women were ordered not to leave their quarters for any reason."

Jacques paused for a moment and looked at the baron who was sitting with his elbows on the table and his face in his hands. It was obvious he was in shock. When the baron didn't speak Jacques asked, " Shall I continue, Sir?"

"Yes, please continue," he said, without looking up.

"We encountered heavy seas for about a week, this slowed our progress.

One evening I was called to the bridge by the captain and told that Marguerite wanted to talk to me. I agreed if the admiral approved. The captain said that was not possible, that the admiral would never permit it. I asked the captain to try to find out what she wanted to tell me and he agreed. The next evening he called me to the bridge again and gave me Marguerite's message. She told him to tell me if I got back to France I was to tell you the whole story about her uncle and what he did. I made a promise to her that I would.

"A few days later we sighted land, everyone aboard ship was told it was the Labrador or New France, but the captain informed me secretly after everyone left that it was the northern tip of Newfoundland.

"When we got close to land, the admiral transferred to another ship and left the area. He ordered our ship in close to the land to put them ashore in the after-boat you had specially built for Marguerite.

"We took our lieutenant out of the stocks and brought him on deck. Sir, it was a sad sight to see three of France's loyal citizens tossed upon the rocky desolate shoreline of North America with nothing, not even a roof over their heads. I sent some of my men ashore and they pulled the after-boat up and turned it over to provide a little shelter for them. While my men were ashore they saw tracks of wolves and other strange animals everywhere. We were allowed to give them enough food for two or three months then we sailed away and left them. It was the most inhumane thing we had ever witnessed in our whole lives."

The baron was weeping uncontrollably. Tears ran down his cheeks.

Jacques felt guilty after delivering his message to this elderly gentleman. "I should have forgotten about the whole thing," he thought. But he knew he had to fulfill his promise to Marguerite, whatever the outcome.

He realized it was a risky undertaking to bring a complaint against one of France's greatest admirals, especially one who was very popular with the king and had started a colony in the New World and, above all, was the most feared man that ever sailed the seven seas. However, Jacques didn't care. He had been a good friend of Pierre de Val, and had watched a princess go to her doom, as far as he was concerned. When his report went to army headquarters, not a question was asked. A few weeks later, he was called in front of the top brass and told to keep his mouth shut or else. He waited several months after being told to keep quiet, and then took early retirement. Now, he was out of the army and he'd made up his mind that heads were going to roll, especially that of Admiral de Roberval.

Jacques looked at the baron, who was wiping his eyes with a table napkin. He waited for him to speak.

"Major, your news has broken my heart," the baron said as he folded his hands on the table. "In my wildest dreams I never thought that my brother would do such a cruel thing to my daughter, my only child. And to Violet. Why would he cast them off on a desolate shore then sail away and leave them? Only some bloodthirsty pirate would do such a thing. Good grief, I will never ever live through this." The baron shook his head in disbelief.

"We were just as shocked about this as you are. I didn't sleep for months after it happened. I'm still having trouble sleeping," said Jacques.

"Do you know the exact location where they were put ashore?" asked the baron.

"No, I am not a navy man, but I know they were put ashore on the first land we sighted in the New World. I heard the men in the crow's nest calling to the bridge that they had sighted land. There was much excitement about the first sight of land after such a long time on the sea," said Jacques.

"Do you know where the admiral is now, Major?" asked the baron.

"No Sir. When we were discharged from the *Valentine* in late August, the captain informed me in a private conversation that the three ships were leaving immediately for the North African coast on a two-year voyage. The admiral and his three ships are somewhere cruising the Mediterranean Sea. Marguerite and company are the last things on the admiral's mind," said Jacques.

"I just can't understand it, Major," said the sorrowful baron. "I'm the one who financed the expedition for my brother. I never dreamt he would do anything like this." He was about to say something else when Jacques held up his hand, indicating he wanted to speak.

"Captain Fonteneau told me he overheard a conversation between the admiral and his two other captains," said Jacques. "They talked about attacking the English colonists around Newfoundland and said it was time to ditch their passengers, namely your daughter and Madame Violet. It was indicated this was the plan from the beginning."

This news hit the baron like a ton of bricks. He knew then he had been a fool. The impact of Jacques's words was such that the baron had to steady himself to keep from falling off his chair. He rang a bell and a butler appeared.

"I need a pan of cool water and a towel as quickly as possible," he told the butler. "I think I am going to faint."

The butler hurried out, and the baron looked at Jacques.

"You have brought me devastating news, Major," he said. "It's like hearing about the death of my daughter and Violet. I never thought I would receive such news when I got out of bed this morning." The baron started weeping again.

The butler came back into the room, accompanied by two older women who were close to panic. They hurried to the baron's side and asked what was wrong. "Are you sick, Sir? Where do you have the pain?" they both inquired.

"No, ladies, I'm not in pain. It's just that my heart is broken," he replied in a weak voice.

The women turned to Jacques with wild eyes and asked, "What's going on, Sir?" It appeared they were ready to attack him.

The baron held up his hand. "I will tell you what's going on in a minute," he told the women, as he wiped his forehead.

One of the women took the towel, soaked it in the water, wrung it out, and placed it on the baron's bald head.

He briefly told them what had happened to Marguerite and Violet, adding, "The major here was on board the ship when it happened." The women started to cry and had to be led out of the room by the butler.

Jacques felt as though he had committed a crime as he shifted on his seat. For a moment he didn't know what to do; he had not been expecting this. He'd thought he was going to talk to someone who was as hard and as tough as the admiral himself. But this man, Baron de la Roberval, was like a lamb, or was he?

Jacques looked at the tear-stained face of a broken hearted father. For a moment, he felt like running out the door, but he couldn't and he didn't. Justice had to be done. The admiral would have to pay for this mortal crime against three of France's finest citizens, no matter what the consequences.

When Jacques was alone with the baron, he saw a sudden change come over the elderly man's face.

The baron stood up and walked the length of the room and back. When he turned to look at Jacques, his face was filled with hate and rage. His eyes bulged as he slammed his fist on the heavy oak table. His voice was one that Jacques hadn't heard before.

"Someone is going to pay for this with their life, Major, as sure as there's a holy God in the Heavens, I will make them pay for this, supposing it's the last thing I do on this earth," he said.

The baron sat at his desk and picked up his quill pen. He wrote the date and time on a sheet of paper.

"Do you have the exact date that the three were put ashore?" he asked, not looking at Jacques.

"Yes, I have it registered on my very soul," Jacques responded, as he told the baron the correct date.

The baron wrote it down and asked, "What do you think of their chances of survival?"

"It is hard for me to say, Sir," Jacques said after a moment's thought. "We left them some provisions, two guns, ammunition and a fair quantity of salt. There's plenty of fish in the rivers and in the ocean near the place where they were abandoned, so it's possible they may not starve to death. We put ashore all of their personal belongings so it's possible they may not freeze to death. However, the area where they went ashore is one of the coldest places on earth. Captain Fonteneau says during the winter the temperature drops to forty below zero, and sometimes the wind is as high as one hundred miles per hour, tearing everything apart." Jacques realized his answers were very negative, but there was no other way to answer the questions.

"What kind of a man is Lieutenant de Val? Is he capable of braving these conditions?" asked the baron.

"The lieutenant is one of the best men I have ever served with. He is strong, a hard worker and very intelligent. Of all the men on board the *Valentine*, if I had to pick someone to go with them to help them survive, it would be Lieutenant Pierre de Val," answered Jacques.

The baron looked closely at Jacques, then asked, "Tell me the truth, Major, what is your opinion? Do you think they could survive a winter under these conditions?"

Jacques paused for a moment. "There is a possibility they could survive if they could get enough wood to keep a fire going night and day, but without that they would not last long," he said.

The baron stood up and walked around, then came back to the table. He was thinking hard.

He finally looked at Jacques and said, "It's November with snow on the ground and the seas are rough. It will soon be freezing-up time. Do you think it is possible for me to get a ship or ships to go to North America at this time to search for my daughter and Violet?"

Jacques thought for a moment then answered, "I am not a sailor and have no knowledge of sailing the ocean. However, there are many captains who have traveled to North America from France and would know the route."

"Do you know of someone I could get who would make the trip across the ocean to search for them?" asked the baron.

"I only know of one captain who might take on the job and that would be Jacques Cartier. He is familiar with that route into New France." Jacques paused, then added, "You might not get him to go at this time of the year because it would be next to suicide to make such a trip. The rough seas and the northeast gales that rage there in the fall would cause ships to ice up.

The thought of such a trip would cause fear in the heart of any mariner."

The baron knew he was right. He also knew that his daughter and Violet were doomed to spend another winter with Lieutenant de Val in the wilds of the New World, that is, if they were still alive. With those thoughts in his mind, he put his hands to his face and wept.

"Major," he said as he wiped away tears and looked straight at Jacques, "You said you were no longer in the army, what are you doing now?"

"I am not employed at the moment. I may seek a job in the south of France later on," said Jacques.

"I can offer you a job trying to find my daughter, if you will accept it," said the baron.

Jacques was not in a position to take on such a job. However, he said he would let him know in about a month. He said he was on his way to the city of Lille to see Henry de Val Cormier, the tailor, and tell him the same story he'd told the baron.

The baron thanked him and told him to come back as soon as possible. "On your return trip from Lille I want you to spend a night with us and update us on your meeting with the tailor," he said, and Jacques promised he would.

The two men shook hands and Jacques departed. It was the last time they met. The baron died a few days later, and most people said it was from a broken heart.

CHAPTER 20
The Trip To Lille

The journey from Paris to the city of Lille in the northeast of France took Jacques more than a week. Bad weather and rain-soaked roads made the going tough. The horse drawn coaches were stuck almost continually.

The meeting he'd had with the baron was very distressing because he took the news of his daughter in such a way it almost broke his heart. Jacques was hoping Henry de Val Cormier would react to the news differently.

It was late at night when Jacques arrived in the city of Lille. He was dropped off at one of the local hotels and went straight to bed without asking any questions. The next morning was sunny and fairly warm for late fall. After breakfast, he informed the hotel manager he might be staying for another night. He asked the manager if he could tell him the directions to a tailor shop owned by Henry de Val.

"Yes, the shop is just two blocks down the street. Anyone you meet will tell you where it is. It's the biggest shop in the city," he said.

Jacques thanked him and headed down the street. Within a short time, he arrived at the tailor shop; it was a busy place. As soon as he walked in the door a man met him, asking his business.

"Are you a customer, Sir?" the man asked politely.

"No, I came to see the owner if possible," said Jacques.

"Do you have an appointment?"

"No I don't, but if you would give him a message he may see me," said Jacques.

The man looked him over and realized he was no ordinary person. "I will try and get word to him that you want to see him. At the moment he is expecting company. That's why I am here now, waiting for them to arrive."

The man disappeared, but in a couple of minutes he came back and asked Jacques what his business was.

"The boss would like to know," he said.

"I am Major George Jacques from the French army. Tell your boss it is important that I speak with him."

The man disappeared again.

In a few minutes a well-dressed man came into the room.

"How do you do, Major?" he said as he held out his hand.

"I am fine. You must be Henry de Val Cormier," said Jacques as he shook his hand.

"Yes, I am," he said.

"I'm ex-Major Jacques from the French Army."

Henry de Val raised an eyebrow and asked no more questions.

"Come to my office, I have a few minutes to spare before my company arrives," he said.

When the office door was closed, Henry asked Jacques to sit down. Jacques refused.

"What can I do for you this morning, Major?" asked Henry.

Jacques looked at the aging businessman, trying to determine his character.

"I have come here bearing news of your son, Lieutenant Pierre de Val," he said, coming right to the point.

"Yes, he has gone to New France, on the other side of the Atlantic. I received a letter from him just after he set off. That's more than a year ago... do you have any news?"

"Yes, I have news, but it may not be the kind you want to hear," said Jacques.

At this point the two men were standing, but when he heard those words, Henry pulled out his chair and sat down.

"What is it, Major?" he asked, his face suddenly pale.

Jacques reached for a chair and sat down.

"I want you to listen to me very carefully because it may take some time to tell you the whole story," he said, as he leaned his elbows on the table and looked into Henry's eyes.

He outlined the whole story to the tailor without being interrupted. There were no questions asked as he talked. The only thing Henry did was take a few notes.

After Jacques finished speaking, Henry let out a deep breath and sat back in his chair. He was obviously mad, but trying to remain calm.

"I want to ask you a question, Major," he said.

"Yes go ahead, I will answer anything I can," said Jacques.

"What is your personal opinion as far as their chances of surviving a winter under the conditions you just described?" Henry asked.

"There is a possibility they may survive if they could get enough firewood to keep a fire going night and day during the winter, and if they could kill enough wild game. There is no doubt that Pierre is a man with a tremendous amount of stamina. He will survive when no one else will," said Jacques.

"So, as far as you're concerned, all is not lost. They could still be alive, even under these conditions," said Henry.

"Miracles do happen, but they were put on a barren island with few trees, not far from the edge of the cruelest waterway in the world, the Labrador Sea. We over-wintered about one hundred miles inland, surrounded by the forest, and in a fort, and even there men froze their feet and hands. But I have great confidence in Pierre. He may be able to fight the elements and survive for one winter, but the second will be doubtful," said Jacques.

"Do you know the exact location where they were put off, Major?" asked Henry.

"No, not the exact location. The admiral warned Captain Fonteneau if he told anyone the exact location, he would throw him over the side. But I do remember it was just before we entered the Gulf of St. Lawrence. Roberval got on another ship and sailed ahead while the three were put ashore."

The tailor thought for a moment then asked, "Do you know if any French fishermen are in that area? Did you see any sign of anyone there?"

"No, Captain Fonteneau and I talked about that many times during the winter we were at Fort Charlesbourg-Royal. He said he knew of no fishermen from any nation using that area," said Jacques.

"Do you know if all the ships going to North America use the same route as Captain Fonteneau? If they do, then there is a possibility they may receive their signal and get rescued," said Henry.

"We thought about that and hoped it would be a possibility. However, most of the ships these days go around the south coast of Newfoundland then take a course straight to France. We know of one fishing company that has a fleet of fishing ships going to Acadia every year under the command of Commodore de Mont. They have several stations around the Strait of Belle Isle. In the late summer, after they secure their voyage, Commodore de Mont goes to each station and collects his vessels and heads back to St. Malo in a convoy. He may be the right person to contact," said Jacques. He stared at the tailor. When Henry didn't reply, he knew he was deep in thought.

"You said you were ex-Major Jacques, or something like that," said Henry, as he looked at Jacques.

"Yes, I was a major in the French army with a thirty year career. It's like I told you, I could not be muzzled any longer so I got out."

Henry looked at the ex-Major then asked, "Would you like to work for me, Major? If you say yes, you can start now?"

"It all depends on the job. What I will be doing?" asked Jacques.

"You will be required to find my son and bring him back to France," said the tailor.

Jacques had not been expecting to hear that. He had only come to deliver a message to a family about what happened to their son, a soldier under his command. He had no plan to search for him. He only wanted to report the incident. But now he knew he was caught between a father who loved his son, and a young French officer tossed out on an isolated island by an admiral, a man who was a lunatic and had no regard for human life.

Jacques paused for a few seconds, then replied, "If I take on the job I may have to travel to many parts of France to see different people. Will you pay for my travel?"

"I will pay anything to get my son back safe and sound," said Henry.

"Okay, I will take on the job, but I know it will be a tough one. I may even have to go across the Atlantic," said Jacques.

"I don't care where you have to travel or who you have to talk to, just as long as you find Pierre," said the distraught tailor.

"I will do whatever has to be done and keep you up to date on what happens," said Jacques.

"I will be doing something about this too. I have friends in high places in France. I will keep you informed as well," said Henry.

Jacques stood up and held out his hand. They shook hands, but before Jacques left, Henry said, "I don't know how to tell my wife about this, it will destroy her. She is looking forward to Pierre coming back from the New World very soon."

"I hope everything turns out well for all of us," said Jacques, as he left to go make his plan of attack.

Jacques went back to his hotel and wrote down what he would do to try and locate the three missing people.

He knew it would be impossible to even try and get a ship to sail to North America at this time of year. No captain would risk it for any amount of money. His plans would have to be made for early next spring. In the meantime, he would have to alert every fishing skipper and every company who sent ships to the New World.

Jacques knew that St. Malo would be the right place to go to talk to fishing skippers because this was the hub of the New World's fishery.

He planned to stop at the castle and tell the baron about his plans, and inform him as well that he was under the employ of the tailor with orders to try and locate the three castaways.

In the meantime, he would talk to Captain Fonteneau and attempt to find out the exact location where the three had been put ashore.

Jacques had heard Henry say he had friends in high places. Perhaps he could write the king and have him get Admiral Roberval go to the New World and pick up the castaways and bring them home.

Jacques knew he would become the most unpopular man in France if he verbally attacked Admiral Roberval without people knowing the true story, so his top priority was to let the public know the facts about what had happened.

Before he left the city of Lille, he had another meeting with Henry and gave him a copy of his plans. Henry was pleased, and gave him a letter okaying his travel expenses. He also informed him he would be going directly to the king.

Early the next morning, Jacques headed for the castle to see Baron de la Roberval.

It took close to a week to make the trip from Lille to Paris. Freezing rain, sloppy snow and mud made traveling difficult.

After a day's rest in Paris, Jacques rented a carriage to take him to the baron's castle. When he got to the castle he saw no one around the grounds, but he saw tracks in the overnight snow and knew someone was inside. He knocked on the door for some time before he received a response. The butler finally opened the door and asked him to come inside.

Jacques told him who he was and why he was there, "I have come to see the baron, if it's possible," he said.

The butler hung his head for a moment then slowly said, "Haven't you heard, Sir, the baron passed away over a week ago. You must be the gentleman who brought the terrible news about Marguerite."

For a moment, Jacques didn't know what to say. He was about to turn and leave when a woman's voice broke the silence.

"I want to talk to you, Major, please," she said from a doorway not far away.

Jacques turned and saw a tall slender woman who was wearing a long dark dress and a veil that covered her face. Jacques thought she must be a member of the baron's family.

"I am shocked to hear this news, Madame," he said. "I offer you my most sincere condolences."

"Thank you, Major. We are broken hearted about the loss of the baron. He was a great man who loved everyone."

The woman invited Jacques into the parlour. He followed her without any hesitation. He was invited to sit at a table near a large fireplace that burned brightly. He was appreciative of the warmth.

After they were seated, the woman lifted the veil and revealed a face that was wrinkled and filled with grief. She rang the bell and asked the butler to bring ale. The elegant lady sat up straight and looked closely at Jacques before beginning to speak.

"My name is Madeline de la Rocque de Roberval," she said. "I am the sister of Baron Charles de Roberval whom you met here recently and is now deceased. May God rest his soul. I am also the sister of Admiral Francis de Roberval, whom you have also met and now hate, and I don't blame you for that." She paused for a moment, looking at Jacques. "If you will permit me, I'll tell you the whole story. It may take a while, but it's important that you know it."

Jacques nodded and she continued.

"My father was Bernard de la Rocque de Roberval. He was an ambassador and governor, a gentleman of the king's household who belonged to an old noble family in the south of France, in a city called Carcassone. He was very wealthy. My mother died a few years ago. She was the daughter of Alix de Popincourt who was a relative of the Queen of France. We came from the de le Rocque family, but added the name Roberval to show our connection with the king's household.

"There were three children, Charles, Jean, and I. As a young man, Charles went away and became a monk, while Jean joined the French navy and became a naval officer.

"My father knew the king well and as a result Jean rose in rank very quickly. He became an admiral at an early age.

"Although Jean rose to the rank of admiral, Charles was still the one that Papa most admired. Jean didn't like that.

"This castle was a monastery when the church put it up for sale. Papa bought it and turned it into the mansion it is today. He moved from the south of France and lived here.

"The thing you have to realize is that Mama didn't want Charles to be a monk. She was against it from the beginning, so when the word came that he was seeing a girl while posted in Normandy, she was very happy and encouraged him to give up the priesthood and this he did.

"Papa was not happy about the girl and threatened to change his will. He wanted Charles to marry into the royal household, not to marry a commoner.

"Jean came home a very furious man. He wanted Papa to change his will immediately and leave everything to him. Papa, of course, would not hear of this and told him so. Jean left and didn't return home for a very long time.

"Not long after this, Papa received a letter from the king informing him that he needed him at the palace for a meeting immediately. When Papa arrived he met an angry king who informed him that Jean had been tripped of his rank of admiral and discharge from the navy. Papa was shocked to hear this and asked why.

"His Highness told him that Jean had forsaken the holy Catholic Church and become a Calvinist. In other words, he was now a Protestant and could no longer be trusted. The king led Papa to believe that the royal household would no longer favour the Roberval family.

"Papa told His Highness that Jean was bitter because of the will he'd made and was just trying to seek revenge on him. He said he would get him to change his mind.

"The king told Papa if Jean repented and came back to the church he would reinstate him as admiral of the fleet.

"With Papa's urging, Jean forsook his Calvinist beliefs and came back to the Catholic Church. He was then made Admiral of the French fleet.

"Jean never forgave Papa or Charles. Even though Papa changed his will and left Jean a large sum of money, Jean vowed that someday he would get his revenge on Charles. We never dreamt he would take it out on Marguerite. It was the news you brought about her that killed Charles."

Madeline paused for a minute before continuing with her story.

"Charles stopped seeing the Norman girl because of Mama and Papa's objections. He went to Paris, where he met a young noblewoman who was third in line to the throne of France, and married her. We were all very happy because she was beautiful and kind.

"She soon became pregnant with Marguerite, and this caused much excitement in the household. Before the time arrived for the child to be born, Charles took his wife to Paris to be near the best medical care available. But, sad to say, she died when Marguerite was born. We were all devastated.

"After the funeral, Charles brought the baby back to the castle and placed it in the care of Mama and I. A few days later he went away for a week, not telling anyone where he was going.

"A week or so later, he returned. With him was the girl from Normandy, Violet Chalifoux, the girl he had fallen in love with when he was a monk, the same girl Mama and Papa hadn't wanted him to marry. Papa and Mama said nothing more about that, however, because Violet was an outstanding woman who came from a good family. They agreed she was the right person to raise young Marguerite."

Madame Madeline was interrupted when the butler and a maid arrived with the ale she'd ordered.

After being served, Jacques asked the question, "Is this the same Violet who went to the New World with Marguerite?"

"Yes it is. She is the only mother Marguerite ever knew, and accompanied her to the New World because she wouldn't let her go alone. Charles was sure Marguerite would be safe with her.

"We all knew for years that Charles was having an affair with Violet, yet no one said anything about it because he was in love with her. They loved each other very much.

"In Papa's will it stipulated that Charles should establish a colony in New France in North America. That was why he fell in with Jean, who knew the way there. Charles trusted him."

She paused, and then said, "The rest is history, Major."

"It's quite a story, but there is another question I would like to ask you, if I may?" Jacques said.

"Go ahead. Ask me whatever you like," she said.

"Did Marguerite ever hear the story you just told me?"

"No, not to our knowledge. She only knew Violet as a nurse and always called her 'Madame Violet.'"

Jacques stared at the ceiling as his mind went back to the admiral's actions, especially on the day he abandoned three passengers on an island in the New World, but also on the manner in which he dealt out punishment to some of the prisoners at Fort Charlesbourg-Royal. Was it possible that he was so cruel as to seek revenge against his brother by abandoning his only daughter on a desolate shore and sailing away as though nothing had happened.

"What do you intend to do about it, Madame Madeline? " he asked.

She paused before replying, "When Charles wrote his will, the day after you left here, he added a clause which stated that you were to receive part of his estate. It is in the form of money to settle the score between him and Jean, and there is no limit on the amount to be spent. It's all written in the will."

For a moment Jacques didn't know what to say. He wondered if this elderly woman wasn't trying to set him up. After all, it was her two brothers they were talking about.

"I have been hired by Henry de Val Cormier, the tailor, to investigate the whole matter regarding his son, Lieutenant Pierre de Val, and report back to him," said Jacques.

"That's wonderful, Major. I know you can get something done, because I know Henry and I am aware he has a lot of influence with the king. If you work for him, you will be protected."

Jacques was not surprised to hear this because everywhere he went people knew about Henry de Val, the tailor, and Pierre de Val, the fiddle player.

"Okay, I'll take the job,' he said to Madeline, " but only because these people have to be found. As for settling the score between Admiral Roberval and your family, I will have no part in that."

"We understand how you feel now. But if you find three bodies, things could change. I have a feeling that Pierre de Val was more to you than just a fellow soldier, and Marguerite was more than just a passenger. Let's wait and see what happens."

Jacques didn't speak as he stood and started to put on his coat. Madeline de Roberval was impressed with this retired army major. He was a tall powerful man who spoke well, and, above all, he was no fool.

"I will give you money for your expenses, and would like you to report your progress every month, if that's possible. We will be at the castle until spring, then we move out and the buildings all go to the Catholic Church. That is in Charles' will," said Madeline, as she rang a bell for the butler.

She wrote a note and gave it to the butler who immediately left the room.

Jacques and Madame Madeline walked to the front door.

"I am behind you every step of the way, no matter what," she said. Jacques knew she meant it by the sound of her voice.

As he turned to leave, the butler arrived and handed Madeline a brown envelope, which she took and passed on to Jacques.

"Here Major," she said, "this is yours, spend it as you like for your travel. I bid you God's protection and will be anxiously waiting for good news."

Jacques thanked her as they shook hands, and then he left.

CHAPTER 21

Major Jacques Goes To Work

After leaving the de Roberval castle, Jacques headed back to Paris. On the way, he counted the money Madeline had given him. It was a large sum, much more then he should carry around with highwaymen on the scene, robbing people and coaches. When he arrived in Paris, he would put the money in a safety deposit box.

Jacques was convinced that no captain could be persuaded to cross the Atlantic Ocean at this time of the year. It was now November and he was sure the three who had been abandoned would not be found until next spring or summer, if at all.

In Paris, he went to the Admiralty and inquired about the whereabouts of explorer Jacques Cartier. He was told Cartier was on a voyage to North America for two years. He enquired about Captain Fonteneau of the *Valentine* and was told he was with Admiral Roberval somewhere near the west coast of Africa, and would not be returning till spring.

Jacques left a letter at the Admiralty for Captain Fonteneau, asking him to contact him as soon as he returned.

After receiving no help in Paris, Jacques decided to go to St. Malo and try to track down the fish merchants who sent ships to the New World each spring.

He knew he would have to move quickly. When snow and freezing conditions came in December, travel around France all but shut down. During that time, horse drawn coaches became clogged in mud and snow.

It was December when Jacques finally reached St Malo, and he went straight to the Country Inn, which was owned by Madame Frances Palchier, the woman he loved.

When he arrived, she hugged and kissed him. "You will never leave this place again," she said, with tears in her eyes.

Jacques was very happy to see her again. "I will be staying for a while, at least two weeks," he said.

She was happy to hear that and took his heavy coat and hat.

"Before you tell me all the news, I want to get you settled away and fed. We will talk later," she said.

Jacques was very much at home here. He had known this woman for many years. She, like him, had never married. He had lived for the army; the inn was her life.

When dinner was ready, they sat down to a beautiful meal.

She asked about Princess Marguerite and her trip to the New World, also if she and Pierre de Val were still having an affair.

Jacques related the whole story to her from the beginning. He told her he had been hired by the two families to search for them, even if it meant having to go to the New World.

When he finished telling Frances the story she was very sad. "I am not a bit surprised about Admiral Roberval's actions. Every sailor who comes in here has a tale of horror, especially those that have spent winters with him. He is very cruel," she said.

"Have you heard any news about his ships returning to France since he left here this summer?" Jacques asked her.

"No. He hasn't returned to St. Malo. He may have returned to the south of France and kept his ships at a port there for the winter," she said.

"I doubt if the Admiralty will allow that because they are fighting ships. Our enemy is England and it's wise to have our most powerful ships close by, just in case they attack us."

"I'm sad to hear you got out of the army, but it's the proper thing to do. You can stay here now with me," Frances said as she held his hand.

"It's possible I could be here for most of the winter because this is where I may be centering my search. St. Malo is the port from which fishing vessels go to and from the New World."

"Jacques Cartier stopped here in September on his way to New France," Frances reminded him. "If you could have talked to him before he left and told him the story he may have gone searching for them. It would be a star in his crown if he found them. He's got a terrible hatred for Admiral Roberval for some reason."

"I know the whole story. It's about the colony in New France, Fort Charlesbourg-Royal. One night, Cartier slipped away from Roberval and came back to France with a load of what he thought was gold and diamonds. It turned out to be fool's gold. For whatever reason, since then Roberval and Cartier have become arch enemies," said Jacques

"I've never met Roberval. But everyone who comes in here gives him a bad name about some atrocity, so some of what they say must be true," said Frances.

"All of it is true," Jacques said in disgust.

Following their meal, Jacques decided to visit the waterfront. He wanted to talk to the fish merchants and get the names of their fishing skippers and ship's captains. He thought they might be able to tell him where Marguerite and company were put ashore.

He rented a horse and headed downtown.

Jacques went to a stable and tied the horse up. While there, he asked the stableman if there was a pub nearby.

"Yes Sir, one just around the corner," answered the man.

Jacques found the pub and entered. Several men were at the bar while others sat at tables scattered around the sides. Everyone was talking. Jacques bought a drink and sat down.

St. Malo was a fishing town, a friendly town, a place where people stopped to say hello to each other. Jacques had not been sitting in the pub for long before an elderly man with snow-white hair approached him. Without even speaking, Jacques knew at once he was a fisherman.

"Good day, Sir," the man said in a friendly manner. "Are you alone?

"I am all alone. Please sit down," said Jacques.

The old man grinned and took a seat.

"I'm Maurice," he said, holding out his hand.

"I'm George Jacques," he said as they shook hands. "Would you like a drink?"

"No thanks, Sir. I don't drink. I just come here to pass some time and have a yarn, and get the news if there's any."

"I suppose there's always lots of news flying around here?" said Jacques.

"You can find out anything you want to know if you ask the right questions," said Maurice.

"Are you from around these parts?" asked Jacques.

"Yes, from here, St Malo. I was born here."

"So I'd say you have heard it all," said Jacques.

"I've seen it all and heard it all," Maurice said.

Jacques took out his pipe and lit it. He felt comfortable; it was good to be in out of the cold wind.

"What did you do for a living all your life?" he asked.

"I spent most of my life fishing. Before that, I was in the French army."

Jacques held out his hand. "Here, shake my hand again. I retired from the army three months ago, retired after thirty-five years service," he said.

"In that case," said Maurice as his face lit up, "I will have a drink to the army with you, if you'll buy."

"Order whatever you like," said Jacques, pleased that Maurice was in a talkative mood. "Where did you fish? Did you ever go to the New World?" he asked him.

"Yes," answered Maurice. "I fished around Newfoundland and Acadia for twenty years. Fished for cod mostly. Did some herring and mackerel fishing, but cod was the main fishery."

"Did you ever go through the Strait of Belle Isle and into the Gulf of St. Lawrence?"

"Yes. Whenever we went to Acadia, that's the course we'd take. It's the shortest route. It's much closer between Cape Bauld and the west coast of Ireland than it is from the south coast of Newfoundland and France. When we were coming back we would all congregate at Quirpon Island and then we'd leave together to cross the Atlantic, it's safer that way," said Maurice.

"Then you know a lot about the Degrat area"? asked Jacques.

"Yes, I went there several times."

"Tell me something. If you leave the west coast of Ireland and sail directly west, what land would you see first when you get to the New World?"

"If you sailed due west you would see an island called Belle Isle to your right. It's just a huge square rock with cliffs going straight down into the water. It has no harbour or coves, nowhere to get ashore. Straight ahead you can see land, this is Rangellett Mountain, and under it is Degrat Harbour, which has good anchorage. Not far away there's a smaller harbour called L'Anse au Pigeon which is on a large island. Behind is Quirpon Harbour, where we waited to cross the Atlantic together on the way home," said Maurice.

Jacques thought for a moment, then said, "In other words, you're saying that if I were to sail to North America on a westerly course and wanted to go ashore on the first land I saw, it would be in the area you just described."

The old fisherman looked inquisitively at Jacques and asked, "Why are you so interested in North America? Are you intending to go there?"

"I am but I'm not sure how soon I can get there. It may be impossible for me to find someone to sail across the ocean this time of the year. I came back from the New World in August, I was aboard the *Valentine* with Admiral Roberval and Captain Fonteneau. We over wintered at Fort Charlsbourg-Royal in New France," said Jacques.

Maurice looked at Jacques with surprise. "You were under the command of that tyrant, Admiral Roberval," he said. "There are a lot of bad reports about him. He mistreated some prisoners on his ship, even shot some of them, and threw some over board alive, according to the stories his crew told about the voyage."

"Yes, I was under the command of that mad man. What you've just said is all true, and there's much more to tell. Before it's all over everyone in France will know about it," said Jacques, with anger in his voice.

The old man sat up straight in his chair. He leaned forward with his elbows on the table, knowing this stranger had more to tell than he was saying.

"What rank did you have when you left the army?" he asked.

"I retired three months ago with the rank of major," answered Jacques.

"In that case, do you mind if I call you 'Major'?" Maurice asked.

"No, it doesn't matter. Major is fine. I have been called worse."

The old fisherman laughed.

"Well, it's obvious you've got an axe to grind with someone, so I think you and I should have a long talk. I might know something. You can trust me," he said.

"If you want to listen, I'll tell you all about it because the faster the news gets around the sooner something might be done to solve it," said Jacques, as he relit his pipe and started to relate the story of Marguerite, starting from the beginning.

Three other people sitting at the next table overheard the conversation and moved closer. They knew Maurice.

None of them had heard what had happened to Marguerite and her companions. While they could hardly believe what Jacques was saying, they said they were not surprised to hear of such cruelty from Admiral de Roberval.

"I am telling you men this story so you can spread it around," said Jacques. "I am telling you in hope that someone may be able to rescue those three people stranded in the New World."

"It's unlikely that anyone will be returning to France this time of the year. The sea gets too rough and icing up is a dangerous monster that every captain fears," said one man.

"You're right," said Jacques. "I know I would be wasting my time to try and get some captain to sail across the Atlantic to Newfoundland in search of three stranded people this time of the year. But what I would like to do is meet with all the fishing companies that send fishing ships to the New World each spring. I'd like to ask them to request their skippers keep an eye out for any signal from someone stranded in the northern part of Newfoundland, along the Strait of Belle Isle, and even along the Labrador coast."

Maurice held up his hand to get attention.

"I know the owners of every fishing company that sails out of this part of France. I've fished for them all and know them well," he said.

This was the kind of information Jacques wanted. It was what he had planned to find out before he left the city of Lille. He asked Maurice if he wanted to make some money.

"Yes," Maurice answered.

The old man was more then willing to help him locate all the fish merchants, especially if he was going to get paid. "I am ready to start whenever you are, Major," he said.

Jacques and Maurice went to a couple of fishing firms and talked to the owners. Jacques related the story of Marguerite and everyone was shocked. The merchants said their fishing crews fished along the south coast of Newfoundland and were never near the Strait of Belle Isle or Labrador, and had no intention of going there due to the late Arctic ice conditions and the storms that swept the area.

One fish merchant told Jacques to go and see Commodore Pierre de Mont because he accompanied his large fishing fleet to Acadia every year.

"His route to Acadia takes him through the Strait of Belle Isle going and coming. He may see something unusual happening around that area. At the very least, he can tell his skippers to be on the lookout for signs of anyone stranded," said the merchant.

Jacques thanked him for his time and left.

He and Maurice decided to wait until the following morning before going to see Commodore de Mont. It was late and Jacques was not yet fully settled in at the Country Inn. He said good evening to Maurice after giving him some money, then headed back to the inn located on the outskirts of the city.

Madame Palchier was overjoyed when Jacques walked in. She greeted him as though he had been gone for months.

"Have you found out anything new about Marguerite and Pierre?" she asked.

"No, nothing that is important, although I've talked to several people, including a couple of fish merchants who go to the New World, to Newfoundland, that is, every year. They go to the south of the island to fish. They stay away from the Arctic ice. Marguerite was put off in the north near the Strait of Belle Isle. The last merchant we talked to gave us the name of a fish merchant who owns a large fleet of ships that go to Acadia every year. He travels the same route as we did when we crossed the Atlantic. I plan to try and see him tomorrow if it's possible. His name is Commodore Pierre de Mont," said Jacques.

"Pierre de Mont," she said, looking at him. "I know him quite well. He's a friend who comes here sometimes when he travels, a fine man."

Jacques was happy to hear this. "Maybe you should give me a letter of introduction when I go to see him tomorrow morning."

"I will go with you if you like," said Frances.

"This will be wonderful. You and I can go to some of the stores in town after we talk to him. I will buy you a nice present, a souvenir to remember me by," Jacques said with a laugh.

"I have you now, that's all I want. I don't need any souvenir," she said as she hugged and kissed him. "You will never leave me again, my darling."

Jacques didn't sleep well. He got out of bed just as the sun's rays lit up the St. Malo countryside. He noticed the ground was white with snow. The blue of the sky and the frost in the air gave him a restless feeling. As he stared out the window he thought about Pierre and Marguerite and Violet. This would be their second winter in the New World, that is, if they had survived. In his mind, he could almost see them, living in that small over-turned boat covered in beach rock and mud, just barely hanging on at the edge of the cruel Labrador Sea. His heart sank as he thought of them.

He thought too about the damage he was doing to his reputation. He was aware that almost all of France believed Admiral de Roberval was a great man who protected France and its people. He knew he could get arrested and thrown in jail for telling the truth.

"Where was this mess going to end?" he wondered, thinking perhaps he should forget about it and head back to Paris. He could get a job in Paris or settle down here with Frances and transform the Country Inn into a grand hotel. "But no," he said to himself. "Admiral de Roberval will pay, supposing it's the last thing I do on this earth."

He pulled on his clothes, hoping that today might be a good day. He decided to take his release papers and identification card with him just in case anyone wanted to verify who he was.

Commodore de Mont was delighted to see Madame Palchier. He welcomed her with open arms and gave Jacques a hearty handshake after their introduction.

Commodore de Mont was very surprised to see Frances and told her so. "You should have notified me yesterday that you were coming to see me this morning. I would have arranged to have lunch prepared for us," he said.

She explained that she and Jacques were seeking information about a very important matter.

"Madame, Monsieur, if I can be of any assistance, I am at your service," the commodore said politely.

Frances told him Jacques would like to give him information that might be important if he was sending ships to the New World in the spring. De Mont said he was sending his fleet of fishing ships back to the New World in the spring and was anxious to hear what Jacques had to say.

Before beginning the story about Marguerite, Jacques told the commodore about his background, his career in the French army and his early release a month ago.

"Sir, my early release is tied in with what I have to tell you. I hope you understand," he said.

Jacques related the whole story to the commodore, who listened very quietly to every word. When Jacques was finished, de Mont said, "Unbelievable. That's the only word I can find to describe what you have just told me. I have never heard such an inhumane story before. If the public hears about this, there will be a terrible uproar."

"I met Princess Marguerite when she was on her way to join the naval ship *Valentine* for her voyage to the New World. She stopped at the inn. She was a very beautiful girl. We shared a glass of wine," said Frances.

"I met Baron de Roberval a few years ago. We were at a business convention in Paris. He seemed to be very interested in the New World. He told me he hoped to visit there one day. I was very sorry to hear of his passing. It's a great tragedy," said de Mont.

"It's hard for me to figure out what to do until I talk to Captain Fonteneau of the *Valentine*. I've been told he is somewhere along the coast of North Africa and may not return until next year. He would know the exact spot where the party was put ashore," said Jacques.

Commodore de Mont thought for a moment then asked, "After the party was put ashore, did you stay on deckand observe the goings on and the location?"

"No. I noticed we were passing a lot of scattered icebergs and heading through the Strait of Belle Isle. That was what Captain Fonteneau said. Shortly after we got underway, I went below to speak to my men. They were talking about taking over the ship and going back to pick up the three castaways. They would have done it right away if I had given the word," said Jacques.

"Are you sure it wasn't on the Labrador Coast? There are places down there that people sometimes mistake for northern Newfoundland, especially if they are not familiar with the coast. One area is Harrington Island. A lot of ships sight this area first, especially if the weather is bad and visibility is poor," said the commodore.

"I can only go with what Captain Fonteneau told me. He said it was the northern tip of Newfoundland," said Jacques.

De Mont leaned back in his chair and looked at the ceiling. He was lost in thought. " I'll tell you what we're facing," he said. "When I leave here with my ships around the last week of May or the first week in June I head on a westerly course. If we strike the Arctic ice, we change course and follow the edge south and go to Acadia along the south coast of Newfoundland. When we get our ships loaded with fish in Acadia, we start heading back to France through the Strait of Belle Isle, collecting our ships at their summer stations as we move through. When we get to Quirpon near Jacques Cartier Island we wait for everyone to catch up to cross the Atlantic together. If the three castaways were in that area for a year, someone would have seen them because there are Eskimos and Indians in that area. They may even have contacted them."

Jacques didn't know what to say. Perhaps the commodore was right, but he could only go by what Captain Fonteneau said. The castaways were put off on the northern tip of the island of Newfoundland.

"Can you offer any suggestions, Commodore de Mont?" he asked.

"My advice is that you'd better be careful. I know Admiral de Roberval personally. He is not a good man to have as an enemy; they say even the King worships him. However, if the word was spread throughout France that he left Princess Marguerite to die on an island off Labrador in North America, there would be a lot of sympathy from people in high places. That would not go well for the admiral upon his return to France from North Africa," said de Mont.

"There is no doubt about it, Sir, Henry de Val will be going to the king and queen of France with the story I've just told you, and demanding that something be done with Admiral Roberval," said Jacques.

"There is only one thing I can do at the moment and that is to tell all my skippers to be on the lookout for any sign of human life in that area when they are passing through next summer. As for repeating your story in public, although I believe you, it would not be a wise thing for me to do. I have thousands of employees and a business to protect. I'm sure you can understand," said de Mont.

"I know full well what you are saying. But you have been very kind for listening to what I had to say and offering to tell your captains to be on the lookout for signs of stranded people in that area. I want to thank you very much," said Jacques.

Commodore de Mont shook hands with Jacques and said, "I have never heard such a story. It's heartbreaking and unbelievable. If the right people hear about this there will be trouble for someone, you wait and see."

Before leaving, Madame Palchier invited the commodore and his wife to a special dinner at the Country Inn during Christmas.

He accepted the invitation and thanked them for coming.

CHAPTER 22

Arrest And Jail

It is said bad news travels fast, and indeed it did with the news of Marguerite, Pierre de Val and Madame Violet. Despite what he'd said, Commodore de Mont did not hesitate to spread the information he had been told.

By the time the sun came up next morning, every person in the city of St Malo and the surrounding towns and villages were discussing the story about Marguerite. The more people told the story, the faster and further the news traveled, and the worse the horror became.

Everyone wanted Admiral de Roberval hung for such an act.

Two days after Major Jacques and Frances saw Commodore de Mont, they were visited by the navy police. Three men came late in the evening and arrested Jacques. They told him he was under arrest for slandering the reputation of a naval officer and spreading lies, therefore damaging the admiral's career. No time was wasted in removing him from the inn. Immediately, his hands were tied and he was thrown into the back of a two-horse carriage and whisked away to an unknown military prison somewhere in central France.

The plans he was making to go to the New World to search for Marguerite and her companions in early spring were put on hold. Nothing could be done until he got out of prison, if he ever got out. He was in a state of shock.

Madame Palchier went to Commodore de Mont for help, but was told very little could be done until a hearing was held sometime during the late winter or early spring.

As the winter wore on, she was told nothing could be done as far as releasing Major Jacques from prison until proof was presented that Admiral de Roberval intentionally put the three people off on a desolated island somewhere in the New World and left them.

Major Jacques asked to write letters to Henry de Val and Madeline de Roberval but was denied his request. He told the naval authorities to contact Captain Fonteneau of the *Valentine*, but was told it would not happen. Frances tried without success to find out where he was in prison, but it appeared nothing could be done for him. He would rot in prison unless someone took his case directly to King François I.

When the fishing fleets left St. Malo in early May, ex-Major George Jacques was still in prison.

CHAPTER 23

The Commodore meets Marguerite

Due to the wind and a heavy tide, it took several hours for the fishing schooner to sail back to Quirpon Harbour with Marguerite aboard. After the vessel got underway, the captain ordered the men to hoist the flags to the top of the mast to indicate something good was happening aboard.

As the ship entered the outer harbour, Marguerite noticed several schooners anchored side by side, their black hulks were deep in the water, laden with loads of salted codfish.

Marguerite stood near the companionway as the men reefed the sails and prepared to tie onto the anchored ships. She could see the bearded faces of the men in the other schooners as they stood by to catch their lines. They stared at her in wonderment.

There were close to twenty vessels anchored in the harbour. They were all owned by Commodore de Mont and waiting for him to arrive. It did not take long for word to spread from vessel to vessel that the young French princess was rescued and was aboard the schooner that had just came into the harbour with flags flying.

Everyone wanted to see her and hear the full details.

As the news reached each vessel the captains ordered all flags to be hoisted and bells to be rung, giving Marguerite a grand welcome.

Marguerite had no intention of leaving the captain and his ship and the men who had rescued her.

"I am not leaving this ship until you say so, Captain," she said.

The captain told her she would stay with him until the commodore arrived, no matter how long it took.

That night, she slept alone in the captain's quarters. It was like paradise to her after sleeping for over two years on bags of hard bread in the hut.

Just before noon the next day, the lookout on the high hill on Jacques Cartier Island signaled that four ships were approaching the harbour. There was no mistake. Commodore de Mont's ship was in the lead.

A stiff breeze was blowing as he approached and this caused a delay so it wasn't until 2 p.m. that the four ships finally entered the harbour.

Commodore de Mont was surprised to see all of his fishing ships with their flags flying and their bells ringing when he arrived. He had never seen this before; he was proud that his good fishermen were welcoming him into Quirpon Harbour.

He came in on the south side, swung into the wind for about one kilometer, and then dropped anchor. The other three ships followed him and tied onto each side.

After the sails were reefed and securely tied, the commodore asked his skipper to ring the bell as a 'thank you' to his fleet and the men on the high hill.

In a few minutes, a boat was launched from the vessel that rescued Marguerite and the captain was on his way to give the commodore the news about whom he had rescued.

Commodore de Mont stood by the rail and greeted his fishing skipper as he came aboard.

"How are you, Captain Le Moine? And thanks for the welcome. I guess the men are anxious to be going home," he said.

"Sir, the flags are not flying to welcome you into the harbour. It's because we have found Princess Marguerite. I have her on board my vessel. We found her at L'Anse au Pigeon yesterday afternoon," the captain said, as he gasped for breath.

"You must be joking, Captain. Are you serious?" asked de Mont.

"I am serious, Sir. I'm the one who found her. It's truly unbelievable; I can hardly talk about it without crying. You will have to excuse me," said the old skipper, as tears ran down his face.

"Dear Lord," said de Mont as he stared in disbelief at the captain. "How is she?"

"She's fine. She stayed aboard our vessel last night."

"The other two people who were with her…are they okay?" asked the commodore.

"No Sir. She was alone when we found her. The other two people who were with her have died. I visited their graves with her before we left L'Anse au Pigeon," said the captain.

"Good grief," said the commodore. "War will surely break out when this news reaches France."

"The princess knows she will have to come aboard with you for the voyage back to France," said the skipper.

"Yes," said the commodore, "we can accommodate her better than the fishing vessels. Some of the smaller boats will tow your vessel over to mine; that will be the best way to transfer her to our ship. In the meantime, we will hoist our flags."

Captian Le Moine asked the commodore what his plans were for sailing across the Atlantic.

"When the princess arrives on this ship, I want all the skippers to come aboard for a meeting and we will brief them about the Atlantic crossing. We have to start the voyage this evening while the weather is in our favour. We will leave at once," said the commodore.

"Yes Sir. I will inform them immediately," said the skipper as he left the ship.

It didn't take long for the group of small rowboats to tow the fishing schooner carrying Marguerite to the side of the commodore's ship, where everyone was excited to see her. The men had not seen a woman since leaving France in May, to say nothing of a real princess.

The men cheered as Marguerite came aboard the commodore's ship. Most of them had been on the lookout for her ever since they arrived in the New World. She had been the main topic of conversation for everyone.

When she stepped on the deck, Marguerite was welcomed aboard by the commodore and his captain. De Mont told her he was preparing living quarters for her voyage home to France. He escorted her to his dining room while this was being taken care of. He ordered his steward to bring her ale and make her comfortable.

The commodore excused himself and went on deck to meet his fishing skippers to brief them on the voyage across the Atlantic.

Marguerite sat in the dining room and looked at herself in the mirror that hung on the wall. She could hardly believe what she saw. She no longer looked like the carefree young woman who had departed France two years ago. She had lost weight, her hair had turned a darker color, lines had formed around her eyes, and the happy smile that had always on her face had disappeared. As she sat at the table and thought about the things that had happened during the last two years she couldn't fight back the tears that welled up in her eyes and ran down her face.

She thought about Pierre who had suffered and died a horrible death from blood poisoning. She recalled the suffering and death of Madame Violet. Then there was the death of her baby girl, the little daughter who had only lived a day. She thought about the horrible living conditions, trying to stay alive in an overturned boat while wrapped in animal skins and huddled around an iron stove with a temperature of forty below zero. Her heart sank as she recalled the howling sounds of the wolves and the roar of polar bears, as they rattled the stovepipe while trying to break through the roof of the hut and grab her.

Marguerite was weeping when she felt a hand touching her shoulder. She looked up and saw the face of the skipper who had found her. The commodore was standing not far away with four other fishing captains. Everyone looked as though they would break down and cry.

"Don't weep, My Lady, you're safe now. We'll take care of you and bring you home, back to France. You don't have to worry anymore," the old skipper said as he put his arm gently around her.

Marguerite dried her eyes and asked to be excused. "It breaks my heart when I think about my two companions who suffered a terrible death and died. Only God knows what they went through," she said.

The men looked at her with pity and told her they would do everything in their power to make her as comfortable as possible on her voyage home.

The commodore told her that her quarters were ready and said a steward would show her the way. He said he was representing the French government and anything that could be done for her would be done.

"I am responsible for you until we dock at our home port of St. Malo," he said. Marguerite thanked him, and followed the steward to her quarters.

CHAPTER 24

The Voyage Back to France

It wasn't easy to frighten Marguerite. Although she had been through hell for more than two years, she hadn't lost her nerve, and neither did she develop any bitterness toward her beloved country.

As she sat on the bed in the best berth aboard ship, she could feel the love of her countrymen around her. It was the first time that she had felt this way since Violet died. As of that moment, she realized she was rescued and on her way home.

She heard a lot of commotion outside and knew what it meant; men were getting the ship underway. The anchors were hoisted and secured, the canvas was hoisted high in the rigging as orders were shouted from every part of the deck.

She looked through the porthole and saw the headlands leading out to Cape Bauld, not far from L'Anse au Pigeon. She took one last look at the land then pulled the curtain across. It was the last glimpse she would ever have of the North American continent.

After the ships were under way and far out to sea, the flagship carrying the commodore swung back and took up the rear. The ship was an old naval vessel converted to a supply ship; it was much faster than the fishing schooners, with a lot more canvas in the wind. The ship still maintained several of its heavy guns, just in case the fishing fleet encountered pirates looking to plunder any vessel carrying valuable cargo.

After darkness settled, a lamp was lit in Marguerite's quarters. Shortly afterwards, a steward came and invited her to dinner with the commodore and she accepted. "I will be back to accompany you to his quarters at eight," the steward told her.

By this time, Marguerite had time to have a sponge bath. She was feeling much better now, after freshening herself up in a civilized manner. She spent a lot of time arranging her hair and making herself presentable. She thought she might be asked to tell the commodore about her two-year ordeal. She hoped she would be asked about it as she wanted to tell everyone what had happened. She also wanted to find out how the fishing captain who had found her knew that she was stranded in the New World. Who had told him about her?

Dressed in a gown she'd pulled from her trunk, Marguerite looked at herself in the mirror and thought she looked quite presentable after such an ordeal.

Just before eight, the steward came and escorted her to the commodore's dining room. De Mont welcomed her as if she was a queen, and led her into the dining room.

Marguerite was surprised and happy to see the skipper who had rescued her standing at the table when she entered. She hugged him and thanked him. The captain of the flagship was also at dinner with them, and two other officers.

After introductions, everyone sat down to eat. De Mont told Marguerite how overjoyed he was that one of his fishing captains had found her. But he said he was saddened by the news that Lieutenant Pierre de Val Cormier and Madame Violet had passed away during their terrible ordeal.

"It is possible that if we could have sailed this route in May, instead of having to go the southern route because of ice, we may have found you then. Or, if a ship had been sent to search for you in the spring they may have found you even earlier," said the commodore. He paused for a moment, then continued, "When I received word last December that you and your party were put ashore somewhere along the Labrador coast or maybe around the northern Newfoundland coast, which was the area where we found you, we could not get anyone to pinpoint the exact location. I called all our fishing skippers to a meeting before we left France and told them to keep a sharp lookout for you or any distress signals. We are happy Captain LeMoine saw your flag and recognized it. It was a superb move on his part. We thank you, skipper."

Marguerite thanked the commodore and the skipper.

"May I ask you a question, Commodore?" she asked.

"Yes, by all means, go ahead," he said.

"You said you received word that we were put ashore somewhere along the north coast of the New World. May I ask who gave you this information?"

"Yes, and I will gladly give you that information. Last year in early December a gentleman by the name of Major Jacques — although he had actually left the army a month or so before — came to see me. He was accompanied by Madame Palchier, owner of the St. Malo Country Inn. Major Jacques said he had been on the *Valentine* when you and your group were put ashore, however he wasn't sure of the exact location. He said he was waiting for the *Valentine* to return from Africa in order to get the exact location from Captain Fonteneau, who was captain of the *Valentine* at the time."

"Did Major Jacques tell you if my father, Baron Charles de Roberval, was contacted and told of our fate?" asked Marguerite.

For a moment the commodore didn't know how to answer. He didn't want to tell the princess her father had passed away with a broken heart after hearing the news about her. He thought she'd be better off hearing about it when she arrived back in France, so he decided not to tell her.

"I don't know if Major Jacques had contacted your father or not. I do know he spread the story around France that you were put ashore by your uncle, Admiral de Roberval, with very little provisions and left to die. All of France was talking about the cruel act. We know for a fact that the Admiralty took action and had Major Jacques arrested and thrown in prison somewhere in France," said the commodore. "Some time in March, Henry de Val, Pierre's father, came to me while he was in St Malo and said he had been in contact with the chief admiral of the navy. He said he was advised that Major Jacques had been sent to Africa as a prisoner to work out his sentence for slandering Admiral Roberval."

Marguerite could hardly believe what she was hearing. It was unbelievable.

After hearing what the commodore had to say, she told him and his dinner party the whole story. How her uncle had threatened to throw her and Violet and Pierre overboard, far out in the Atlantic Ocean, and would have done so if he had not feared a mutiny by the army soldiers aboard the *Valentine* at the time.

"Then," she concluded, "He put us ashore on the first land he saw, with no regard for us, leaving us to die in the wilderness of North America."

No one at the table could believe what they had heard.

When dinner was finished, the men offered Marguerite all the assistance they could give and guaranteed her a safe passage back home to France. She gratefully thanked them for their concern and was escorted back to her quarters.

CHAPTER 25

Henry de Val Cormier Goes To The Queen

After Jacques left the office of Henry de Val Cormier there was quite an uproar. Henry called all his staff and workers together and told them what Jacques had just told him. It was devastating news for everyone. Some did not believe it. Others said they had heard about Admiral de Roberval's cruel acts. Everyone wondered if it was possible for Jacques to do anything to rescue the party.

Henry told his workers he was going to Paris immediately to see the Queen of France, if need be, and demand an investigation and that something be done.

One of his foreman asked the question, "How reliable is the story that this Major Jacques reported to you? Don't you think you should check the story out with the Admiralty before going to His Majesty?"

The man said the Admiralty should have a report registered, and if that was the case Henry would know the story was true. Henry thought for a moment and replied that he would check before heading to Paris.

After the meeting was over, Henry thought long and hard about it all. He wondered if it just might be that Major Jacques had an axe to grind with someone because of his early retirement from the army? Or if he just wanted to cause trouble for Admiral de Roberval? For these reasons, he decided to wait until the New Year. He waited until the end of January, hoping to hear news from Major Jacques, but none came.

When February arrived, he decided to go to Paris and inquire at the Admiralty about Admiral de Roberval's whereabouts. He would also try to arrange a meeting with him to see if the story Major Jacques had told him had any truth to it.

Traveling in France during the winter was very difficult, especially when snow covered the countryside.

Every night along the way, Henry de Val stayed either in a country inn or a rooming house.

He arrived at the Country Inn the night before he got to Paris. The inn was full of travelers heading for the capital city. After he had checked into his room and freshened up, he heard the call to dinner.

He felt tired after a long day on the road and thought he should rest instead of going to dinner. However, he decided to eat first and rest his weary bones later.

He arrived at the dining room and was seated at a large table filled with people. During the meal, Henry overheard a conversation between two women seated not far from him. They were talking about Marguerite de Roberval and the horrible thing her uncle, Admiral de Roberval, had done to her.

Henry tried to get their attention by asking them to pass vegetables that were out of his reach. They did so without noticing him.

Finally he said, "Excuse me, ladies, are you traveling to Paris?"

"Yes," one of them replied.

"So am I," he said, "If the weather stays favorable tomorrow and if the sled doesn't fall to pieces. We had a rough ride today."

That was enough of an introduction to get a conversation going. The weather was a concern for everyone at the inn. Henry found the two women to be very talkative and polite. They were both from the St. Malo area.

"I couldn't help but overhear your conversation a few moments ago, when you were talking about the young Princess Marguerite and how she was stranded in the New World, left by some admiral," said Henry.

For the first time, one of the women really looked at Henry de Val and saw that he was a very distinguished looking gentleman. She fixed her eyes on him and said, "Yes. We were discussing Princess Marguerite. It's the latest gossip. Haven't you heard what happened to her? All of France is talking about it."

"I come from the city of Lille in the north of France. I suppose the news hasn't reached that far north yet. But what happened?" Henry asked.

Both women wanted to talk at once, however, one decided to be silent while the other spoke. "It happened almost two years ago. Admiral de Roberval cast Marguerite ashore on a rocky island and she hasn't been seen or heard from since. The story is that an elderly nurse and a young army lieutenant were put off with her. People swear the story is true."

Henry looked at the two women for a minute. He could tell from looking they were well to do.

"Ladies," he said, "maybe it's just a rumour started by some drunk in one of the seaside pubs. And then people spread it around, you know how it goes."

"A rumour, my eye. I was told the whole story by an innkeeper who knows the man who was aboard the ship and saw it all happen. And that's not all," the woman leaned towards Henry and lowered her voice to a whisper. "The man was an officer in the French army. A few days after he told the story and it traveled around, the naval police came to the inn where he was staying and arrested him. He hasn't been heard from since. I was told by a good reliable source that Marguerite's father died of a broken heart after he heard the news."

Henry de Val was taken by surprise when he heard this. It certainly sounded like Major Jacques. Maybe this was why he hadn't heard from him since he'd left his office around the last of November.

"This is an unbelievable story, but maybe there is some truth to it. I intend to go to the St. Malo area in a couple of weeks. If I had the innkeeper's name and address, maybe I could stay at his place and talk to him," said Henry.

"That's not a problem because the Country Inn is located on the main road leading to the city. The innkeeper is a woman, Madame Palchier," said the woman.

Henry wrote the name down. He thanked them both and told the waiter to put their dinner on his bill.

"They are friends of mine," he said.

The women thanked him and invited him to have a midnight snack with them. He accepted their invitation.

After Henry went back to his room he got paper and made notes. He knew where he would have to go when he got to Paris. To the Navy department. He would demand to be taken to Major Jacques. If his request were denied, he would take the matter to the highest office in France.

Henry de Val was no fool. He knew how to get a meeting with people in high places.

After he arrived in Paris in the early afternoon, he went to a first class rooming house and checked in. He refreshed himself, had a bite to eat, then headed straight for the office of French naval headquarters. He was in possession of certain papers that got him directly in to see naval dignitaries, no appointments required.

He went straight to the office of the Chief Admiral of naval operations. When he approached the office, he was stopped by an armed guard who asked to see his papers. Henry showed him his papers and was escorted into the office.

The Chief Admiral was a short burly man who had seen better times. He wore a uniform that needed pressing and was surrounded by used ale mugs that were scattered on his desk.

"Good afternoon, Chief Admiral," said Henry, as he stepped in front of his desk.

"Good afternoon, Sir," said the chief admiral, in a voice that sounded as though he had several frogs caught in his throat.

"I'm Henry de Val Cormier from the city of Lille," said Henry as the two men shook hands.

"Have a seat, please," said the chief admiral.

Henry seated himself in an armchair facing the chief admiral.

"Your name rings a bell. I've heard it before," said the chief admiral.

"Yes you may have. I own a tailoring business. I've designed uniforms for many military dignitaries and my company makes all the royal gowns."

"Oh yes, now I know where I met you. It was at the coronation ball of King Francois I. You were there."

"Yes, I designed the coronation gowns."

Those remarks opened up doors for Henry that would have been otherwise barred.

"Please have a glass of wine with me," said the chief admiral.

"No thank you. I have to attend two other meetings this afternoon and time is of the essence," said Henry.

"Very good, Monsieur Cormier. What can I do for you today?"

Henry de Val was a smooth talker. He told the chief admiral how his son Pierre went to the New World as a young lieutenant almost two years ago on the *Valentine*, a French man-of-war.

He said he had not been heard from since except for rumours going around the French countryside. He went on to tell the story that Major Jacques of the French army had reported regarding his son and Princess Marguerite being cast ashore on an island with nothing but the clothes on their back.

He also told the chief admiral that his naval police had arrested the major and were holding him in jail somewhere in France because he had reported what Admiral de Roberval had done.

The chief admiral listened to Henry very quietly. When he finished telling the story the chief admiral cleared his throat and said, " Monsieur Cormier, this is the first I've heard of the incident and to say the least I am shocked to hear of such a thing, if it's true."

"There is a way to find out if it's true or not. All we have to do is locate the prison where the major is being held, then you and I can go and interview him."

The chief admiral thought for a moment then said, "If we locate this person you are referring to, how will we know if he is telling the truth or not?"

"That should be easy. All you have to do is have the *Valentine* return to France and talk to her captain, Captain Fonteneau. He was ship's captain at the time of the incident. He will know what went on."

The chief admiral sensed anger in his visitor's voice. He was aware that the man had influence with the royal household and could get an appointment with His Majesty, so he would have to be careful.

"I will immediately have someone check this out and see if there is such a man as Major Jacques in one of our prisons. I will let you know the moment I find anything," he told Henry.

"I will only wait twenty-four hours for your reply. I have factories operating in several French cities that need me. However, my son is missing because one of your admirals committed a breach of the law against French citizens. If that is true, heads will roll," said Henry. "I intend to be in Paris for two days, during which I have personal business with Her Majesty the Queen. After that, I will be traveling to St. Malo before returning to Lille."

"I guarantee you I will have a written report to you at your room before this time tomorrow," promised the chief admiral.

With this, Henry de Val bid him good afternoon and departed.

At noon the next day, a runner from the chief admiral arrived with a written message for Henry de Val. It said a prisoner by the name of ex-Army Major George Jacques had been among several prisoners shipped to one of the African colonies for a year, to serve his sentence. However word had been sent to have him returned, and it was expected he would be back sometime before June.

Henry de Val used a lot of foul language after he read the message. The messenger had orders to wait for a reply.

Henry quickly wrote a reply stating he would take his complaint directly to the royal household and call for an investigation. He sealed the envelope and gave it to the runner to be delivered.

It is not recorded, and I suppose it may never be known, what went on during the meeting between Henry de Val and the royal household regarding the Marguerite affair. However, the chief admiral of naval operations received direct orders not many days after to have Admiral de Roberval and Captain Fonteneau, who were both somewhere along the east coast of Africa, return to France immediately. The letter also stated that Admiral de Roberval was to be relived of his duties immediately upon his arrival back in France.

Henry knew this would take months. He would not wait in Paris until Major Jacques and Captain Fonteneau, now known as Admiral Fonteneau, returned. He would travel on to St. Malo and try to see Madame Palchier.

CHAPTER 26

Henry goes to St. Malo

Henry de Val arrived at the Country Inn on the outskirts of St. Malo. It was a cold drizzly day in March, with melting snow creating mud and slush, which clung to everything.

Passengers didn't have to knock at the inn. It was common practice here that whenever a horse and carriage stopped, someone from the inn was there to greet the passengers.

Henry stepped inside and asked if there was a room for one person. The concierge said there was, and Henry asked to kindly book him for the night.

He removed his bags and paid the coachman. It had been a long hard ride and he needed rest. The concierge showed him to his room. As soon as the concierge departed, Henry took off his clothes and got into bed. Any business he had to do could wait until tomorrow.

He awoke just after daybreak to a rainy, windy morning; he felt well rested but very hungry.

He washed, shaved, and dressed in clean clothing.

He could smell the aroma of fresh bread just out of the oven.

Locking his room, he followed the delicious odour all the way to the dining room.

The maid greeted him and showed him to a private room just off the kitchen. Henry thought it strange that he had bypassed the big dining room where overnight guests ate breakfast.

"Would you like ale, Sir?" asked the maid, who was wearing a white apron that hung almost to the floor.

"Yes, please," he replied.

She disappeared into the kitchen for a minute then returned and stood beside him.

"Excuse me, Sir, but Madame Palchier would like to join you for breakfast if it pleases you?" she said.

"May I ask who Madame Palchier is?" Henry asked.

"She is the owner of the inn," said the maid. "Last night when she saw your name on the register she left word that she would like a meeting with you this morning, if possible. She asked me to tell her when you arrived for breakfast."

"It will be a pleasure to have breakfast with Madame Palchier," said Henry.

He remembered what Jacques had told him about Madame Palchier. She had been friends with Pierre and Marguerite and was upset when Jacques told her what Admiral Roberval had done to them. He was anxious to meet her.

The maid brought the ale and set another place for Madame Palchier across from Henry. She then left the room, closing the door behind her.

He decided to question Madame about what Jacques had told her. He would compare her story with that of Jacques to see if it was the same. By then, he would have sufficient information to demand action by the royal household.

Henry was surprised when Madame Palchier came into the private dining room. He was expecting to see an older woman and this was not the case. He saw a very attractive lady, tall and slender, and wearing a gown that showed her graceful form. She had a pleasant smile that made him forget about the rain and drizzle outside.

Henry stood and greeted her, pleased that he was looking his best.

"Good morning. Monsieur Henry de Val Cormier. I am Madame Frances Palchier. I hope I am not intruding, especially this early in the morning," she said with a smile.

"I am pleased you are intruding this morning, especially after my terrible three-day trip from Paris. It gives me great pleasure to have such a beautiful lady invite me for breakfast," he said, as he held out her chair.

Madame Palchier thanked him and sat down.

The maid came in to take their breakfast order then left.

Frances knew Henry de Val Cormier was a very wealthy man and well known throughout France. He was well known in high society, so much so that he could visit the royal family. She felt privileged to have breakfast with such an important figure.

As she looked at him, she was reminded of his son, Pierre de Val. Father and son were both good-looking men.

Their conversation began with the weather and the many problems experienced while traveling through France.

"Are we behind closed doors, Madame Palchier?" Henry asked after a few minutes.

"Yes, this is a private dining room. No one else can hear our conversation and no one will ever know what we've talked about," she said, as she invited him to call her 'Frances.'

"Thank you, and please call me Henry," he said.

"I am anxious to know if Major Jacques came to St Malo after he visited me at Lille in late November?" he asked.

"Yes, he came here around the tenth of December and spent a week," she said.

"Did he tell you anything about the voyage he took to North America with Admiral de Roberval?"

"Yes, he certainly did, in every detail," said Frances. "In fact, the party was here before they departed. A couple of days before they left, Major Jacques, whom I have known for many years, came here for lunch. He was accompanied by Princess Marguerite de Roberval and they were on their way to the firing range. After they left the inn, it was discovered that Major Jacques had left his saddlebag in the dining room; he sent Pierre back for it, and Marguerite came with him. That was the first time I met the princess. She and your son came here several times before they left for the New World."

"So, in other words, there was an affair going on?"

"I can't say if they had an affair or not. All I can say is that they spent a considerable amount of time together here. But no one knew anything about it, only George and I," she said.

"I see," said Henry, as he looked up at the ceiling.

"As for the trip across the Atlantic with Admiral de Roberval, I know more of what went on than anyone because I spent days discussing it with George. When he returned, as soon as he left the *Valentine,* he came directly here. He was accompanied by a lieutenant who had sailed to the New World with him, and he told me the same story."

"You will have to tell me all the details. I want to know," said Henry.

"I certainly will tell you all the details and everything I know. However, the story is too long to begin while having breakfast. We can continue upstairs in my apartment; it could take several hours" said Frances.

Henry thought for a moment then asked, "May we please talk this morning? I have an appointment this afternoon."

"Better still, we can have the maid bring our breakfast to my apartment rather then eat here. We can go there now, if you'd like," said Frances.

"That will be excellent," said Henry, as they left the dining room.

In Madame Palchier's apartment, Henry was seated at a lovely hardwood table. They were there for a few minutes before the maid arrived with

their meal. Henry was very hungry and ate silently. When breakfast was over, Frances began telling him what George Jacques had told her about Pierre's voyage across the Atlantic. It was the exact story he had told Henry when he visited Lille. Frances went on to tell him about Jacques's arrest by the naval police and how he was carried away to some unknown destination and locked up.

"I have been trying to get news of his whereabouts ever since I received the news, but have been unsuccessful. And, to make matters worse, I don't know who to turn to for help; it seems all doors are shut," she sadly said.

Henry stared at her. It seemed she was almost at a breaking point and he sensed she was in love with Major Jacques. He knew Frances was telling the truth, but wondered how she would take the news when he told her where George Jacques was. Finally, he had to tell her.

"Frances, I know where Major Jacques is, or at least I think I know. The chief admiral of the navy gave me the information as to where he is being held."

Frances was wide-eyed as she looked at Henry. "Where is it?" she demanded.

"I was told by the chief admiral that just after they arrested him, he was sentenced to ten years for slandering Admiral de Roberval and sent to one of the African colonies to work out his prison term. The chief admiral didn't say where in Africa he was being held. When I told the king this, he ordered him returned immediately," said Henry.

Frances covered her face with her hands. Henry could see tears roll down her face as she wiped her eyes.

"It is not likely we will ever see George again. If the high officials in the navy want to protect Admiral de Roberval, they will have him silenced forever," she said.

"I don't think you're right about that because His Majesty has ordered Admiral de Roberval back to France and has taken his authority away from him. A ship has left France in search of the *Valentine* and did you know that Captain Fonteneau has been promoted to admiral," said Henry.

"Well, at least a few things are moving in the right direction." Said Frances. "When is the *Valentine* expected back in France?" "I'm not sure. The chief admiral wasn't certain where the *Valentine* was. The last time he heard from de Roberval he was off the east coast of Africa."

"You and I should go see Commodore de Mont. He has fishing ships fishing around South Africa. It's possible he may know the whereabouts of the *Valentine*. And he may have some suggestions as to where to look for the castaways in North America," said Francis.

"Do you know the commodore?" asked Henry.

"Yes, I know him well; he is a fine man."

"Very well. We will travel there as soon as you're ready," said Henry.

In less then half an hour, the two were on their way to see Commodore de Mont at his office near the waterfront in St. Malo.

De Mont was very pleased to meet Henry de Val Cormier. He had heard much about him as his wife had often purchased the clothing he made. He welcomed Henry with open arms.

The commodore informed them that the *Valentine* was last sighted by his ships heading east into the Indian Ocean. He said one of his captains reported receiving the *Valentine's* signal that the ship would be returning to France in July.

"What do you think about sending a ship to North America in May to search of the three people abandoned there?" asked Henry.

"It wouldn't be wise to send any ship unless Captain Fonteneau is in charge; he knows where they were put ashore. I will be sending twenty or thirty fishing vessels to North America in a couple of months. We will be keeping a careful watch for the three wherever we go," said de Mont.

"I appreciate that very much, but that's not good enough. I'd like to send a ship to search along the Labrador coast and the northern part of Newfoundland," Henry said.

"I agree. But without knowing where they were put ashore, it would be like looking for a needle in a haystack. Ask His Majesty if he will send the *Valentine* with Captain Fonteneau back to the area where they were abandoned as soon as he arrives back in France," suggested de Mont.

Henry thought for a moment then said, "I agree. That would be the best thing to do." Henry told the commodore that the king had ordered the chief admiral of the navy to strip de Roberval of his title. He said too that Captain Fonteneau had been promoted and was now Admiral Fonteneau.

The commodore was very surprised to hear this. "I hardly know what to say," he said. "There will be a lot of happy people when this news gets around."

The three concluded their meeting. The commodore invited Henry and Frances to dine at his home but they refused. De Mont gave Frances a hug and told her that everything would be fine.

"I certainly hope so, and we thank you very much for meeting us on such short notice," she said, as she and Henry left.

The commodore told her it was a pleasure to be of service, and assured her he would do all in his power to help find the three castaways.

CHAPTER 27

Marguerite Comes Home

While the ship carrying Marguerite headed for the west coast of Ireland, she spent many hours telling the commodore about her ordeal while living in L'Anse au Pigeon. She told him about the winter weather and the huge storms that swept the area, and of what happened to Pierre and Violet and how they died. She told him everything, even how she got pregnant and gave birth to a baby girl who only lived one day. She told him about the boat that came into the harbour more than a year ago and left again, the sailors acting as though they'd seen the devil.

De Mont and Marguerite became good friends. He was like a father to her, giving her comfort at every opportunity.

He told her about his meeting with Major Jacques and Madame Palchier, and the meeting with Henry de Val Cornier. He told her everything, except that her father had passed away. This news would come later, after they arrived at St. Malo.

"We left St Malo the middle of May and headed for North America. Up to that time, the *Valentine* hadn't arrived back in France. According to reports received from the Admiralty, the ship will not arrive back until the middle of August, or later. We might be back in St. Malo before that," said de Mont.

By the time the fishing fleet reached the west coast of Ireland, the commodore and several of his officers had plans made as to what they would do to give Marguerite a rousing welcome home.

When they reached the Irish coast, they sent their fastest schooner ahead to St. Malo. In the meantime, the rest of the fleet slowed down so that before they arrived the word would be spread that Marguerite was rescued and would soon be back in France.

De Mont gave the captain of the schooner orders to tell everyone to have French flags flying to welcome Princess Marguerite home.

The commodore also wrote a letter to be delivered to the Country Inn, in which he told Madame Palchier that only Marguerite had survived the ordeal in the wilderness of North America. He said he would accompany her to the Country Inn as soon as he arrived.

The following morning, the commodore asked the steward to help Marguerite prepare for the arrival in St. Malo.

As the fishing fleet got close to the harbour, they could hear ships' bells ringing and see flags flying. Much to their surprise, the commodore announced that the *Valentine* was moored at the pier with all her flags flying.

Sailors from the three naval ships were lined on the dock and they all gave a rousing salute and three cheers as Marguerite came ashore, accompanied by Commodore de Mont and the captain who had rescued her.

The mayor and Admiral Fonteneau met them. The mayor shook Marguerite's hand. Afterwards, Admiral Fonteneau held her in his arms and wept. He whispered that Major Jacques was at Madame Palchier's Country Inn.

"You will be going directly to the inn with me as soon as your baggage is put aboard the carriage," he said, as Marguerite accepted a salute from the navy sailors.

Marguerite hugged the commodore and thanked him for his hospitality and kindness.

"I will tell my father how well you treated me on your ship. He will be contacting the king," she said.

De Mont thanked her. This was the time he had planned to tell her that her father had passed away, but he didn't have the courage. Someone else would have to do it.

Marguerite ran to Captain Le Moine, the fishing skipper who had rescued her. She hugged and kissed him on the cheek and the old man cried as he held her.

"My father will reward you for what you did in rescuing me," she said, as she hugged him again before saying goodbye.

In a horse drawn carriage with Admiral Fonteneau by her side, Marguerite drove to the Country Inn, through streets that were lined with people eager to welcome her home.

Marguerite was silent as she rode through the outskirts of the city. Her mind went back to the days when Pierre raced with her on horseback along the same road. She had to banish the thought, because now she was back in France, rescued from the wilds of the New World.

From a distance, they could see the flags flying all around the inn and a big sign saying 'Welcome Marguerite" hung over the gate. She saw Madame Palchier standing near the gate with a man she did not recognize.

The commodore helped her down from the carriage and ordered her bags to be taken off. He stepped aside as Madame Palchier rushed to embrace Marguerite, with tears running down her face. Marguerite returned her embrace, and told her she was happy to be back in France.

The man with Madame Palchier had a noticeable scar on the left side of his face. He reached out and put his arms around Marguerite. For a moment she didn't know what to say. She hugged him as if she knew him, but who was he? Marguerite had no time to ask questions. Everything was moving so fast.

Madame Palchier asked everyone to come inside. Commodore de Mont excused himself, saying he had to return to the waterfront to attend to business.

As he was leaving, he said, "Marguerite, I want you to go to my store and get yourself a complete wardrobe, with my compliments."

Marguerite thanked him again.

The commodore turned to the man who was holding Marguerite and asked, "Are you Major Jacques?"

"Yes, I am," replied Jacques.

"Good grief, what ever happened to you?"

"It's a long story. I plan to visit you soon and tell you all about it," said Jacques.

"Come tomorrow evening," said de Mont.

"Maybe I will," said Jacques.

Marguerite heard the conversation and looked again at the man who had just embraced her. She could not believe her eyes.

"My God, my God," she cried. "Major Jacques, I can't believe it, I just can't believe it." Tears rolled down her face as she spoke.

The commodore boarded the carriage and left as Marguerite linked arms with Major Jacques and walked into the inn.

They joined Madame Palchier in the dining room. Marguerite took off her shawl and hung it on the back of a chair, then looked at Jacques and asked, "Have you been to see my father, Major?"

Jacques said nothing for a moment, then replied, "Yes, I was at the castle and saw your father. I told him the whole story of what happened. He was devastated with the news."

He tried to look away but couldn't. She was looking straight at him as if sensing something. Jacques had hoped he wouldn't have to have this conversation. But looking at Marguerite's face, he knew that she had not been told the news of her father's death.

"What did my father say or do when you told him about what Uncle Jean did to us?" she asked.

Jacques gathered all the strength he had. As it was, he was not feeling very well, having just returned from the labour camps in Africa where the beatings and lack of food had almost killed him. But, no matter what he felt like, he knew he would have to tell Marguerite about her father.

"Marguerite, I want you to sit down because I have bad news," he said.

She knew immediately it was about her father, but she sat down and asked him to tell her whatever it was.

"I went to see your father in November. I told him what his brother did to you, Pierre de Val and Madame Violet. He was broken hearted when I left. I told him I would visit him again on my return from the city of Lille where I was going to see Henry de Val, Pierre's father. When I returned two weeks later, I got the shock of my life. I was told he had passed away two days after I left. They said he died of a broken heart."

Marguerite wept as she told Jacques she wasn't surprised to hear this news. She said during the time they were stranded in L'Anse au Pigeon, she and Violet had often discussed how her father would react when he heard what had happened to them. They suspected the news might kill him. But now, her beloved father was gone, and for the first time Marguerite felt like an orphan with no place to go.

Madame Palchier sat near her and held her hand. In just a few minutes, a servant brought mugs of ale. There was no doubt about it, this would be a day that would long be remembered by the three people sitting at the table of the Country Inn.

In a little while, Marguerite dried her eyes. "I suppose it's no use for me to weep," she said. "Papa is gone. Madame Violet, the only mother I ever knew, is dead. Pierre and my baby are buried in the New World, in a place where the salt briny ocean washes their graves every day. And, as for me, I am home in France and at the Country Inn where it all started. This is the first place I found love, the kind of love that will stay with me forever. While I was in the New World, I saw hate. Violet developed such a terrible hatred for Admiral Roberval that she put a curse on him that will follow him to his grave. That's what she said when she was dying."

Frances looked at George Jacques then back again at Marguerite. It was time to tell her some good news.

"Marguerite, there is news that you should know and I think George is the one to tell you," she said.

Jacques wasn't sure if Marguerite was in any mood to hear good news, after just being told about her father's death. However, he proceeded:

"Pierre's father went directly to the king and told him the story about what Admiral de Roberval had done to you and Pierre and Madame Violet," he said. "The king then ordered de Roberval to return to France and took away his title of 'Admiral' and threw him out of the navy. The king seized all his assets and ordered him to live in the south of France, where he grew up. I am still trying to find out where he is."

"At least something good is happening," Marguerite said.

Food started to arrive on the table as the three settled in for a long conversation about Marguerite's ordeal in the New World.

Marguerite spent several days at the Country Inn, where she was fitted with a complete new wardrobe, courtesy of Commodore de Mont. The commodore and his wife invited her to dine with them. She also received an invitation to dinner with the mayor of St. Malo, and was showered with gifts from all the fishing captains for miles around.

The story of her rescue was on everyone's lips and people flocked to see her.

Marguerite decided it was time to go back home to the castle. She didn't know how it could be possible to walk in the door and not be greeted by her father. She told Madame Palchier that in one way she was glad he was gone, because she was sure when he heard about Violet's death the pain would have been too much for him to bear. It was best for him not to know.

Jacques told her he would be traveling with her to Paris. He said he was an employee of her father's estate and had to give Madame Madeline a full report on what had transpired, and see if she had further orders. Madame Palchier also went with them. She planned to spend a few days in Paris.

The trip to Paris took close to a week.

Marguerite, Frances and Jacques arrived at the castle late in the evening. They were met by Madame Madeline, who welcomed them with open arms.

After talking to her niece for several hours, Madeline invited Jacques to a private meeting where she read part of the will left by the baron.

The will stated that Jacques was to receive a large sum of money. The money, however, could only be given after certain tasks were completed.

The first part of the will stated that half the money could be paid upon Marguerite's safe return home.

"She has returned safe and sound, therefore I'm now giving you half the money. Even this amount is enough to last you for the rest of your life," said Madeline.

Going to a large safe, she took out a metal box and placed it on the table. When she opened the top of the box, Jacques saw it was filled with gold coins.

"This is yours. It's half the money you are to receive," she said, as she tipped the coins onto the table.

Jacques saw the box also contained a sealed envelope with his name on it. The envelope was marked 'Private.'

"Major, I don't know what is in that envelope," said Madeline. "But I do know what has to be done to collect the other half of the money."

She and Jacques exchanged meaningful glances. Madeline then closed the cover of the metal box and locked it. Jacques put the gold coins she'd given him in his moneybag. He tucked the envelope in his inside pocket.

"Six months from this date, this castle is to go to the Holy Catholic Church and be used as a home for retired monks. Marguerite has a new home that the baron purchased a few years ago on the outskirts of Paris. Her father's wish was that she become a schoolteacher and teach orphaned children," said Madeline.

After a tearful farewell to Marguerite, Jacques and Frances said goodbye. Jacques put his luggage, including his moneybag, in the carriage and disappeared down the long dusty road leading to Paris, with Frances by his side. He would never see Marguerite again.

CHAPTER 28

The Assassination

Jean Francois de la Roberval became a condemned man after the King of France stripped him of his naval title and seized his assets. He was ordered to live in the south of France for what he had done to Marguerite and her two companions.

After he received this humiliation from the king, he became bitter toward the monarchy and the Catholic Church. He decided to rejoin the Protestant religion and become a Calvinist.

One rainy night in 1560, he was coming out of a Calvinist meeting when a lone assassin attacked him.

In the ensuing scuffle, he was pierced with a sword in the heart three times, and fell like a dog in a mud puddle on the sidewalk.

If you are ever in L'Anse au Pigeon on a rainy, windswept night when the clock strikes eleven, you might hear a woman's voice upon the nearby hill putting a curse on a cruel admiral.

And, if you listen hard enough you may hear a whispered 'thank you,' followed by the clink of gold coins and the closing of a metal box as payment is counted out.

For what?

We don't know.

EPILOGUE

One day, years after Marguerite had become a schoolteacher, she took out Violet's diary, the one she'd written for the baron, but which he'd never had the opportunity to read. The diary, with its brown leather cover, was weather worn and almost falling apart. Marguerite opened the diary and wept as she read of Pierre's death and that of their baby girl in L'Anse au Pigeon.

She sat up straight and red spots of anger came on her cheeks as she continued to read and discovered how Violet had disposed of her baby. Tears flowed and she cried aloud as she thought of her daughter's tiny body ravaged by wild animals. Her daughter never had the privilege of a Christian burial. She had been poked away like a dead animal. Marguerite wept until her eyes were red and stinging. She fell asleep finally and dreamt of her baby, bloody and torn. Marguerite cried again when she awoke. But as the days and weeks and months passed, she felt less angry at Violet and her tears fell less often. It took time but there finally came a day when she was able to accept what Violet had done and to forgive her.

Marguerite talked about her and Pierre's baby when she visited Henry de Val Cormier in Lille. They wept together as they talked about the baby and Pierre and when she gave him Pierre's personal belongings, including his beloved violin.

Over the years, Marguerite and Henry continued to stay in touch, mainly through letters, but occasionally they would meet for what Henry called a commemoration of their lost loved ones.

There came a day when, with twinges of guilt, Marguerite also decided to open the letter Violet had written in L'Anse au Pigeon. The envelope was addressed to Baron Charles de la Roberval and marked 'confidential.'

She slit the envelope open and slowly pulled out Violet's letter, as tears filled her eyes and memories flooded through her mind. She wasn't at all surprised to find it was a love letter to her father. She had always had a feeling that her father and Violet were more than just an employer and an employee.

'Charles, mon amour,' the letter began.

Violet went on to say how much she'd always loved the baron. She said theirs had been a love affair that had brought her peace and contentment and much happiness. She spoke matter of factly of her illness and said she doubted she would ever see him or France again. She spoke of her sorrow at what had happened to Marguerite and Pierre. She told of Pierre's death. And she said how very sorry she was that she would no longer be there to care for and protect Marguerite.

She ended the letter with the words, 'Yours till death us do part.'

Whatever happened to Marguerite's ring?

The story has been told and retold many times how a strange ring was found close to the salt pond near L'Anse au Pigeon by some children who were playing in the muddy bottom. To tell it once more may shed some light on the story surrounding Marguerite and the Isle of Demons.

One foggy afternoon three young children in L'Anse au Pigeon were playing near the shoreline at low tide. They were having a mud ball fight. The mud on the shoreline was four inches deep. As they rolled mud into balls and threw it at each other, the children discovered there was clay below the mud that would make better balls, ones that would stay together when traveling through the air.

As they scooped up the clay and rolled it into balls, one of the children saw something sparkling in the clay. The child looked closer and discovered it was more than a pebble. He walked down to the river and washed his find and knew at once it was a ring. "It looks nice," the children thought. "We should trade it for something."

They went to the nearest house, not far from the liver factory, where an old woman and her son lived. Opening the door, they called "Hey Auntie, Auntie Lotty, some and see what we found. It looks like a ring." Aunt Lotty came to the door and saw the boys covered in mud. "Your mothers will kill you if you go home like that," she said. "But, Aunt Lotty, we found something in the clay that looks like a ring. We thought you might give us something for it, maybe some molasses bread."

Aunt Lotty took the ring and looked at it. "One slice of bread each for the ring and then it's mine," she said finally. The boys agreed and figured they had a bargain.

When the boys left, Aunt Lotty went to the washstand and poured water in the wash pan. She swished the ring around for a bit, removing most of the mud. Her eyes were not good so she went and got the magnifying glass. After closely examining the ring, she was convinced it had some value. Aunt Lotty had never seen a diamond, but after staring at the ring for some time she was convinced it had diamonds on it. She put the ring on and was surprised that it fit her finger perfectly.

At dinnertime, her bachelor son, Stan, came home from fishing and she showed him the ring she was wearing.

"Mom, this ring looks to be of great value. Take it off. I want to get a better look at it," he said

Aunt Lotty took off the ring and let Stan look at it. He got a toothbrush and carefully cleaned the ring. He knew it was a golden diamond ring.

"Mom, this ring is worth a fortune. I can see letters of some kind on the inside part but I don't know what it says," said Stan.

"It fits me perfectly," said Aunt Lotty as she put the ring back on her finger.

As Stan ate his supper and talked about the struggle he was having trying to make a living for him and his mother at the fishery, he wondered aloud if there was a better way to make a living.

Aunt Lotty told him she wished there was.

It was then Stan took another look at the ring on his mother's finger.

"Mom, that ring you've got on, let's sell it. We might get a lot of money for it," he said in excitement.

"No, Stan, I'm going to keep it," Aunt Lotty said, as she put her hand under her apron.

There was a lot of excitement about the golden diamond ring in the little community of L'Anse au Pigeon and the surrounding area. People came from miles around to see the ring that Aunt Lotty refused to remove from her finger.

Shortly after Aunt Lotty started wearing the ring, she became ill. She had dizzy spells and weakness came over her. Sometimes she would have a problem getting up in the morning to cook and clean her house.

One night, she went to bed not feeling well. She had a headache and felt dizzy.

Aunt Lotty had a dream. She dreamt she was sitting near the shoreline at L'Anse au Pigeon when a young woman walked up to her and very pleasantly said 'hello.' The young woman said she was a French princess. She admired Aunt Lotty's ring and said it was hers.

"I don't know anything about this being your ring. Some children found it in the mud near the shoreline. I gave them molasses bread for it," said Aunt Lotty. "Do you want it back?"

"No, no it's yours now. But I have something to tell you. You had better not take off the ring for anyone or for any reason, because if you do and you die without it on you go in the grave and you will not go to heaven. So, make sure you keep it on forever."

Aunt Lotty woke up and sat up straight, her eyes wild looking. Stan made his mother lie back on the bed while he got a cold cloth and placed it on her forehead. He knew she was having a nightmare.

Aunt Lotty told her dream to anyone who came along.

One day, two strange men came to her house and knocked on the door. Stan went out and asked if he could do anything for them.

They told Stan they wanted to talk to his mother about buying the strange ring she had. They said they would pay a fortune, enough money to keep him and his mother for the rest of their days.

"You will never have to fish again," they said.

Stan invited the men in.

It was impossible for them to talk to Aunt Lotty about selling the ring. She went into her bedroom and closed the door.

The man became very angry. They again offered Stan a large sum of money. When he refused, they told him they would be back again. They said next time they wouldn't leave without the ring. Stan asked them to leave.

For several weeks, a strange vessel was seen hanging around Quirpon Island, but no one knew who it was.

After the two men left, Aunt Lotty became very worried and, of course, at her age worry made her frightened, miserable and ill.

There was no doctor or nurse available to attend Aunt Lotty so the midwife was called. She examined Aunt Lotty and announced that death was not far away.

After hearing this, Stan went and got the minister to prepare his mother for her journey to the Great Beyond.

When the minister arrived, she asked Aunt Lotty if there was anything she wanted done before she passed from this life, or if there was anything she wanted to tell anyone.

Aunt Lotty sat up in bed and said, "Oh, my yes, there is something I must tell you. I have to be wearing my ring when you put me in the grave. If I don't have it on when I get to heaven's Gate St. Peter won't let me in. So make sure the ring is on my finger when I'm put in my casket. Will you make me a promise?"

Stan vowed the ring would be on her finger when the casket was closed and the minister promised Aunt Lotty faithfully that she would oversee and see it was done. They would nail the cover down and not have it opened after it was shut.

In less than two hours, Aunt Lotty passed from this life, wearing the French princess's ring.

They laid out Aunt Lotty and dressed her in her long black dress. Her hands were folded and tied on her chest with the golden diamond ring clearly showing on her finger. A casket was made of rough board and her body placed inside. The cover was nailed down tight under the supervision of Stan and the minister. The casket was then taken to the church and placed on the altar for burial the following day.

A lot of people came into the community when the news spread about Aunt Lotty's death. Even strangers came to town.

It was a custom in those days not to leave relatives of a departed soul alone when their loved one died. So, when Aunt Lotty died, a few young men went to stay with Stan.

Moonshine was passed around and some songs were sung. "Go and look for a few girls to come and join us. We might as well have a good time," said one of the young men. Stan gave the okay.

All was going well until around 1 a.m. when a loud scream was heard outside, and then came banging on the door.

"Stan, open up. Open up, Stan, as quick as you can."

Everyone stopped. It was a woman's voice they heard.

"Who is there?" roared Stan.

"For the love of St. Peter, Stan, open the door and let me in. It's your mother. Them two men got the ring off my finger. Open up."

Stan got frightened. He knew it was his mother; there was no else who could fake her voice. Stan started shaking at the knees.

The three young fellows with him opened a window in the kitchen and jumped out, leaving Stan alone.

After some time, Stan went to the door and let his mother in. As she came through the door, he fainted.

Aunt Lotty tells the story that around midnight the same two men came and opened the casket and grabbed the ring off her finger and dashed out the door. With this, she came alive again and got out of the casket and ran for home.

Aunt Lotty lived another three years and went back to central Newfoundland where she died and was buried at her home of Lushes Bight.

Acknowledgements

Special thanks to Iris Fillier and Alvone Sutton for
their editing contributions.

And to Junior and Eileen Canning for their advice and research.

Thank you as well to the following people for their help with
research: Baine and Nancy Pilgrim, Caesar and Barbara Pilgrim,
Nelson and Sharon Roberts.

Special thanks to Norm Tucker of St. John's, who was born just a
stone's throw away from the hut in L'Anse au Pigeon which provided
shelter for Marguerite, Violet and Pierre in the sixteenth century.

Special thanks to Wallace Maynard & John Kennedy

As always, I would like to thank my wife Beatrice for
her help and assistance

About The Author

Earl B. Pilgrim, Newfoundland and Labrador's favourite storyteller, was born in Roddickton in 1939 and still lives there with his wife, Beatrice. They are the parents of four children.

Earl started his working career in the Canadian Army where he became involved in the sport of boxing and went on to become Canadian Light Heavyweight Boxing Champion.

Following his stint in the forces, he worked as a Forest Ranger with the Newfoundland and Labrador Forestry Department. After nine years as a Forest Ranger, he became a Wildlife Protection Officer with the Newfoundland Wildlife Service.

Awards Earl has received for his work include the Queen Elizabeth II Golden Jubilee Medal; the Safari International Award; the Gunther Behr Award; and the Achievement Beyond the Call of Duty Award.

Earl and his son, Norman, have a wilderness lodge in the mountains of the Cloud River on the Northern Peninsula, near Roddickton. They offer big game hunting for moose, caribou and black bear in the fall and snowmobiling in the winter. During summer, they offer salmon and trout fishing. The area where they have their lodge is one of the most successful on the island for all of these endeavours.

Earl can be reached by calling 709-457-2041 or cell 709-457-7071 or email earl.pilgrim@nf.sympatico.ca
Web address is www.boughwiffenoutfitters.com